The Fae's Bride

Silveri Sisters
Book 1

R. L. Medina

For my family. Through the hard times and the good times, you've always been there for me.

Contents

Chapter 1

Market Day

Alessia Silveri stood in the kitchen and savored the smell of caffé and cherry biscotti. The large window was open, the sky beginning to lighten outside. Candles glowed from their holders, casting her shadow against the stone wall.

Despite the cool morning air, heat spread across Alessia's skin. Her chest felt tight and her stomach queasy. They'd been preparing for market day for so long, yet she still didn't feel ready. What if they didn't sell enough to cover the repairs needed? Their villa needed a new roof, the stable doors needed fixing, and there was a worrisome crack in their staircase, among other things.

The villa seemed to groan in agreement.

A little grunt sounded, catching Alessia's attention. Bruno, their house elf, hopped onto the table to inspect all the packed crates laid out. He nibbled a biscotti, dropping crumbs on the wrapped breads and pastries. He reached for one of the packages.

"This is for market," Alessia told him, blocking his little hand.

He turned his beady, dark eyes on her and rattled something off in Elvish. Judging by his cross look, he didn't like her answer.

"I'll bring you something back," she promised.

At this, he grinned and rubbed his bearded chin. Alessia turned her attention back to the crates, making sure everything was secure.

The vegetables and cherries were packed tight, chilled jars of fresh milk secured, and the bundles of fresh and dried herbs filled the kitchen with their clashing scents. She just needed Liliana to pack up the potions and salves she'd made. Then everything would be ready.

"All set for market?"

Alessia looked up to find her mother, still dressed in her silk robe, entering the small kitchen. She walked in, holding her chamber stick up and filling the room with the candle's light. Her mother looked beautiful even with her wearied look and dark circles under her eyes. Her bronze skin, which Alessia had inherited, seemed to glow in the candlelight, and her mass of black curls hung loosely around her.

"I think we're as ready as we'll ever be. How are you feeling?" Alessia answered.

"I'm fine," Mama said, her dark brown eyes roaming over the loaded crates.

It was the same answer she always gave. Even when Alessia knew it was a lie. As a seer, her mother suffered from headaches, but lately, they seemed to be more frequent and stronger.

"Whatever we don't sell today, we can always sell at the Strawberry Festival in a few weeks," Mama said.

Alessia sighed. "The produce and milk won't last that long, Mama. We need to sell as much of it today as we can."

"It will all work out. The girls aren't up yet?" Mama asked mildly, setting her chamber stick down on the table.

"They'll be up shortly."

"Yes. Well, I should get dressed. I'll make sure the others start getting ready, too."

"You should stay home and rest, Mama. I can handle things just fine."

Her mother clucked her tongue. "You've been working yourself too hard, *amore.*"

Alessia fought the urge to roll her eyes. Unlike her mother and sisters, Alessia didn't have magic. No visions of the future like Mama. No skill with brewing potions like Liliana or baking magical treats like Pamina. She couldn't understand animals like Serafina or make them do her bidding, and unlike Fiorella, her plant magic was limited to planting, watering, and pruning.

All she had were her *wits and grit*, as Mama said. Hard work was just as important as magic, Alessia was told.

"There's something I want to discuss with you, Alessia," Mama said, pulling her out of her thoughts.

The seriousness of her mother's tone startled her. She met her eyes, suddenly feeling the chill of the early mountain air. Even Bruno stopped eating, watching the two warily from the table.

"What is it?" Alessia asked, gripping the top of the wooden chair in front of her.

A troubled look passed across Mama's face, but it was quickly masked with an unreadable expression. "I want you to take some of today's earnings to Signora Savelli. See if she can set up a match for you."

Alessia laughed, cutting her off. Signora Savelli was the

town's matchmaker and notorious for pairing beautiful young women with rich, old men.

Her mother didn't laugh.

Alessia frowned. "You can't be serious. A match for me? I'm nearly twenty and five, Mama. Well beyond marrying age."

"That hardly matters," Mama replied, shrugging Alessia's words off. "We could at least go and see her list of eligible matches," she continued.

Had her mother lost her mind? Were things really that bad for them to resort to... marriage? Alessia's mind raced, forming a proper response. She needed to put a stop to this before her mother got too carried away with the idea.

"Even if we could afford her prices, Mama, it would be all for nothing. My chances of finding a prospect are... well, impossible. No one in Zamerra would be willing to overlook... my patronage. Besides, I don't even want to marry."

Her mother gave her a long, hard look. Alessia met her gaze, fighting the urge to squirm. If Mama was going to be stubborn about it, she would push back just as hard.

The whole idea was preposterous. What she'd said was true. With Signora Silveri being a seer and unmarried herself, and Alessia's father a mysterious rogue long out of the picture, her chances of finding a prospective spouse were abysmal.

No one wanted to marry into the strange, scandalous Silveri family. They were witches, even if Alessia didn't have magic.

Mama opened her mouth to say something but was cut off by a shrill squawk and clamoring. The others were up and battling over the bathroom, by the sound of it. A door slammed and footsteps pounded above them.

Noisy bunch. The villa seemed to say with affection.

Alessia had always sensed their home was alive with its own feelings and thoughts. She imagined its voice sleepy and gentle, like a wise, older man. Though, given her upbringing, she wasn't sure why she thought of it as male.

"Alessia—ooh," Mama said with a hiss of pain.

She held a hand up to her head and lowered herself into a chair. Alessia turned to the cupboard and grabbed a glass to fill with water. After filling it up, she walked over to her mother and handed the cup to her.

Mama nodded her thanks as she took a small sip. A groan escaped her, her eyes shut tight, and one fist clenched atop the table.

She shook her head slightly, dark curls shaking at the movement. "I'm afraid I don't feel up to going today after all."

Alessia nodded in agreement. "No. You should stay home and rest, Mama. Don't worry about market. I can take care of everything."

Like always. She thought to herself with a sigh. That was another reason her mother's idea wouldn't work. If Alessia were married, who would take care of Mama and her sisters? They needed her.

As if on cue, the others swept into the kitchen in a flurry. All thoughts of marriage matches were soon forgotten as Alessia hurried the others through breakfast and packed up the last of their wares to sell. Mama, still caught in the throes of her headache, gave them her blessing, took her medication, and returned to her room.

Outside, the sun was beginning to rise, melting the dew from the tall grass. It was the start of what looked to be a beautiful Spring day, but Alessia couldn't shake the worry. Why had Mama's headaches returned so forcefully? They were usually accompanied by a vision, but her mother hadn't had a vision in so long. So, why weren't the headaches going away?

Pushing away these thoughts, Alessia loaded the last of the crates onto the wagon and turned her attention to her sisters.

Liliana, the second oldest, twisted a tight, black curl around her finger, frowning at the potions she'd packed. Pamina stood in front of the wagon, stuffing one of her cherry tarts into her mouth whole.

Serafina came marching down the path from their villa, her dark auburn curls falling loose from her ribbon. Fiorella trailed behind her with an excited look on her face.

"We're coming too," Serafina announced.

Her dark eyes narrowed at Alessia as if daring her to argue.

"Fina, no—"

"Mama said so," Serafina cut her off with a triumphant little smile.

Alessia glanced at Fiorella, the youngest Silveri sister. She nodded, confirming Serafina's words.

All of them going to market? Why would Mama agree to that? Didn't she know how much trouble it was for her to manage all of them?

Liliana groaned. "Don't you two have chores to do?"

Serafina turned to her. "Already finished."

"Ha! The sun's barely risen, so I highly doubt that," Liliana said.

"Mostly done"—Serafina rolled her eyes—"Mama said we could finish the rest tomorrow."

They all looked at Alessia. Alessia glanced back at the stone villa. Mama did need her rest. Perhaps it was better for them all to go and let her rest in a quiet home for a change.

She turned back to her sisters and gave them her sternest look. "Very well. But no wandering. You stay with us the entire time. Understood?"

Fiorella squealed, hands clasped together as she nodded. Alessia looked at Serafina. She was the one who always gave her the most trouble.

"Yes, we know," her sister responded with a dramatic sigh.

Liliana snorted and shook her head at Alessia. "This won't end well. Do you remember why she was expelled indefinitely from school? She sent snakes to slither up that poor boy's trousers."

Serafina scowled. "Angelo? He called me freckle face. Besides, they were harmless little garden snakes," she lifted her chin, "and I was thirteen then. A child."

"Hey!" Fiorella, who had just turned ten, piped in.

"Yes. Well, you *do* have a freckled face, and you're still a child," Liliana pointed out.

"I'm fifteen!" Serafina said with a huff.

"That's enough, you two. It's time to go." Alessia shot Liliana a warning look.

There was enough to worry about without Liliana and Serafina's bickering.

"I wish I could go back to school," Fiorella said with a faraway look.

"No, you don't. It's stupid and a bore and—"

"Mama and I can teach you all you need to know, Ella. Now, let's go," Alessia said, cutting off Serafina's tirade.

"Oh, one moment!" Fiorella shouted, dashing back up the path.

Alessia frowned. "Where is she going now?"

She turned to the others. They were suspiciously quiet. Her eyes fell on Serafina. Her sister bit her lip, refusing to meet Alessia's gaze. Serafina holding her tongue? *That was very suspicious.*

"Mama said she could," Serafina finally blurted.

"Said she could what?" Alessia asked.

"Oh, Santos." Liliana groaned and rubbed her forehead.

Pamina smiled. "I think it's admirable," she said, turning to Alessia. "She wants to do her part."

Before Alessia could respond, Fiorella sprinted toward

them, carrying a small wooden crate filled with little sacks. They were all neatly tied at the top with thin vines and a tiny red rose tucked into each.

She smiled at Alessia, green eyes looking so hopeful. "Seeds."

Alessia hesitated.

Fiorella's smile faded. "Mama said..." she looked to Serafina.

"Put it in the cart, Ella," Serafina said gently.

Alessia sighed. "Alright," she agreed, not meeting Liliana's disapproving glare.

"They look lovely," she added as Fiorella nestled her crate next to the tomatoes.

"Thank you," her little sister replied, beaming.

"And what happens when a man-eating plant sprouts from one of those seeds? Or a singing flower?" Liliana shook her head, arms folded across her chest.

Serafina scoffed loudly. "You should talk. You and all your putrid poisons."

"Medicinal potions," Liliana corrected icily, "we shouldn't risk drawing more attention."

Fiorella sniffed. "But these are just tomato and pepper seeds. They're not..." she faltered.

Alessia glanced at the dirt path before them, trying to tune out the arguing. The sun was creeping higher, and the morning mist had lifted from the mountains. If they didn't get there soon, all the best spots would be taken.

"Enough," she finally said. "Fina, you know Liliana's potions and salve help people. Ella, they're just seeds from regular plants and vegetables, right?"

Fiorella nodded.

"Mama said she could pack them up and sell them. They're just seeds. Non-magic, regular seeds," Serafina said, turning to

Alessia. "We're wasting time arguing when we could be setting up right now."

Alessia sighed and motioned for them to start moving. She could worry about it later.

"They'll be running us away with pitchforks if those go bad," Liliana murmured beside her.

Pamina rolled her eyes. "Don't be so dramatic. They haven't run us off yet. I don't know what you're so worried about. The townsfolk are harmless."

"Brainless, more like," Liliana sneered.

Fabrizio whinnied, stomping his hooves.

Serafina smiled. "He agrees," she nodded toward their old horse.

Alessia pointed in warning. "Don't do that in town."

"Do what?"

"Talk to the animals," Liliana answered before she could.

Serafina frowned. "I wasn't talking to—"

Alessia threw her hands up in exasperation. "Enough! Let's go. Remember, everyone, act normal."

Chapter 2

The Letter

Massimo Gallo read the letter for possibly the fifteenth time. The king's fancy scrawl was unmistakable, and the envelope was stamped with the official royal seal. All of that was genuine. It was the contents inside the letter that perplexed him.

His uncle Count Domenico had died and his successor, Massimo's distant cousin Alberto, had also passed away suddenly. Apparently in some duel. This left Massimo next in line for inheriting the title of count. Surely, a mistake. Didn't they know of his fae heritage? Everyone knew about the fae blood in his mother's line.

"Pardon me, Signor Gallo. Signor Lazaro is here. Should we show him in?" Signora Gabon, the housekeeper asked, pulling him out of his thoughts.

"Dante is here? Oh, yes. Thank you. Show him in," Massimo answered, nodding politely.

He turned his attention back to the letter, setting it down with a huff only to pick it up again. There had to be something he was missing. Maybe he had a family member who he didn't know about that could take his place. Someone better suited to such a high rank.

Him, a count? The idea made him snort aloud.

"Meow?"

Massimo glanced down at Lucia, his fluffy gray cat who was curled upon her cushion. She stretched and looked up at him with an irritated look. Massimo smiled and held out his hand to stroke her. She only stared at him.

"I suppose we'll have to pack, Lucia. One doesn't ignore a royal summons. I'm sure once they get a good look at my pointed ears, they'll see the mistake they've made, and I'll be dismissed." He set the letter down on the little side table once more.

"Could be fun, yes? I've never been to the palazzo before. Food should be good, anyway." Massimo drummed his finger on the wood, lost in thought.

His eyes rested on the crowded bookshelves behind him. It would be a long trip and he should travel light, but he'd need at least a few books. How many could he fit into his trunk without weighing it down too much?

Massimo sighed and shook his head at her. "You're lucky, Lucia. They never ask cats to be counts. Though perhaps somewhere in the world, cats are allowed to be counts. A land of cats, maybe, where of course a cat could be a count. Who else would they appoint? A dog?"

He chuckled at the idea before dismissing it. "Oh, I'm ranting again, aren't I?"

Another prime example of why he shouldn't be count. The thought of addressing an entire crowd made him shudder and his skin itch.

Ignoring him as she usually did, Lucia yawned and curled back onto her cushion, her back to him now.

"Ahh. I thought I'd find you here. Holed up in your library

as usual," a familiar cheery voice rang out behind Massimo, startling him.

He turned to see his closest friend, Dante Lazaro, enter the room. The warlock was dressed in a puffy, royal blue jacket and matching trousers that suited his dark complexion. His black curls hung haphazardly around his face, though Massimo knew just how much work and time it took his friend to achieve this 'effortless' look.

Dante fixed Massimo with a brilliant smile and strode toward an open seat.

"Ooh. Honey cakes. My favorite," he exclaimed as he sat beside Massimo.

"Yes. Of course. Help yourself," Massimo waved a hand, gesturing to the plate of untouched pastries and the carafe of caffé.

The sound of Dante pouring himself a cup filled the silence. Golden sunlight streamed in through the wide double windows and the smell of old books mixed with the strong caffé gave the library a cozy feel. It was Massimo's favorite room.

He had lived his entire life in his family's grand villa. It held so many memories, both good and bad. He couldn't imagine leaving it behind. If he became count, would he be able to stay?

"What's got you so gloomy this early in the day, Massimo?" His friend's question pulled him back to the present.

Massimo turned toward Dante. The warlock fixed his dark eyes on him, calculating and sharp.

"Alberto is dead," he replied bluntly.

Dante paused mid-sip and frowned. "Who?"

"My cousin."

"Oh. My condolences."

"No, that's not why I'm upset," Massimo said.

Dante's dark eyebrow arched at him. "No? Your father's side then, I imagine?"

"Well, yes. I mean, I'm upset about his sudden passing, of course. It's just that he was next in line for the countship, so apparently it... Well, it's fallen to me. Can you believe that?"

"You're going to be a count?"

Massimo shook his head, picked up the letter, and handed it to his friend. He watched in silence as Dante read.

The warlock finished with a long whistle and handed the letter back to Massimo.

"Well?" Massimo asked.

Dante smiled. "I think it's a wonderful idea."

"You do?" Massimo couldn't hide the surprise in his tone.

"You never find a good enough reason to leave your home. Now you have one."

Massimo frowned. "I leave home. I go on my morning walk every day."

Dante snorted. "Yes, but this will be an opportunity to see more than your street. And think of all the people you'll meet."

"People? People don't like me, Dante."

His friend scoffed. "Nonsense. I like you."

Massimo shook his head. "You know what I mean. I'd be forced back into society. With the upper class, and I've had enough of them."

With their fae heritage, he and his mother had often been shunned or ignored by the upper class. Even the supposed friends his mother had made would talk behind her back.

Dante nodded sympathetically and sighed. "They're not all bad, Massimo. I know this might not be what you want to hear, but you can't just spend the rest of your life in mourning. In hiding. This isn't what your Mama wanted for you."

Silence stretched between them. Massimo's chest tightened at the memory of his late mother. It had only been a couple of years since her passing, but the pain was just as fresh as ever.

He sighed, pushing away the emotions. "What she wanted was for me to marry. Have a family."

"You? Married?"

"She thought my father's lineage and our wealth would be enough for people to overlook my faults. It wasn't."

"Things are changing," Dante said softly.

"Yes. Well, after several failed marriage attempts, she gave up. But we were happy, you know. Just the two of us here."

Massimo looked around the library. His mother had made sure he would be comfortable in life before she passed, and he would be forever grateful for that. Though the villa, as elegant as it was, didn't feel like home without Mama. When he wasn't lost in his books, Massimo was sharply reminded of her absence.

"Yes, well, this could be your second chance at happiness, my friend. You shouldn't let it go."

Massimo turned Dante's words over. There was some wisdom there, but the thought of taking on this role made his stomach churn.

'Meow'

Massimo looked down and smiled as Lucia rubbed herself against his legs. He knelt and stroked her fuzzy, warm head. As much as she ignored him, the cat was also remarkably in tune with his moods.

Lucia, unlike others, was unbothered by his fae-ness and his mumblings and strange ideas. All she cared about was being fed on time and pet when she wanted it.

Cats were understandable. Fickle at times, maybe, but he could anticipate her needs.

People were much harder.

"Besides, think of all the good you could accomplish as count," Dante added, reaching for the last of the honey cakes. He took a bite and washed it down with his caffé. "It's about time we had someone decent in charge of things. You could be at the helm of change, so to speak."

Massimo's mouth went dry. Such a role would involve a lot of speaking, he imagined. Something he was ill-equipped at.

"Do you want to come along with me, Dante?" Massimo asked hopefully.

Dante's nose crinkled. "Me? What would I do at the palazzo? The king is a bore and I highly doubt they would let a commoner, not to mention a warlock, fraternize with the royal court."

Massimo pointed to himself. "Well, if they're allowing fae to be counts, I couldn't imagine a warlock in the palazzo would be any worse."

Dante gave him a mockingly serious look. "Oh, but I could poison the king's cup."

"You wouldn't do that."

His friend set his mug down on the table beside them and shrugged. "I might. If I was bored. Which is why I think it would be much better if I stay here." He swept his hand around at Massimo's library. "I can look after things while you're away. And I'm sure Lucia will appreciate my company. You can't leave her alone."

"Of course not. She's coming with me."

Dante's head snapped toward him, his lips turned up in amusement. "You're bringing your cat to see the king?"

Massimo frowned. "Why, yes. Of course, I am. I couldn't leave her behind."

They turned to look at the feline in question. She stared blankly back at them. Massimo stroked her head and smiled.

If the king could overlook Massimo's fae heritage, then he could surely overlook him bringing his cat to the palazzo. Besides, Lucia was no trouble. As long as she got fed and petted at the precise moment she wanted, all would be good.

The gray cat meowed as if in agreement. Tired of Massimo's affection, Lucia shrank away from his reach and sauntered out of the room with a swish of her tail.

"So, you're going then?"

Dante's question brought Massimo's head around.

Seeing Massimo's questioning look, Dante continued, "You're going to be a count."

Massimo tapped his fingers on the side table. "Well, I never imagined I would inherit my cousin's title. I still don't know if it's for certain, but one doesn't ignore a royal summons. By the time I arrive, I'm sure everything will be sorted out, and I'll be free to leave."

He glanced out the window. "Truthfully, some time away does sound appealing. Even if it's just for a short time."

Dante grunted. "Yes, a change of scenery does sound nice. I've been contemplating it myself, lately. I'm tired of the constant dinner parties and the same dreary old faces. And the gossip has grown stale."

"You could always turn down the invitations as I do," Massimo suggested.

"Then what would I do to amuse myself? The only reason I'm invited to such events is because of my friendship with you. That and you know, I'm one of the few warlocks they know. They are very curious about our... wild ways." Dante's dark eyebrows waggled.

"What wild ways?"

Dante grinned. "You should come with me next invitation. The whispers you'll hear are quite entertaining. Did you know there's a rumor going around that you have a secret bride? A fae bride. Now that you've been called out of hiding, everyone will be anxious to see who... or what she is."

Heat spread up Massimo's neck. "A secret fae bride? That's preposterous. Where did they get such an idea?"

Massimo knew the people found him strange, but how could they think he was keeping a bride in his home like some jailer? Did they think him a monster?

Dante waved away his questions. "People will believe anything. I'm sure they will be quite overjoyed to find the rumors are false."

"Why is that?"

His friend laughed, dark eyes twinkling. "My dear, Massimo, don't you know? Your new status has now made you the most appealing, most sought-after bachelor on the market."

"The market?"

Dante nodded, grinning. "Yes. The marriage market."

His words rang in Massimo's ears. *Marriage?* Massimo had been so caught up with the whole count business, he hadn't expected this additional problem. Ill-suited to be count, he was even more so to become somebody's husband. He'd been told so on several occasions.

"Don't fret, my friend. No one is going to force your hand. And if the king should try..." Dante gave him a wicked grin, "just tell him you know a warlock who specializes in the dark arts."

"I thought you were a healer. Don't you make medicinal potions?"

"Potions. Poisons. I can do it all. For the right price, of course." Dante folded his arms across his chest and smiled.

Massimo glanced at the sunlight streaming in and sighed. "I suppose we should break for lunch. Then I can send a reply to the king. You'll stay for lunch, won't you?"

Dante grinned. "Of course. What are we having?"

"I'll go check with the cook," Massimo said as he rose to leave.

Massimo left the library and paused in the hall. His conversation with Dante replayed in his mind. *A change of scenery.*

Yes, but that wouldn't be the only thing changing. All the responsibilities that came along with becoming count already felt numerous and heavy.

The voices of the servant girls downstairs pulled him out of his thoughts. Had he already missed lunch hour? No one had come and told him. Silly as it was, he would forget to eat if it weren't for the reminder.

He could spend hours in the library. The giant portrait in the hall caught his eye, making him pause once more. It was an oil painting of him and Mama when he was young.

Her warm amber eyes he'd inherited held him captive.

It's time for something new, amore. It's time to move on. She seemed to be saying.

How a painting could say anything, Massimo didn't know, but he knew, without a doubt, that she was right. It was time. Maybe Dante was right, too. Maybe this was his second chance.

Chapter 3

Zamerra

T he town wasn't far from their villa but navigating the
mountainous path with a heavy cart and old horse
made for a slow journey. Fabrizio liked to take his
time and snack on the tall purple flowers that grew wild along
the dirt road.

Zamerra was a beautiful place. Nestled in the valley
surrounded by forested mountains and the river, it was also a
quiet town. There was only one road in and out, and most of the
townsfolk never left.

There had been no newcomers since Gloria Silveri came
with her brood of girls and their peculiar abilities. Alessia
remembered that day well. They had traveled and lived in
many places before arriving in Zamerra.

To her, it had seemed a haven from the chaos of the outside
world. Mama declared it home, and that was that. There were
many questions in the beginning. To this day, no one quite
knew how the Silveri family inherited the villa just outside of
Zamerra. Even Alessia herself didn't know the whole story of
how they came to be there. Mama liked her secrets.

Pushing the memories away, Alessia glanced at her sister walking beside her. Liliana's face was hard, her expression unreadable to those who didn't know her.

"You're worried about the seeds," Alessia said quietly, not wanting the others to hear.

Liliana's brown eyes met hers. "You're not?"

Alessia shrugged. "There are other things to worry about."

"Such as?"

"Nothing. I shouldn't have said that."

Liliana frowned. "We're keeping secrets now?"

"No. Of course not." Alessia glanced at Pamina, who had slowed down to join them.

"I'll tell you later," she added quickly, pasting a smile on her face.

Pamina joined them, catching a flyaway mahogany curl and tucking it behind her ear. Her light brown eyes lit up. "Do you think we'll make enough to get some fabric? I'd love to make a new dress for Ella. Poor thing is always left with our hand-me-downs."

"What's wrong with hand-me-downs?" Liliana asked.

Pamina shrugged. "Nothing, but it's time she had a new dress. Don't you think, Alessia?"

"We'll see how it goes at market," Alessia replied evenly, not wanting to get anyone's hopes up.

Satisfied, Pamina smiled and fell into step with them. Now, Pamina, she was definitely more fit to be a bride than Alessia. At only twenty years, she was the proper age too. Her honey-colored skin and mahogany curls paired with her easy smile and generous curves drew the men in almost as much as her magical pastries did.

Her bakery items were always the first to go and most readily accepted by the town. After all, who didn't like sugar?

If her mother was so set on making a match, maybe Pamina

would have a chance. Though that idea made Alessia cringe. No matter their circumstances, Mama would never force any of them into a marriage. Where had the idea come from, anyway?

A fit of girlish giggles startled Alessia out of her thoughts. The younger two were walking ahead, snickering and whispering together.

Alessia couldn't help but smile at their excitement. She just hoped they wouldn't be too upset when some of the more cantankerous town folk hurried past or snubbed them. The girls were old enough to understand the reputation the Silveri name held.

"Signor Salvatore! Hello." Serafina's voice cut through the air.

Alessia looked up to see their neighbor walking down the dirt path from his villa. He waved at the sisters and gave them one of his dazzling smiles.

Salvatore Rossi was one of the handsomest men in Zamerra and he and his husband were the closest thing to friends that the sisters had.

"Good morning, signorinas. Lovely day for market, no?" He took a puff on his beautifully carved pipe and gave them a wink.

"You're up early. Where is Signor—" Serafina was cut short as the door to the villa slammed shut.

Adriano Rossi, Salvatore's faun husband, walked stiffly toward them, carrying a rather large tote bag. He stopped at the little gate and smiled at the sisters, tipping his straw hat in greeting.

"Good morning," the sisters returned.

Adriano turned to his husband and sighed. "I suppose there's no talking you out of going now, is there?"

"Not a chance," Salvatore replied cheerfully, motioning for Adriano to lead the way.

"Alright, then," Adriano said, accepting defeat.

They closed their gate behind them and joined the sisters on the dirt road. The sun was still rising, leaving reddish-orange streaks in the sky. Though it was spring, the chill of night clung around them.

"Don't you want to go to market?" Serafina frowned, looking up at the giant faun.

"No."

"No? Why not?"

"I like home. Home is better," he answered, glancing back toward his villa and down at his hooves that peeked out of his woven trousers.

"But you're always home. Don't you get bored there? What do you—"

"Fina," Alessia stopped her before she could keep pestering their poor neighbor.

The girl meant no harm with her questions, but she was getting older now, and she needed to learn some propriety. The Rossis, like the Silveri sisters, lived outside of town for a reason. In their villa, they were free to be together without raised eyebrows or rude whispers about Adriano's furry legs and hooves.

Alessa would have to explain things to Serafina later.

"What are you selling today? Any of that strawberry wine?" Salvatore changed the subject, eyeing their loaded cart hopefully.

"No wine today, I'm afraid, but we'd be happy to make you some as a special order. We could have it ready in time for the Strawberry Festival," Alessia answered.

The men exchanged quiet glances. No doubt, remembering the last time they had bought a bottle from them. Strawberry wine made from the Silveri garden was known for improving stamina and passion.

Salvatore smiled, dark eyes twinkling. "Sign us up for a bottle, please."

Fabrizio brayed loudly, hooves clomping along the dirt road. Serafina laughed and whispered something to Fiorella, whose face turned red with embarrassment.

Alessia gave them a silent warning. Whatever Fabrizio had said was probably not something to repeat. The old horse had a dirty mind, it seemed, and an even dirtier mouth.

Serafina couldn't help but use her magic any better than Fiorella could. As the youngest, they still had a lot of learning to do with Mama, but lately, their mother had grown more and more lax with the girls' training.

Helping them control their magic was another task that Alessia would have to add to her never-ending list. Never mind that she was ill-equip for such a job.

"I don't suppose you have heard the news? About the count?" Salvatore asked, breaking the silence.

Alessia shook her head. "No, what is the news, signor?"

She gave him a polite smile in encouragement, though secretly, she didn't give a witch's wart about the old count.

"He's dead," Salvatore finished bluntly.

"Oh, my. That's dreadful," Pamina answered right away, frowning.

Guilt flooded Alessia. How was she supposed to know that he'd gone and died?

"Yes, how awful. We hadn't heard," she said.

"Who's going to be the new count, then?" Liliana asked, seemingly unmoved by the news.

Salvatore stopped to smoke his pipe before answering with a shrug. "That's the big question. Nobody knows. Apparently, the next in line is also dead. Some foolish duel or something."

"Oh, Santos," Pamina clucked, shaking her head in pity.

Alessia didn't hear the others' responses. Though her heart went out to the count's family and loved ones, she had many more pressing matters to worry about than who was next in line to be count.

"Look!" Serafina called out excitedly, racing ahead.

Alessia didn't need to look to know what her sister had seen. The dread unfurling in her stomach was clue enough. They'd made it to town.

Fiorella ran to catch up with Serafina, her faded green sundress billowing out as she did. She clapped her hands excitedly as they stood at the top of the hill, looking down at Zamerra.

Early morning sunlight streamed into the valley, casting a golden glow on the stone and brick villas and streets. Water gushed from the giant stone fountain in the middle of the town. The noise was muffled by the loud voices and clamor of the townspeople.

Men and women moved along the plaza, children darting between them as they set up for market. The sweet smell of freshly baked breads and brewed caffé drifted toward them, followed by the sharp smell of garlic.

Serafina and Fiorella raced down the hill with delighted squeals.

"Wait!" Alessia called after them, a hand on the wagon to help Fabrizio.

Liliana grabbed the other side of the cart and met Alessia's eyes. "You shouldn't have let them come."

Alessia scoffed. "Let's just make it through today."

To her relief, Serafina and Fiorella stood waiting for them at the bottom of the hill. Fabrizio halted suddenly, making the cart jerk. He turned his head toward the young girls and bent to nibble some of the tall grass beside the road.

"Come on," Alessia gently nudged him forward.

He spit the grass onto her boots and snorted loudly before moving.

Salvatore laughed. "Your horse is quite the character."

"Yes. Quite," Alessia agreed, glaring at Fabrizio.

The horse paid her no mind as he continued down the dirt road. Alessia followed, doing another headcount of their inventory. She'd already counted and calculated everything, but performing the task helped keep the anxiety at bay. If her head was filled with numbers, it couldn't be filled with worries, right?

"Just once around the plaza. That's what we agreed." Adriano's deep voice startled Alessia out of her thoughts.

She turned to see the giant faun staring miserably at the town. His fingers were curled into fists and his mouth set in a grim line. He looked even less thrilled than she was about going into Zamerra.

Salvatore pulled the pipe out of his mouth. "Yes, *amore mio*. It's not a sin, you know, to let yourself enjoy these things."

Adriano gave him a flat look and kept walking.

The dirt road ended at the edge of town. A dry patch of grass and weeds stood between them and the bright cobblestones. As soon as Fabrizio's hooves clomped against the stones, Alessia braced herself for the coming reception.

Heads swiveled toward them, eyes wide with curiosity. Adriano's hooves echoed Fabrizio's as they moved toward the fountain.

"Good morning!" one of the friendlier folks called out to them.

"Morning," Alessia returned with a polite smile. The signors and her sisters murmured their own greetings.

They made it to their usual spot behind the fountain and parted ways with Salvatore and Adriano. Alessia turned her attention to the cart and motioned for Liliana to help. Together with the help of the younger girls, they unloaded all the crates and set them along the cobblestone.

"There you go!" Serafina said as she and Pamina unhooked the cart from Fabrizio.

The old horse whinnied and slowly started trotting back to the grass. Setting out the last of the woven blankets for herself to sit on, Alessia scanned the plaza.

Vendors were spreading out their goods. Mothers were holding back their children, telling them to wait. Several of the storekeepers were clustered together, smoking on pipes and waiting for things to begin.

"Look how big their tomatoes are!" a woman exclaimed, steering her partner toward them.

Her eyes snapped to Alessia. "And zucchini? They're not even in season yet. What is your secret?"

The man with her snickered. "I think you know."

He picked up a zucchini and held it up for inspection before giving the woman a pointed look and mouthing 'magic' to her.

Pamina stepped forward with a smile. "Would you like to buy some? They're perfect for any dish. I have some recipes if you'd like to—"

"No. Come on, Arturo," the woman cut her off, lip curling as she pulled her partner away.

He tossed the vegetable back into the crate carelessly, leering at Pamina as he was dragged away. Alessia stepped in front of her sister, blocking his view with a glare.

"All of this from your garden, huh?" Another woman stopped to look over their crates.

"Yes, Signora Antole. Would you like to sample a cherry?" Pamina offered with a pretty smile.

The older woman leaned heavily on her cane and studied her. "Is it just you girls today? I hope your Mama is well."

She turned her gray head toward Alessia and clucked her tongue. "Such beautiful girls. It's a wonder none of you are married yet," her eyes drifted to Liliana, "especially at your ages. But I suppose it must be difficult given your... unique circumstance. Surely there must be someone who would be willing to overlook your patronage. As pretty as you are."

Alessia cleared her throat. "Yes, well—"

"You look two look just like your Mama. Beautiful woman." She turned her attention to Pamina and the younger girls. "Of course, you are all beautiful. You must take after your fathers, I imagine. Pity none of you know your father. Why—"

"Excuse me, signora, but did you want to sample anything?" Alessia interrupted with a tight smile.

The older woman frowned. "No, no, dear. I'm just looking."

Serafina opened her mouth to say something, but Alessia shot her a warning look. As much as she wanted the old busybody to leave, they needed any sale they could get.

"What about a tart? I baked these fresh for market yesterday," Pamina said, holding out a tray of pastry samples.

"Oh, no. I shouldn't. I suppose one won't hurt, though. Thank you," Signora Antole said as she took one of the tarts and hobbled away.

"Good riddance," Serafina muttered under her breath.

Before Alessia could chide her, more people walked up to take a look at their items. Pamina took the lead, greeting them cheerfully. The townsfolk were starting to line up to have a look at the Silveris and their goods.

Alessia watched as Pamina and Serafina went to work, chatting up the customers amicably. Even shy Fiorella was doing her best to engage the curious onlookers. Liliana stood watching as well, her arms folded over her chest and eyes narrowed on the young men buzzing around her sisters.

Alessia caught her eye. A silent understanding passed between them. Between the two of them, they'd look out for the others. Without Alessia there, the task would be too much for Liliana alone. Another reason Mama's idea was ridiculous. Her sisters needed her.

Chapter 4

The Palazzo

The day of departure had arrived, and Massimo learned very quickly that cats and carriages were not a good mix. Even with Massimo's gentle assurance and her favorite sardine snacks, poor Lucia went into full panic and clawed the fancy cushions and curtains to shreds.

If the coachman had heard the yowls and chaos coming from within the carriage, he didn't say. Though he gave Massimo a startled look when he opened the door for him. Massimo thanked the man and held the trembling Lucia tightly against his chest as he stepped out.

Sweat coated his forehead, his hair had fallen loose from its tie, and his traveling suit was a rumpled mess covered with cat fur. Surely, the royal court wouldn't find his pointed ears any more scandalous than his disheveled appearance.

"Hello," Massimo said, greeting one of the men who came toward him.

He started to reach out his hand to greet the man properly but remembered Lucia was occupying it at the moment. As he pondered the best way to switch her to the other side, the man walked past, eyeing him curiously.

Three other men joined him, unloading Massimo's trunks from the carriage. They nodded when Massimo thanked them but remained silent.

Massimo turned away from them and marveled at the towering castle before him. White stone stuck out starkly against the blue sky. Palazzo delle Stelle was only one of the king's many dwellings, and it was one of the smaller ones, too. *What a life.* Massimo couldn't imagine such a lifestyle. How did one find the time to enjoy all that they had when they had so much?

"I wonder how big *his* library is," Massimo muttered aloud.

One of the men snorted beside Massimo, startling him. He made a note to check himself before speaking his thoughts aloud. It wouldn't do to offend the royal court on his first day.

"Ah. Signor Gallo, welcome," a deep baritone voice called from the other side of the courtyard.

The voice was attached to an older man dressed in a similar uniform to the men who were carrying his luggage.

"Thank you, Signor..." Massimo replied to the greeting, waiting as the man took in his appearance.

Apart from a slight twitch, the older man showed no reaction to his messy appearance or Lucia's unexpected presence.

"Excuse me, Signor Gallo. I am Signor Santino and I'll be your valletto," he paused and swept a hand over the retreating carriage, "unless you've brought your own manservant?"

Massimo shook his head. "No. I don't have a valletto."

Santino's arched eyebrow and the surprised looks exchanged by the other men were acute reminders of Massimo's impropriety. His status and position came with many traditions and customs he found silly and tedious. He'd spent so much time to himself that he'd forgotten about the formalities of the outside world. Would he be able to get away with such independence as a count?

Massimo was beginning to worry that the answer was no. But there was still a chance that this whole thing was a mistake and someone else would be brought in to take up the reins, freeing him to return to his comfortable life.

"Very good, signor. The king is expecting you, but first, shall we get you"—Santino's eyes skirted Massimo's clothes and snagged on Lucia—"and your... cat settled?"

"Yes, thank you," Massimo answered with a nod. He stroked the cat's head reassuringly as he followed the older man toward the wide castle doors.

He glanced at the servants carrying his trunks and hoped for their sakes that whichever room they had readied for him wasn't too far off. What if there were stairs involved?

"Once you've freshened up, I'll escort you to the king's council chambers."

Massimo was startled at the man's words. *The king's council chambers?* Why did it sound so ominous? Foolishly, Massimo had been hoping to have some time to explore the palazzo before having to report to the king.

Find that massive library he'd been dreaming about. *Oh, well.*

All thoughts of the king's bookshelves vanished as they entered the castle. Massimo's head spun, trying to take it all in. True to its name, the palazzo's décor was made up mostly of stars. Tapestries of starry skies and large, dark blue banners with silver studs in the shape of constellations covered the stone walls. Marble statues of centaurs, fauns, and fae lined the long hallway as they went.

Santino and the other men slowed to allow Massimo a better look at it all. Remembering the heavy books packed away in the trunks the poor men were carrying, Massimo hurried on his way.

"Here we are, Signor Gallo," Santino announced with a slight bow.

He opened the door with a large brass key and held out the key to Massimo. Massimo shifted Lucia to his side and took it with a nod of thanks.

Santino nodded in turn and motioned for the men to bring the trunks in. Massimo moved out of their way and thanked them again before they left.

He glanced around the fancy furnished room and worried how Lucia would do left alone in an unfamiliar place. There were far too many priceless looking cushions for her to shred. There was also the matter of the carriage, which he would have to explain and apologize for once he met with the king.

"Should you need me, signor, I'll be right out here."

Massimo turned to Santino. "Yes. Thank you."

The door closed behind the valletto, leaving Massimo and Lucia alone in the suite. It was much fancier than his rooms at home, and though there was much to admire, Massimo couldn't help but feel overwhelmed by it.

"Now, please behave yourself, Lucia," he said, setting the cat down.

She sat for a moment in the middle of the room and stared hard at him. Massimo watched her carefully, wishing he could read her mind. Though the quick turn of her head and haughty meow she leveled at him gave the impression that she was warning him as well.

Put me in a carriage again and watch what happens, she seemed to be saying.

Not wanting to keep his royal highness waiting, Massimo went straight to his trunk to retrieve a change of clothes. Should he go with the muted trousers and crisp shirt, or would the king prefer something more colorful? He sighed. Choosing an outfit fit to be seen by the king was going to be the least of his worries.

King Carlo D'Avalos was much more jovial in person than he appeared on the various posters and cards Massimo had seen. He was also, it turned out, a man of cats as well and was delighted to meet Lucia. Perhaps even more delighted to see her than her fae master.

Lucia, in turn, showed as much enthusiasm at meeting royalty as she did watching raindrops. A mild curiosity at first, but then boredom as she realized he had nothing of interest to offer her.

Massimo sat, back straight, in the stiff chair in the king's council chamber. There were other officials of the court seated at the table, watching their exchange in haughty silence. Santino watched from his post by the door and waited patiently. Massimo knew the valletto couldn't join them, but he felt bad making the poor man stand for so long. Would they allow him a chair at least?

"How much time will you need to get your affairs in order?" King D'Avalos's question interrupted Massimo's thoughts.

"My affairs, Your Highness?"

Lucia, now nestled back in his lap, stared blankly up at Massimo and purred unhelpfully.

The king nodded. "Yes. I imagine you'll need some time to sort out your estate and staff. Draw up a new will."

"You'll want to come out and assess your new estate as well. And the lands that accompany it," another council member added.

Everyone looked to Massimo. Heat flooded his face as it occurred to him that by accepting this title of count, he would have to move. What would the new place be like? Would it have a room fit for a library where he could sit by the window and drink his caffé as he liked to do?

Not only would he be inheriting a new estate, but land as well. *Land*. With towns and villages and no doubt people. People he would be responsible for. The thought of strangers relying on him for anything made him want to tuck Lucia into his arm and bolt out of the room.

Why did he think coming there would be a grand idea? Returning home to his quiet life and his books sounded much more appealing. Less stuffy and... *less 'peopley'*, that was for sure.

"Count Gallo?" one of the men, one of the younger ones, asked, pulling him out of his thoughts.

Another man, older, snorted. "He isn't count, yet. Let's not rush things."

Massimo found himself nodding and agreeing with the man. Surely, they would realize this was a big mistake. He thought his mere appearance would be enough to disqualify him, but he hadn't expected everyone to welcome him so openly and warmly.

Was having fae blood in fashion these days?

Realizing everyone was still waiting for his reply, he cleared his throat and tried to sound like he knew what he was talking about. "Of course. I should return home and organize my affairs. And I quite understand, should someone else step up to accept this inheritance... I never expected it would be me. Not that I'm not just as capable as the next fellow, but I'm certain Your Highness could find someone better suited. Oh, but I wouldn't want you to think I'm ungrateful for the opportunity or worse, that I would question your sovereignty and..."

The quick swipe of Lucia's paw against his lap cut Massimo off. He glanced down at her gratefully. He'd been rambling again.

The men stared at him, dumbfounded. Well, he hadn't intentionally meant to sound like a blabbering fool, but perhaps it would be in his favor. There could be no question now that they had the wrong man for the job.

"Yes, of course. Take as much time as you need, but not too long. There is much to be done," King Carlo said, seemingly unfazed by Massimo's ineptitude.

He took a long drink from his mug, filling the awkward silence with loud guzzling. Dante's words replayed in Massimo's mind. *I could poison the king's cup.*

Massimo pushed the memory away, annoyed with his brain for bringing it back up. What he needed his mind to do was figure out a way out of this situation. One that wouldn't anger or offend the king.

How did one tell a royal *thank you, but no?*

"I suppose the next order of business would be to publicly announce... the count?" another man spoke up.

The others murmured their agreement. Massimo shifted uncomfortably in his seat but couldn't find a good reason to reject the inheritance. Not one that would satisfy the king and the others, at least.

Everyone fell quiet once more, their eyes studying Massimo. Could they tell he wanted to run from the room? He stroked Lucia's fur, swallowing down his anxiety. Sitting in the council chambers with the few advisors was hard enough for him; how could he face the public?

A new fear gripped him. What if they asked him to give a speech? It wasn't that he was afraid to talk. No, what Massimo feared most was that he wouldn't know how to stop talking. He would make a fool of himself. Though he didn't usually spend much time worrying about what others thought of him, he didn't like the idea that they would find him an idiot.

Count Gallo. The blabbering fae.

Massimo forced his face into a polite smile and nodded in acknowledgment to the king. Though he had missed the last thing the man had said. He glanced at Santino and the door, ready to be done with the whole affair.

"So, you are wed then?" One of the councilmen frowned.

Massimo startled, jostling Lucia, who promptly glared at him.

The man's words snapped him back to attention. Marriage? Was that what the conversation had turned to when he wasn't listening?

"Married? Me? Oh, no. I apologize. I misheard. No, I'm not wed."

Surprise and confusion flickered on everyone's faces. Only the king seemed unbothered by Massimo's statement.

He waved his large hand in the air as if swatting away his words. "No matter. You have the year to reconcile that as well."

"A year!?" Massimo's voice heightened.

Surely not. How was he supposed to find someone to marry within the year? He looked down at his cat, who stared up at him with a look of boredom.

"Sometimes I wish I were a cat." The words left him before he could stop them.

Everyone gaped at him. The king chortled and raised his mug at him in agreement.

"Your Highness, should we show the patrizios in now?" one of the king's servants asked.

"Yes. Yes. Bring them in," King Carlos said with a mouthful of grapes.

Massimo watched as the doors opened and ten finely dressed men strode in. Voices clamored together as everyone greeted him at once. The sound echoed in the long room. Massimo nodded and responded to every greeting as politely as he could. Servants milled about, offering caffé and light sandwiches for the guests.

"Pardon me, Count Gallo, I'm Patrizio Foncello. Do you like strawberries?" a large fellow to his right asked.

Massimo turned his attention to him. "Strawberries? I suppose I like them as well as any other fruit. Though they do leave a bitter taste when they're too tart."

A look of uncertainty flashed across the man's face, but he pushed on. "Oh, well, then I'm sure you'd love the Zamerra Strawberry Festival. We have much to offer besides strawberries as well. There is dancing and music. Pie-eating contests, goat wrangling, treasure hunting, and so much more."

"Sounds... eventful. I'm sure it will be a splendid event," Massimo replied evenly. What in the fae was goat wrangling? It didn't sound like something he'd enjoy.

The man grinned. "Yes. Yes. You must come!"

"Oh, no... I..." Massimo let the words die on his lips. Was this the sort of thing expected of him now as count?

"Oh, but you must! My wife, the patrizia, will be so thrilled. The whole town will be."

"That sounds... lovely," Massimo forced out.

Patrizio Foncello was practically glowing. How could he say no now? The others watched with a mixture of surprise, jealousy, and calculation. Massimo groaned inwardly. What had he agreed to?

Chapter 5

Mama's Vision

"Why didn't they want my seeds?" Fiorella asked as they started up the mountain home.

"Do you think I should have labeled them? Maybe I should have painted a picture on the outside?" she continued, frowning.

Serafina gave her a sympathetic look. "It's fine, Ella. We can sell them at the Strawberry Festival."

"Yes. Of course." Pamina nodded encouragingly and handed the youngest Silveri one of the sugary candies they'd exchanged some of her tarts for.

Alessia shared a look with Pamina. Poor Fiorella. It wasn't her fault she couldn't control her magic. Plant and earth magic were some of the hardest crafts to master. It would be years before their sister could harness it well enough to grow something without unknowingly altering it.

"Pamina is right, Ella. We can try again next time. Signor Fratelli did say once he had more room on his shelves, he'd be interested in buying them to sell in his store," Alessia added.

Liliana scoffed. "We shouldn't have traded with him. We

could have gotten full price for our goods if you had just given it more time."

Alessia took a calming breath and turned to her sister. "We needed supplies, Liliana. No one was interested in buying today. Not with this business about the count."

"And what are we going to do about the roof, then? Do you—"

"It's fine, Liliana," Alessia cut her off, growing impatient.

Liliana grunted and shook her head. Alessia could practically feel the judgment radiating from her.

"Maybe Bruno can help us fix the roof again," Fiorella suggested.

"Yes. Maybe," Alessia said.

"Ha! Bruno doesn't know a hammer from a nail. Look what a shoddy job he did last time," Liliana argued.

"That's because you upset him. You wouldn't let him help you mix up your poison, so he was sulking," Serafina cut in.

"Potions," Liliana corrected, "and if I let him help, he'd throw in who knows what and poison the whole town."

"You would probably like that, you cranky—"

"Enough!" Alessia cut Serafina off. Her voice echoed around them. A bird squawked above them, flying toward the trees in the distance. Even Fabrizio paused to give Alessia a surprised look.

Serafina snickered at the bird's call but wisely kept her mouth shut. The sun was setting behind them, streaking the sky with orange and red and the air was growing cooler.

"I'll take care of the roof. There's no need to argue," Alessa said softly, giving Liliana a pleading look.

They walked the rest of the way in silence, Alessia lost in her thoughts. They'd made so little at the market. How were they going to make it to the Strawberry Festival?

A distinct whistling sound came from the trees ahead as the

branches stretched toward them. This was one of the peculiar effects Fiorella seemed to have on the flora. Plants became more active and more alive in her presence.

The Silveri villa came into view, nestled in the forested mountains. Despite their constant tending, the garden and surrounding wood grew wild and nearly devoured their home entirely.

"I'll get the gate," Fiorella offered, rushing ahead of them.

The wood creaked as she opened the ivy-covered gate and Fabrizio led the way in. Alessia waited for her sisters before bringing up the rear and closing the gate behind her.

A cacophony of meows and sharp yapping greeted them. The dozen outdoor cats that had claimed the yard as their home came over to welcome them, along with little Gio, the tiny scrappy dog that they'd adopted into their gang.

Serafina bent to pet them all, greeting them each by name as they rushed her. Fabrizio stomped his hooves, making them scatter out of the path.

Welcome home. Their villa seemed to call out. Alessia looked up at its ivy-covered tan stone face. It was nice to be back home.

Her sisters never seemed to hear the villa, but they were always polite enough not to mock or argue with her supposed theory. Perhaps because they felt sorry for Alessia. She was the oldest, after all, but born with no magic.

Pushing away the thoughts, Alessia turned to the others. "Let's get the wagon unloaded and everything put away."

Birds flew from tree to tree, chirping noisily. Serafina stopped to give them a friendly wave before unhooking Fabrizio and leading him to the stables. Pamina started humming and by the time they finished bringing everything inside that needed to be brought in, they were all singing the same song. Even Liliana was humming along.

Serafina finished the last lines, her face mockingly serious and voice shockingly deep, imitating the man's part. Fiorella and Pamina laughed at her theatrics. Liliana snorted. Alessia smiled, a twisting pain in her heart. Even with all their fighting, she couldn't imagine being away from her sisters. This was where she belonged.

Alessia glanced back at their wild-looking yard and gardens as she followed the others into the kitchen. The smell of garlic and candles enveloped them as they walked in.

Mama was at the table, waiting for them. Candles already lit. "How was the market?" she asked, her voice calm.

Alessia could tell she was probing. *Waiting.* Her sisters exchanged glances and looked at her. They were waiting for her, too.

Mama's dark eyes sought Alessia's. Her bushy brows knitted together, and her lips pursed.

She knew. Somehow, she knew Alessia hadn't seen the matchmaker. Of course, she would know right away. Alessia squared her shoulders back and prepared for the scolding that was sure to come later.

"It was fine. We sold and traded almost everything we brought. We got most of the supplies we needed, too," Alessia said.

"Are you feeling better?" Fiorella asked, walking toward their mother.

"Much better, thank you," Mama said.

"No one bought my seeds, Mama," Fiorella said with a sad little sigh.

Mama spread her arms wide, embracing her youngest in a tight hug. "Don't fret, *amore*. We can sell them at the festival."

"Ooh, and there's going to be a new count, Mama! Old Domenico died," Serafina said excitedly.

Their mother smiled, her dark eyes twinkling with amusement. "A new count?"

Alessia washed her hands at the sink as her sisters told their mother about the day. Pamina stood to help her prepare supper. They could use some of the turning vegetables the storekeeper hadn't wanted. Pasta would be quick and filling.

"Alessia, come with me, please." Mama's voice interrupted her thoughts.

Alessia turned and followed her mother out of the kitchen. Her heart hammered loudly in her ears. Liliana met her eyes as she left, a questioning look on her face. Alessia could only shake her head. She'd have to tell her sister later.

Mama led Alessia outside and started walking toward their garden. Her long, white dress trailed along the vibrant green grass. She paused and looked back, waiting for Alessia to catch up with her. In the glow of the setting sun, her mother looked ethereal and much younger than her years.

"You didn't go to see Signora Savelli," Mama stated, her dark eyes searching Alessia's.

Alessia sighed. "No, Mama. There was not enough money even if I wanted to."

"Hmm," Mama replied, scanning their garden, a worried look on her face.

"Mama, things are not that bad to resort to marriage. We'll be okay. What is this all about?" Alessia asked.

"Are you happy here, Alessia?"

Mama's question surprised her. Happy? Of course, she was happy.

"Yes! Mama, yes. Of course."

"But is this what you really want? This villa? Forever?"

Alessia glanced back at the stone-faced home.

Is this what you want? It seemed to echo in its sleepy voice.

"Of course. This is our home. I could never leave here. Or leave you or the others."

Mama started walking again, staring silently ahead. Puzzled, Alessia followed her, dread coiling inside her. She didn't like where all these questions were headed. Why, after all this time, was Mama questioning her sincerity?

Of course, she was happy. Of course, she wanted to stay there forever. How could Mama even think otherwise?

Maybe she got overwhelmed sometimes with all the things she had to shoulder, but she would never trade that for some loveless marriage match.

"Come sit with me, amore," Mama patted the open space beside her on the wooden bench.

A similar image of a different time flashed in Alessia's mind. The last time Mama had asked her to sit with her on that same bench was when she had told Alessia they were staying there permanently. That Zamerra would be their home.

Fighting the panic trying to claw itself out, Alessia took a seat beside her mother and waited. She glanced at the bell-shaped flowers near the gate in the distance. They were a magical flower, Fiorella had accidentally grown that could produce sound, repeating whatever they heard. They'd brought one of the flowers inside so they could hear if any intruders came into their yard at night.

Hopefully, Alessia was sitting far enough away that the flowers wouldn't be able to pick up their conversation. The last thing she needed was for all her sisters to know her business.

Mama turned to her, her face so serious. "I had a vision."

A million thoughts raced through Alessia's mind. A vision? Mama hadn't had a vision in so long. Was that why her headaches had worsened lately?

The birds, oblivious to the crisis below, chirped happily

with each other as they soared back and forth from the woods to the open sky.

"A vision?" Alessia prompted, hoping her mother would just come out and tell her.

Her silence was beginning to scare her. What had she seen that she didn't want to tell her oldest daughter?

"Yes. As you know, visions are... tricky. They don't always show what will be. Only what *could* be."

Alessia fought back the wave of frustration. "Yes, I know. Mama, what did you see?"

Mama smiled. "It was a vision of your wedding day, Alessia." She paused, eyes watching Alessia's reaction carefully.

Alessia felt her mouth drop open. Of all the things she'd been expecting to hear... a vision of her wedding day was not one of them. There were so many more questions Alessia wanted to ask; she didn't know where to begin. When? Where? Who?

"Are you sure it was... me? Not Liliana?" Alessia asked instead.

Mama gave her a flat look. "You think I would mix up my own daughters?"

She took Alessia's hands in hers and squeezed gently. "You were so happy, amore. So beautiful."

Alessia's face warmed at her mother's words. "But... I'm happy now, Mama. I don't... I don't want to be married."

Letting go of her hands, Mama brushed a curl out of Alessia's face and nodded. "Are those your words or mine?"

"What?"

Mama sighed. "Sometimes I wonder if I've dissuaded you all from finding your own happiness with my... life choices. Listen"—her face grew serious—"I'm happy with my choices. I wouldn't change them for anything, but you girls. You were so young when we came here. This home is all you've known. As much as I love having you all with me, I would never ask you to sacrifice your own dreams for mine."

Her words struck Alessia hard. She felt as if the ground was being ripped from beneath her. Her head spun.

Sensing her panic, Mama wrapped an arm around her and held her close. "Alessia, you look like death. I'm not sending you away, amore. I know you don't like change, but I think you've sensed it coming. Haven't you? Is this what scares you?"

Alessia sank into her mother's embrace, a lump growing in her throat and her eyes growing hot. Mama was right. She didn't like change. Why did things have to change? Things were good as they were. She had the villa, her family, and their work. She was happy.

"Don't you want to know who he is?" Mama's question startled her.

Alessia sat up and met her gaze. "No. Like you said, the visions aren't always true. Maybe you saw something that could have been, but it's gone now. It's too late for that."

Mama frowned. "It's never too late for love, Alessia."

Swiping at her eyes, Alessia took a deep breath and forced a smile she hoped was convincing. "I guess we'll just have to wait for the future to play out, then. I should probably get started on supper. The girls will need help."

She started to stand, but Mama grabbed her wrist. "Promise me, you'll keep your heart open to love, Alessia. Sometimes change can be a good thing, yes?"

"Of course, Mama," Alessia replied quickly, unable to meet her mother's gaze.

She didn't want anything to change. Everything was perfect as it was. Though curiosity did tug at her. A vision of her wedding day? She had daydreamed of such a thing when she was Fiorella's age, but she hadn't thought of it since. Not since she'd heard some of the townsfolk discussing her and her sister's scandalous upbringing.

As if reading her thoughts, Mama only smiled and shook her head, giving up on the discussion. Hopefully, that would be the end of it. Alessia's face heated at the thought of going to see Zamerra's matchmaker. She would be better off responding to a call for a mail-order bride than counting on the older woman's help in finding her a compatible match.

Not waiting for Mama to say more, Alessia started walking back to the house. She glanced back to see her mother still sitting on the bench, a far-off look on her face. The words she had spoken replayed in her mind.

Sometimes change can be a good thing.

A shiver ran down Alessia's spine. Dismissing her mother's revelation, she turned her attention back to the tasks at hand. She had more than enough to keep her busy for the following weeks. Maybe if she kept busy, she wouldn't have to worry about Mama's vision.

There certainly wasn't anyone in Zamerra she was interested in binding herself to. The vision was wrong. There would be no wedding day because there would be no groom. She needed to get her mind back on track—think about the things that were in her control.

Supper. She could start with that.

Chapter 6

The Strawberry Festival

Massimo, having learned his lesson on his prior trip, had Dante mix up a special tonic for Lucia for the travel to Zamerra. The gray cat was curled on his lap, yawning sleepily. An improvement from the last carriage ride they'd taken.

The coachman took them as far as he could up the mountainous road before leaving them. Massimo stood beside his trunk, the only one he'd brought this time, and held Lucia. The man had assured him someone was coming with a horse-drawn cart to fetch them, but he hadn't specified when.

"Well, I suppose next time I should pack lighter," Massimo's voice sounded loud in the quiet.

He glanced around, awed by the surrounding mountains and tall, vibrant green grass. Colorful wildflowers blanketed the ground and a clear sky stretched above him. The sun was slowly making its way to its spot. Far off in the distance, trees dotted the landscape. It was all quite a shock compared to the busy city Massimo was used to.

Even the air seemed different. Fuller. Fresher.

Though he wasn't a full-blooded fae, nor had he inherited any remarkable fae abilities (aside from the pointed ears and superior hearing), Massimo couldn't help but feel something stir inside of him at the nature around him.

It was like a painting.

"No. Much better than any painting." Massimo spoke out loud.

Lucia, still feeling the effects of whatever Dante had given her, blinked and looked around, purring with contentment. Massimo hoped it would last for the ride they had left. Who knew how long that would take?

"Should we start walking? Send someone back for the trunk?" Massimo wondered aloud, glancing back at his trunk.

He couldn't imagine anyone would steal it. The place was so abandoned, he couldn't imagine anyone coming along the road at all. Though supposedly, this famous Strawberry Festival attracted people far and wide. At least, that is what Patrizio Foncello had claimed.

Despite his reservations about the whole affair, Massimo was curious to see what awaited him in Zamerra. Maybe if he busied himself with exploring all the towns he'd inherited, he could delay the other responsibilities placed upon him. *Like marrying.*

A year didn't seem nearly enough time to meet someone, court them, and propose marriage. Just thinking about it made him shudder. Massimo wasn't good with words. How could he ever hope to charm someone?

"It would need to be someone who isn't opposed to marrying someone with fae blood. Do you imagine such a person exists?" he questioned, stroking Lucia's head as he pondered.

The sound of a wagon and horse in the distance interrupted his musings. He turned to see a small figure coming his way.

"Well, that's a relief. At least now we won't have to drag that thing up the mountain," Massimo said, nodding toward his trunk.

Lucia, who'd fallen asleep in his arms, didn't respond.

With his free arm, Massimo waved at the approaching cart. It seemed to take forever before it finally reached them. Of course, mountain travel was probably tricky, so he couldn't fault them.

"Whoa," the driver called out, slowing the horse to a stop before Massimo.

A familiar figure hopped down from the driver's bench.

"Count Gallo! Good morning." Patrizio Foncello gave him a quick bow. He motioned for the driver to retrieve Massimo's luggage.

The young man jumped down, eyes widening when he saw Massimo's ears. "You're—"

"How was your travel?" the patrizio interrupted, shooting the boy a dark look, and pushing him toward the trunk.

"It was... long," Massimo answered.

"Yes. Yes." The older man looked around. "Where is your valletto?"

Massimo followed his gaze to the young driver, who was struggling with the trunk.

"Santino? He has taken ill."

The poor man's fever had come on so suddenly and Massimo hadn't bothered to find a replacement on such short notice. He couldn't imagine any of the upper-class valletti would be eager to leave their posts and travel with him to the little mountain town.

"Oh, my apologies, Count. I shall be happy to find a fill-in for you once we get to Zamerra."

Massimo was about to tell him that was unnecessary when the driver's grunt interrupted them. It had taken two men to load the trunk into the carriage and two to unload it on the ground. Massimo doubted the young man, though muscular as he was, would be able to do it alone.

"Here. One moment and I can help you," Massimo said, walking over to the cart to set Lucia in.

"Oh, no, Count Gallo. Please don't trouble yourself." Patrizio Foncello made a waving motion.

He squared his shoulders back, cracked his knuckles, and bent to help the driver with the trunk. Massimo watched, guiltily, as the two men heaved it onto the wagon with some effort.

"Shall we?" Patrizio Foncello motioned for Massimo to board first.

Careful not to jostle his sleeping cat too much, Massimo climbed in and sat on the bench. The other two men joined him, making the wood sink a bit as they did.

With a slap of the reins, they were off. Pain shot up Massimo's backside as the wagon bumped along the mountainous road. He grimaced. Hopefully, they were very close to Zamerra now.

The sun had fully risen, warming the chilly air. Massimo nodded politely as his guide regaled him with the history and lore of the little town and its inhabitants. Even with his expert fae hearing, Massimo had a hard time catching everything over the noisy wagon and his own chattering teeth.

His head was beginning to throb with the constant bumps. It was a testament to Dante's magical abilities that Lucia, luckily for them all, slept through the whole ordeal.

At least the pain spearing through him provided him with a distraction from the anxiety he'd felt before. The people, whether they liked him or not, deserved a proper count. The sooner Massimo made sure everyone was well and happy and cared for, the sooner he could return home to his favorite chair and books.

That thought made him smile.

By the time they drew nearer, the sun had risen, and large, puffy white clouds floated across a clear blue sky. Massimo took in the breathtaking scenery with a sense of wonder.

He'd never been to a place as untouched as Zamerra before. The surrounding forested mountains and meadows were wild. Bright blue water ran from the creek alongside the dirt road, sparkling in the sunlight. Spring flowers bloomed along the path as they grew closer to town.

Voices rose in the distance along with string music.

"Straight to the Blossom Inn, please," Patrizio Foncello said to the driver.

People stopped to stare as they entered the town. Massimo waved to the onlookers, still holding a sleeping Lucia in his lap.

The townspeople cheered and called out to him as they drove along the cobblestoned streets. Vendors lined the streets and people milled about, dressed in their best festival attire. Bright banners with painted strawberries and strawberry blossoms hung from building to building. Red and pink flowers sprouted in planters that hung outside windows and on doorsteps.

People hung out of open windows, waving and yelling. Even more, people streamed out of the clustered stone and brick villas and shops, blocking their path. It wasn't until their patrizio commanded them to return to their business that they thinned out and gave them enough space to drive forward.

A giant fountain stood in the middle of the plaza, a garland of red flowers and ribbon wrapped around the white stone. Vendors crowded around, their wares laid out on colorful woven rugs and crates.

"Watch out!" A voice cut through the air.

Massimo looked up to find a driverless horse racing toward them, dragging a loaded cart behind him.

"Move!" Patrizio Foncello yelled to their driver, grabbing the reins from him. He steered their startled horse out of the other one's path.

"Fabrizio! Stop!" a woman's voice rose out over the clamor.

The horse brayed loudly, drawing more attention. Two young men followed by a group of young women and girls raced after him.

"Fabrizio, halt!" One of the girl's voices rang out through the street.

Something crackled in the air. The hair on Massimo's neck bristled. *Magic.*

The horse stopped so suddenly, the wagon jerked wildly before coming to a stop as well. Crates slid off and fell to the ground. Glass shattered. The sweet smell of strawberry wine filled the air.

Gasps rippled through the crowd of onlookers. People whispered together, pointing and shaking their heads at the spectacle.

The Silveri Sisters are at it again.

They shouldn't be here. Not with the count present. Troublesome witches.

Massimo frowned at their words.

One of the young girls who'd been chasing the horse broke into a sob. She was comforted by one of her sisters as the rest began picking up the broken glass.

"Oh, Santos," Patrizio Foncello muttered with a shake of his head.

"Here. Careful with her," Massimo said, handing the still-sleeping Lucia off to the older man.

He jumped down from the wagon and approached the

young women. Seeing one of them struggle with a crate, he stretched out his arms to help her as she turned toward him.

"Oh!" she exclaimed in surprise.

The crate fell from her grasp and landed inches from his boots. Bottles shattered upon impact, splashing wine on the hem of his trousers.

She stared at the mess with a look of despair that cut right through Massimo. Her dark curls had fallen from her bun, and dirt smeared across her cheek and blue sundress. She was stunning.

"Well, aren't you going to apologize to the count?" a woman demanded.

Massimo frowned at her haughty tone. He opened his mouth to reply, but the young woman met his gaze, and all words fled.

Her eyes landed on his pointed ears. Confusion and surprise flashed across her face before she hurried into a curtsy and motioned for her sisters to follow suit.

Now that everyone could get a good look at him, Massimo braced himself for their outrage. Whispers echoed through the plaza.

Pointed ears!

He's fae. Do you think the king knows?

Of course, he'd know!

"Are you fae?" one of the girls asked bluntly, dark eyes shining with excitement.

Everyone gasped.

Massimo smiled at her. "On my mother's side."

Her smile widened. "Oh! That's excellent. I'm Serafina Silveri. Are—"

"My sincerest apologies, Count. For the wine," her older sister stepped forward, catching his attention. Her dark eyes met his, sending a wave of heat through him.

Massimo's throat went dry. He shrugged off her apology, still at a loss for words. She knew what he was and was accepting him?

"It was his fault," Serafina spoke up again.

She pointed to one of the young men who'd joined in on the chase.

His face reddened. "I'm sorry! I didn't mean to spook him. It was just a wooden snake. Only a prank. I didn't mean to—"

The girl turned her glare on him. "*Asino.*"

"Serafina!" The dark-haired beauty silenced her. She glanced at Massimo, blushing prettily.

Someone gasped. Murmurs of disapproval followed from the crowd. Patrizio Foncello, who was still holding Lucia, looked flustered as he watched the scene unfold.

"Thank you for your help, Angelo," another sister spoke up, smiling sympathetically at the embarrassed boy.

"And what are you going to do about this mess? We can't have broken glass on our streets." The same pesky woman spoke again.

Others murmured in agreement. The whispers Massimo heard made his skin heat. These poor women had lost nearly all their inventory, and the townsfolk were worried about broken bottles?

"Well, I should think that would be simple, signora," Massimo said, his voice silencing the onlookers.

Everyone was watching him. He bent and started picking up the glass, much to everyone's surprise.

"Oh no, Count! You shouldn't be doing that," another woman said with a horrified look.

"Well, you could always help too," Massimo said, continuing to clean.

The townsfolk exchanged glances before, one by one, they

started helping the sisters. Someone brought brooms out, and the job was over quickly.

"Thank you, Count Gallo," the oldest sister said. She gave him an appreciative smile that made Massimo's stomach lurch.

"I'd offer you some wine if it wasn't all pooling at your feet. I can offer you a jar of jam, though. If you like?" she held out one of the unbroken jars.

"Thank you. It's a pity about your wine. I should have liked to... try it," Massimo replied, rubbing the back of his neck awkwardly.

"Yes. Well, we can make more," she replied brightly.

"That would be lovely, Signora..." Massimo winced, realizing he'd already forgotten her name.

"Silveri," she supplied, eyes darting away from Massimo.

The crowd stood around watching the exchange, some staring open-mouthed at Massimo. Others whispered together.

What is she thinking, talking to the new count?

I heard he's single. Looking for a bride.

Well, he wouldn't want her. Someone should tell him about the witches. Scandalous.

Massimo didn't know what kind of scandal the Silveri sisters were involved in, but he couldn't help but grow curious about them and their magic.

"Well, I suppose I should freshen up. I'm sure the innkeeper would allow you and your sisters to freshen up as well, if you'd like to join me?" Massimo asked.

Murmurs of surprise echoed through the crowd.

"Oh. Thank you," she replied, a hand on her fallen curls.

She glanced at the remaining crates of jam and shook her head. "I think we'll manage just fine, but thank you. I hope you enjoy the festival."

Worried, he's said the wrong thing, Massimo cleared his throat. "I didn't mean to offend or suggest... anything... inappropriate. Forgive me, Signora Silveri. I only meant if you needed to... never mind. Enjoy the festival."

He gave her a quick bow and returned to the wagon. Patrizio Foncello handed Lucia back to him and instructed the driver to continue.

"Trust me, Count Gallo. As lovely as they are, I'd stay far away from the Silveri sisters. They are witches, after all," the older man said with a sage look.

Massimo frowned. "I'm part fae. Would you hold that same advice about me?"

Patrizio Foncello's face reddened. "No! Of course not, Count. I only meant that their ways are strange and they're a tight bunch. Anyone who weds Alessia Silveri would be saddled with the rest of them and their mother as well. Lovely women, but... troublesome."

The young driver nodded in agreement. Massimo didn't hear the rest of Foncello's words. *Alessia. Alessia Silveri.* He glanced back for another look at her, but she was swallowed up by the crowd.

Chapter 7

The Festival Disaster

I'm sure the Innkeeper would allow you and your sisters to freshen up as well.

The count's words echoed in Alessia's mind. Heat spread up her neck. She could only imagine what a sight she and her sisters must make, their hair and dresses in disrepair after chasing Fabrizio through the plaza.

Everyone knew proper signoras didn't run.

Serafina had even hiked up her dress to a scandalous height before Liliana yanked it down. Then there was Serafina's choice word. Spoken right in front of the count.

Count Gallo. He was undoubtedly fae. Fae and handsome. The memory of his amber eyes made Alessia flush. She'd never seen such a beautiful man before. Pushing the thought away, she made her way back to their cart.

The rest of the townsfolk had moved on, though some still stayed, watching the Silveris with mixed looks of pity and disapproval.

"What are we going to do now?" Liliana asked Alessia, meeting her gaze. "Only half is salvageable."

"It took forever to get those strawberries ripe enough for the wine," Fiorella said between sniffles. Her eyes were red-rimmed from crying.

"I know. You worked so hard, Ella," Alessia said softly. She glanced at the others. "You all did. It's going to be all right. I'll make it work."

Liliana scoffed. "How?"

"Excuse me," Angelo said hesitantly, still standing behind them.

They all turned to the young Rossi boy. He had the same dark, wavy hair as Salvatore, but unlike his older brother, Angelo had sea-blue eyes.

He smiled uncertainly as he approached, his gaze darting around and landing on Serafina. She glared back, arms folded across her chest.

Fabrizio whinnied at his approach. Sweat shone from his coat, but the wild look in his eye was gone.

"There, there. It's alright, Fabrizio. I won't let him near you." Serafina calmed the trembling horse.

"I wanted to apologize. For my prank. It was childish. I also wanted to make it up to you. Perhaps a trade?" Angelo continued, seemingly unfazed by Serafina's feral look.

Alessia sighed. "That's very kind of you, Angelo, but I'm afraid we don't have much left to trade you."

"My seeds! My seeds are undamaged," Fiorella said with an excited clap. She turned to grab the crate from the cart.

Liliana shook her head at Alessia. She started to speak, but Alessia shot her a look of warning. The last thing they needed was more trouble.

"What will you trade for the seeds?" Pamina asked, breaking the awkward silence.

Angelo glanced at his older brother, Rafaelo, who'd hung

back after the chase, and back to Alessia. "We could trade one of our stallions. Your horse is aging and—"

"Absolutely not!" Serafina interjected.

Fabrizio snorted in agreement.

"Now, now. What's all the fuss about, Angelo?" Salvatore cut in.

Alessia turned to find their neighbors walking toward them, ignoring the onlookers. With the shock of the new fae count, Adriano, and the Silveri sisters, the town was a buzz with whispers and gossip.

"He scared Fabrizio and made us lose all our wine," Serafina supplied eagerly.

Angelo scowled at her.

Salvatore glanced at the spilled wine on the street and looked at Alessia in alarm. "All of the wine?"

Pamina rushed forward with a bottle. "We still have this one," she offered with a smile.

Salvatore took it with a relieved sigh. "What would be a fair trade then for all this?" he asked, turning to Alessia.

"We can trade two of our goats," Angelo said.

Rafaelo shook his head. "Mama wouldn't approve of that trade. You know she loves those goats."

Serafina's head snapped toward him. "And why wouldn't she approve?"

"Fina," Alessia warned.

It was no secret that Signora Rossi didn't like the Silveri girls. She'd been the one to get Serafina expelled from school after the snake incident.

"My mother doesn't approve of many things. I'm afraid that list is endless," Salvatore said with a frown.

Adriano gave him a sympathetic smile.

"Well, I can pay outright with the little coin I have, but it's not much," Angelo said, steering the conversation back to the trade.

"We can throw in a little coin as well," Salvatore added.

Adriano nodded.

"Oh, thank you, but we couldn't..." Alessia let the words die.

They needed this sale.

"Thank you," she said instead and motioned for Fiorella to hand them the crate of seeds.

"On a happier note, Adriano and I would like to invite you and Signora Silveri for dinner tomorrow. We're going to invite the new count as well. Mama can't turn down the invitation if he comes, can she?" Salvatore turned to Rafaelo and Angelo.

"She could if she finds out he's... you know," Angelo said, glancing around at the plaza.

"What? Fae? Do you have something against our new count, Angelo?" Serafina was quick to demand.

Angelo's eyes widened. "No! Of course not. It's just my mother. You know how she is."

Serafina grunted. "Oh, I do. She's—"

"Fina, why don't you help Pamina? Please," Alessia said, nodding toward their sister, who was talking to an older couple who'd walked up.

"Well, I don't suppose there's a chance of getting another bottle anytime soon, is there?" Salvatore asked, handing the wine to Adriano.

"I heard Signora Molina was making strawberry wine this year. You could try there," Alessia said.

Serafina scoffed over her shoulder. "That old crow doesn't know how to make strawberry wine."

Alessia threw her a warning look. "Mind your tongue. I don't want any more trouble today."

"We'd rather wait for your wine, anyway," Salvatore said.

"And you will come to dinner, won't you? And your Mama? Is she well?" Salvatore asked as he handed Alessia a small bag full of coin.

"She's been having headaches again, so I'm not sure if she'll be up for it, but we'll be there," Alessia replied.

With a final nod and hugs for their younger brothers and brothers-in-law, Adriano and Salvatore said goodbye. Angelo gave Alessia his own small bag of coin and took the crate of seeds from Fiorella.

"We should get back to our goats and Marco. Enjoy the festival!" Angelo said, nodding for Rafaelo to lead the way. He glanced back, his blue-green eyes tracking Serafina as she busied herself with the jam, her back to them.

The young men disappeared into the growing crowd and music started up again, drowning out the clamor and voices around them.

"Can you believe it?" A shrill voice caught Alessia's ears.

She turned to see a couple in conversation by the fountain.

"He has the pointed ears!" The woman's voice carried over the water and the music.

Murmurs followed the lady's loud announcement. Seeing she'd drawn the attention of the crowd, she straightened her shoulders and nodded. "The count! The new count is fae," she finished dramatically.

Alessia fought the urge to roll her eyes at the hysteria. Having fae blood wasn't that uncommon. What was the woman getting so worked up about?

"Excuse me, signorinas, I'm afraid I'll have to ask you to move. You're blocking the street," another woman said, startling Alessia.

Signora Savelli, the old matchmaker, standing beside her, frowned. "Yes, and I should think your poor mother would be beside herself if she'd seen that wretched display of wantonness."

Her friend gave Alessia a pitying look. "Do you really think to snare yourself a count, dearie?"

Their words rang in Alessia's ears, making her flush. Everyone was listening now.

"My sister could snare anyone she wanted, you old toad!" Serafina rushed to her defense.

The women gasped, shaking their heads, and shooting Alessia reproachful looks.

"Stop it," Alessia commanded, whipping toward Serafina.

Fabrizio stomped his hooves, and the street cats had begun to gather, lured by Serafina's presence and riled up by her anger. The flowers and plants that dotted the buildings shook and trembled along.

Alessia grabbed Fiorella and Serafina's hands, squeezing them tight. Pamina and Liliana stood protectively beside them.

"I assure you, signoras, I have no designs on anyone. Least of all our new count. We will move our wagon now. Thank you." Alessia spoke the words loudly, her words echoing in the plaza.

With as much dignity as she could muster, she turned and led her sisters toward Fabrizio.

"Where are we going to go, Alessia?" Fiorella asked.

"Everyone took all the good spots," Serafina grumbled over the noise.

Alessia bit her lip, scanning the busy plaza. Where, indeed?

"There's a spot over there!" Pamina suggested, pointing to an empty corner on the opposite side of the plaza.

Liliana frowned. "No one ever goes that way."

"They will once we're set up. No one else can make strawberry jam like we do," Alessia answered brightly.

She glanced at the spilled wine and tried not to let it ruin their day. They deserved to enjoy the festival after all the work they'd done. She could worry about the loss later.

Letting go of her sister's hands, Alessia gave Fabrizio a gentle nudge. The horse snorted as he trudged toward the spot, casting a baleful look her way.

They made it to the corner without further incident and busied themselves setting up for customers. This time, Alessia tied up Fabrizio so he couldn't wander off. The old horse stomped angrily at this but was quickly placated by Serafina.

Thankfully, the cats stayed away as they set out their remaining jam. Though an alarming thought filled her.

"Serafina, where did all the cats go? You didn't use your magic, did you?" Alessia asked quietly.

Serafina frowned. "No, but I can."

"Don't," Liliana warned.

Serafina scowled.

"What does wanton mean?" Fiorella asked before the two could start fighting.

Alessia shared a look with Liliana and sighed. "Nothing. Don't pay any attention to them, Ella."

"Caffé?" Pamina asked, holding the steaming carafe aloft.

Murmurs of approval rippled through them as Alessia handed each a mug. When it was her turn, she breathed in the rich aroma and sighed. How could she ever live without Pamina's special brew?

Feeling much better after a few sips, Alessia turned to Liliana. "We'll have to make more wine to fulfill the orders we had."

Liliana shook her head. "That will take a while. We used all the strawberries for this batch."

A dull ache was beginning to spread in Alessia's head. What was she supposed to tell their customers?

"We have to make more, though. The count said he wanted some," Serafina said.

Alessia's stomach fluttered at the mention of the handsome count. His face flashed in her mind.

Oh, no, you don't. Enough of that.

This was not the time for such thoughts. It was time to put her mind to good use and come up with a solution. A sigh escaped her. Why was it always on her to solve all the problems?

"We could buy a bottle from Signora Molina?" Pamina offered.

Both Liliana and Serafina snorted.

Alessia shook her head. "No. We'll make another bottle."

Liliana and Pamina exchanged looks as if she'd lost her mind. Alessia didn't appreciate the sentiment, though she was beginning to worry about that herself. There was enough on her list of to-do's. She certainly didn't want to add anything else to it, but they couldn't very well disappoint their new count.

"But there are no more strawberries." Fiorella voiced everyone's concern.

Alessia shrugged helplessly. "We'll grow more then. It will be fine. Yes, everything is going to be fine."

She said this more for her own benefit than her sisters. Meeting the count in such a manner had disrupted everything. His amber eyes flashed in her mind. Deep. Intelligent. Kind. No one had ever looked at her with such intensity.

Pushing away the thoughts, Alessia shook her head. Her attraction to Count Gallo was a surprise, but she wasn't going to let it interfere with what she needed to do.

"Well then, someone should go and let him know." Serafina's words caught her attention.

She gave Alessia a hopeful smile. "I can go tell him we're making the wine custom for him."

Liliana grunted. "You and your poor manners? I should think not."

Serafina scowled. "Never mind my manners! You're one to talk. Your idea of charming a man is to snarl at him."

Liliana made a disgusted sound. "Please. I have no intentions of charming any man. Let alone a count! And do you suppose he would find snakes in his trousers charming? That is your specialty, isn't it?"

"Oh, enough about the snakes! Must you always bring that up?"

People had turned to look at them now, drawn by their raised voices.

Alessia stepped between the two, hands raised in a placating gesture. "Enough! No one is going to bother the count." She lowered her voice. "We don't need any more trouble. Please."

After making sure they looked appropriately contrite, or as contrite as she could hope for them to be, Alessia lowered her arms and straightened her skirt.

"Really. All this fuss over a silly old count. Handsome, yes, but I see no reason to lose our heads over it," she said with a grunt.

Again, it seemed she was speaking for her own benefit more than her sisters. They shushed her, eyes widening in alarm. Alessia's heart leapt into her throat.

The crowd had grown restless around them, and as she slowly turned around, she could see why. Count Gallo had come up behind them, along with Patrizio Foncello. Had he heard her?

Her face flamed. He gave her a polite smile, making her stomach flutter. Alessia's shoulders dropped in relief. He had been too far away to hear her over the people's cheers.

Finally, some good luck.

Chapter 8

The Blossom Inn

The Blossom Inn was no bigger than Massimo's villa, but the tan stone looked far more weathered. Two tall, scraggly looking cypress trees stood on either side of the inn and the wide-set doors underneath the stone arch looked freshly painted with a deep brown.

"Greetings, Count Gallo!" a friendly voice called as Massimo disembarked from the wagon.

Massimo looked up to see a short, bearded man barrel out of the inn, followed by more people. He bowed to Massimo and motioned to a boy, who looked like a younger version of himself, to help the driver carry the trunk inside.

"I'm Signor Giordano. At your service, Count. This is my wife, Signora Giordano, and our children. Luca, Lena, Luigi, Lara, and Leo," he said proudly, nodding to each person in turn.

Massimo smiled politely at them. The oldest girl blushed furiously while the others snickered, earning a sharp glare from their mother. They curtsied and bowed clumsily, lowering their heads respectfully at him.

"My, what a large—and lovely—family you have, signor.

66

Thank you for your hospitality on such short notice." Massimo addressed the innkeeper.

The man grinned broadly and motioned for Massimo and the patrizio to follow him into the stone building. The noise of the crowd faded away as they entered the inn.

Inside, the air was cooler and the smell of fresh caffé made Massimo sigh aloud. Though he was curious to explore the town, a part of him was already homesick. At least he had Lucia and his books to keep him company during his stay. The cat continued snoozing in his arms.

"Here is your room, Count. I hope you find it to your liking. Please let me know if you need anything. Anything at all," the innkeeper said, handing the lock over to Massimo.

"Yes. Thank you," Massimo replied, using one hand to open the door and the other to hold on to Lucia.

He wasn't sure how she would react to being in a new place when she woke. Hopefully, he could have her food ready before then. Before Signor Giordano left, Massimo put in an order for fresh fish for her.

The Blossom Inn was in fact smaller than his home in Via delle Rose, but Massimo appreciated the cozy feel of it. The room they'd put him in could easily fit into his own room. It was modest, clean, and quaint.

Setting Lucia down on the bed, he turned his attention to his trunk. His clothes were rumpled from traveling, but he didn't think the townsfolk would care. This wasn't the high-class society Massimo was used to, and he didn't want to stick out even more than he already did.

"Did you see his ears?" one of the Giordano children whispered outside his room.

"Shh! He'll hear you," another scolded.

"But did you see them? He's fae!"

"So? Father is part dwarf. Which makes you dwarf too, you dolt."

"I think he's handsome. That golden skin and silky hair. Oh, and that jaw!" another girl gushed.

Snickers and jeers followed, fading away as they moved down the hall.

Massimo glanced at the door. He knew Patrizio Foncello was waiting to show him off all around Zamerra, but the temptation of pulling out one of the books he'd brought was nearly impossible to deny. The sunlight pouring in was perfect for lying beside Lucia with a good novel. All he would need was some fresh caffè or perhaps a cool glass of strawberry limonata. Something to nibble on and...

You're here for the festival.

Maybe he could find Alessia and her sisters again. Her warm eyes and full lips flashed in his mind. She was beautiful, but there was something much more to it than that. Massimo frowned. What was it about her that was so... alluring?

Music and laughter drifted in from the open window, catching Massimo's ear. A distinct bleating followed. Had the goat wrangling begun?

Despite his curiosity, something held him back. How long did he have to make an appearance? What if they expected him to make a speech?

Massimo sighed and shook the questions away. He was the count now. He had his duty to the people. At least for as long as they would have him.

Lucia purred in her sleep, pulling him out of his thoughts. Massimo sighed and forced himself to walk away from the trunk and head for the door.

No more stalling.

The sooner he shook everyone's hands and tried all the

strawberry drinks and foods they had to offer, the sooner he could say goodbye to Zamerra.

The inn was quiet. Was he the only guest? Where was Patrizio Foncello? Or Signor Giordano? Unsure of what to do, Massimo made his way downstairs.

A clattering came from the kitchen. Feminine voices talked in hushed tones behind the doors. Massimo didn't want to bother them, but perhaps it was a cook or servant who could tell him where the patrizio had gone.

Clearing his throat, Massimo pushed open the swinging doors. Signora Giordano and her daughter stood at the sink, busy at work. They hadn't heard him enter.

Massimo cleared his throat again. "Excu—"

Signora Giordano let out a sound somewhere between a yelp and a squeal. They turned around in unison to stare at him. The daughter's eyes met his, her face flushing.

"Santos," Signora Giordano murmured under her breath.

"Forgive me, signora. I didn't mean to startle you. I was looking for the patrizio. Did he leave?" Massimo asked.

"Oh! Count Gallo. We were just preparing some fish for your cat. The patrizio went to retrieve his wife. I believe he mentioned something about wanting to introduce you." The woman rattled off, wiping her hands against her apron.

Massimo smiled. "Thank you. I'm sure Lucia will appreciate it. I suppose I should wait here then."

Signora Giordano nudged her daughter toward him with a pointed look.

The girl curtsied, face reddening. "Would you care for anything, Count?"

"Count Gallo! There you are," the innkeeper interrupted, coming through the swinging doors.

"The patrizio is outside waiting for you," he added, frowning at the aggravated look his wife gave him.

"Thank you," Massimo replied, taking his leave.

He pretended not to hear the argument that ensued. The words *bachelor* and *eligible* echoed from the kitchen, making him quicken his pace.

"Oh, your Countship, come meet my wife. Signora Foncello," the patrizio called, waving Massimo over to their wagon.

Massimo nodded politely. "Pleased to meet you, Signora Foncello,"

The middle-aged woman beamed and motioned him to join her on the bench. "We are so pleased to have you, Count Gallo," she gushed.

"Do you like dancing?" she asked as the wagon took off.

"Sometimes," Massimo answered warily.

Signora Foncello smiled. "It's an excellent way to meet eligible young women."

Massimo shifted awkwardly on the bench. "Oh. Well..."

"Frederico told me about that... encounter with the Silveri sisters. I hope that hasn't tainted your opinion of Zamerra. I assure you, our town is quite proper," she continued.

"Of course. I was pleased to see how the townsfolk pitched in to help them. It seems you've built a close-knit community here," Massimo said.

"Oh, yes. We do what we can for the girls. What with their mother's... situation," she hesitated.

Massimo frowned. "Their mother is unwell?"

"Oh, I don't know. They live outside Zamerra, you see. Further up the mountain. Just the girls and their mother," Signora Foncello whispered with a shake of her head.

"I see. Does no one go and check on them?" Massimo asked.

A startled look crossed her face. She glanced at her husband, who was driving the wagon.

"From time to time, but they prefer to be left alone. We

leave them to their business as they wish," Patrizio Foncello answered for her.

After witnessing the townsfolk's harshness, Massimo wasn't surprised to hear that. It seemed people, poor or rich, could be just as awful to those who were different. Memories of his mother being excluded flashed in his mind. His fists clenched in his lap, chest tightening.

"Frederico, stop here. The musicians have just started. Count, you must come and at least watch the dances." Signora Foncello's words cut through his thoughts.

Unable to reject her invitation, Massimo hopped down from the wagon and followed them to the center of the plaza.

Guitars sounded above the cheers and chatter of the crowd. The clashing smell of strawberry perfume and savory meat filled the air along with the sweat of the people pressing in. Massimo held his breath as they weaved their way through.

He was just about to turn back and feign a headache when his eyes landed on a familiar face. Alessia Silveri was there with her sisters. Dancing. Her dark curls hung loosely, bouncing as she swayed with the music. A beautiful smile lit up her face.

Massimo found himself moving toward her, unable to stop himself. He was vaguely aware of the others as they greeted him and moved out of his way. The music came to an end, and everyone clapped. Alessia turned toward him with a startled look.

For a moment, they just stared at each other.

She curtsied, her sisters following her lead. "Count," she murmured.

Her dark eyes met his briefly before flickering away. Everyone was watching them now, but Massimo couldn't make his mouth work. Instead, he just stood there mute, staring like a fool.

"You... are a good dancer," he finally got out.

Alessia's face reddened. "Oh. Thank you."

"Oh, Count Gallo! I thought I lost you. Come, we have a seat reserved over here for you," Signora Foncello interrupted, linking arms with Massimo and leading him away.

More faces greeted him as he sat at the long table with the Foncellos. An assortment of food and drinks were brought before him, but just the thought of eating made Massimo's stomach heave. The sun was beginning to set, and the air grew cooler, a welcome relief from the warmth coming from all the bodies crowding around him.

Voices clamored over the music, the clashing sounds piercing Massimo's ears. It was loud. Stuffy. It was all too much. If it weren't for Alessia, who had moved back into his eyeline, he would have excused himself and returned to the inn on foot.

He watched, mesmerized, as she danced gracefully to the soft notes of the ballad. Other townsfolk danced alongside her and her sisters, giving them a wide berth. The patrizio's words echoed in Massimo's mind.

They prefer to be left alone.

But was that true? Massimo knew that hadn't been the case for his mother. She wanted to be a part of the upper-class society so badly. To be accepted.

Pushing away the dark thoughts, Massimo turned his attention back to Signora Foncello. She motioned for him to lean in closer.

He bent his head toward her. "Signora?"

"As you can see, Count, everyone here is quite skilled with dance and music. I know this must seem trifle compared to the parties you're accustomed to, but we are so pleased to have you celebrate with us. Will you be staying with us long?"

Massimo gave her a polite smile. "Unfortunately, I have to return home shortly. I have much business to attend to, but I'm so thankful for the opportunity to come and see Zamerra. It's a beautiful place."

His gaze lingered on Alessia.

"Of course. Well, I do hope you return soon. There's much you haven't seen yet," Signora Foncello said, waving her hand to get his attention.

"Here, Count! Try some of this strawberry gelato." The patrizio's voice interrupted Massimo's thoughts.

"Oh, thank you," Massimo replied, taking the cone from his outstretched hand.

The gelato was melting fast as Massimo took a taste. Sweet strawberry flavor burst in his mouth.

Unable to speak, he nodded his thanks at the gelato vendor behind them, who was grinning proudly with his missing teeth.

Massimo turned his attention back to Alessia, watching as she twirled along the plaza along with the others. Her movements were smooth and graceful. Funny that he was the one with fae blood, yet she seemed more fae-like than he. Perhaps she was part fae?

That would explain Massimo's fascination with her. Even now, as he watched her, he fought the urge to join her.

"Don't you dance, Count?" Signora Foncello asked, trying once more to draw his attention.

"Oh, yes. I'm afraid I'm rather tired tonight. Perhaps another time,"

"Yes! We'll have to give you a proper send-off," she said excitedly, turning to her husband. "You'll have to tell the musicians and the vendors, of course. A dance for the count!"

"Oh, no. You don't need to go to all that trouble," Massimo replied.

The thought of another dance made him cringe. His eyes met Alessia's. She smiled warmly at him before turning away.

"Well, I suppose another dance would be nice," he found himself saying as he tracked her movement.

Was she leaving already? Alarm filled him. He strained his neck, trying to see her off, but she and her sisters disappeared into the sea of people. Now there was truly no more reason for him to stay.

He rose to his feet and bowed to the patrizio and patrizia. "I'm afraid I've grown tired after my long journey. I think I'll retire now."

"Oh. Well, you don't have to walk. Frederico can take you back in the wagon," Signora Foncello offered.

"Thank you, but I think I'd prefer walking. It's such a lovely town," Massimo said with a smile.

He said his goodbyes to everyone and hurried in the direction he'd seen Alessia and her sisters leave. He searched the crowd and sighed. It was too late. They were gone.

"Well, I guess that's that," he muttered to himself before turning back toward the inn.

Probably for the best.

It wasn't like he'd be in Zamerra long enough to get acquainted with them, anyway.

Chapter 9

The Seeds

"I smell like sour wine," Liliana complained as they walked up the mountain.

Alessia turned to her. "We all do, I'm sure."

The sun was setting, and the air was growing cooler. Music and laughter sounded behind them as they left Zamerra. Most of the townsfolk would stay up all night dancing and drinking. Would the count keep dancing too?

Alessia shook off the thought.

"What do you think of Angelo buying all the seeds to make up for... that mishap?" she asked her sister.

Liliana's dark eyebrow arched. "What do *you* think?"

"I thought it was kind of him, but what is he going to do with them?"

"Grow them, I suppose. And if one turns out to be flesh-eating, well, I'm sure Serafina would love that." Liliana smiled.

Alessia shook her head. "I thought she'd outgrown that silly feud."

Liliana shrugged. "I guess not."

Pamina, who'd fallen back to join them, laughed. "Really,

you two. Don't you know anything about romance? Didn't you ever have a girlhood crush?"

Alessia and Liliana exchanged surprised looks.

"Romance? She called him an—"

Alessia cut Liliana off with a look. The two younger girls who were walking ahead were probably listening to them.

Pamina laughed. "Young love."

Her smile faded, a wistful look flashing on her face. The noise of Fabrizio's hooves and the wagon wheels against the dirt road filled the silence.

Alessia didn't like the longing glance Pamina threw back at the town. When she was Fiorella and Serafina's age, Pamina had many girlhood crushes. All of which led only to heartache and disappointment. Now at the ripe marrying age, Pamina hadn't mentioned anything about romance. Hadn't she outgrown the hope of marrying?

Guilt filled Alessia. Was there someone in town Pamina was still crushing on? An unrequited love that somehow Alessia had missed?

"What did you think of our new count?" Pamina changed the topic.

Liliana rolled her eyes. "Don't tell me you've fallen for his looks like everyone else, Pamina."

She turned to Alessia for support and frowned. "Not you too!"

"Of course not! Don't be silly," Alessia answered.

"Well, he was watching you," Serafina called from ahead. Fiorella giggled.

Alessia scoffed. "Nonsense. I'm sure he already has a betrothed. Someone of noble blood."

"So? Maybe you've changed his mind," Serafina continued.

"No, Fina. That's not how things work," Alessia replied.

"But why?" Fiorella asked.

Alessia sighed. "Because. That's just how things are. Now, enough about the count. Did anyone bring something back for Bruno?"

"I found a gold button for him," Fiorella said excitedly.

"Oh, he'll love that," Pamina said, turning to smile at her.

They fell into silence once more and Alessia took in the beautiful mountain scenery. There wasn't much daylight left and once they reached the villa, there would be the unloading and cleaning to do. Supper to prepare. The cats and Gio yowled and barked ahead as they approached their gate.

Welcome home, the villa greeted.

* * *

Alessia climbed out onto the roof of the bedroom she shared with Liliana. *Finally, some peace and quiet.* As much as she loved her family, there were times when their home felt overcrowded, and the constant activity exhausted her.

The woods that surrounded their villa were blissfully silent and the night air was cold, but she didn't feel like going back inside for her shawl. It was only a matter of time before somebody went looking for her. She'd left the others to clean up after supper, and a part of her felt guilty about it. There was still work left to be done.

There was always work to be done.

Alessia sighed and scanned the horizon. From their roof, she had a good view of the mountainous path that led past their neighbors and into town. She drew her knees to her chest and tried to ignore the worry gnawing at her. She'd been so busy, there hadn't been time to ruminate on Mama's vision. But up there on the roof with the dark, starry sky spread above her, the questions swarmed in.

What if the vision was real? What if she really was to

marry? Alessia tried to envision what married life would be like, but there was no one she could see herself with. Besides, she couldn't leave her mother and sisters. They needed her.

"There you are. I figured you were hiding up here. Can I join you?"

Alessia turned her head to find Liliana standing by the window. She held out a steaming mug of caffé to her. "I brought an offering."

"Thank you," Alessia said, standing up to retrieve it.

It warmed her hands instantly as she held it up to her nose to inhale the sweet, rich aroma. Moving over, she made room for Liliana to crawl out. They sat in silence for a minute, Alessia sipping the hot liquid.

"Do you want some?" she offered it to her sister.

Liliana shook her head and stretched her long legs. "I already had a cup."

Alessia slowly sat beside her, careful not to spill the mug. She took another sip, the noise filling the silence.

"So, why are you hiding up here? Are we getting on your nerves?" Liliana asked teasingly, glancing at Alessia.

"No. Nothing like that. I just..." Alessia shrugged, "needed to be alone for a minute."

Liliana nodded. "I understand that. I come out here to be alone too sometimes. Well, a lot of times, actually. They're so loud."

Serafina's laughter rang out from the house as if to prove Liliana's point.

Alessia smiled at the sound. "What are they doing in there?"

"Pamina is playing the piano, and Serafina is treating Mama to one of her ballads. And Bruno was dancing with Fiorella. That's when I left."

Alessia finished the rest of her caffé and set down the mug.

The smooth liquid filled her with warmth. Pamina made the best caffé, possibly in the entire world. Alessia couldn't imagine going through the day without it.

"So, what is it? What's wrong?" Liliana's question caught her ear.

She turned to her sister and shrugged. "Nothing. I'm just tired."

Liliana snorted. "I know that's not true. You just drank Pamina's caffé, and that stuff works instantly."

"There's something you and Mama aren't telling us. You've been hiding something. I'm not an idiot, Alessia. Tell me what it is." Liliana's face hardened, her dark eyes piercing Alessia's.

"Mama told me about a vision she had. Recently."

Her sister frowned. "A vision? She hasn't had one in so long. That must be why she's been having all the headaches. Well, what was it?"

Alessia's stomach churned. She hadn't discussed the vision with anyone, but Liliana was the most sensible of them all. Surely, she'd see it was a mistake.

"Something bad, then?" Liliana's voice softened.

"It was a vision of my wedding day," Alessia blurted. She winced at the panic lacing her words.

Liliana gaped at her. "Your... wedding day?" She blinked rapidly.

Alessia felt her face flush. "Silly, I know. But you know how Mama's visions work. It could have been a glimpse of a future that's never to be. I mean, can you imagine me married?"

Liliana's eyes searched hers. She reminded Alessia of Mama with her dark, calculating gaze.

"Well, no, but I can't imagine why anyone would want to get married. Saddle yourself with someone for life? Losing your independence. Can you imagine yourself married?"

Her question rattled Alessia down to the bone.

"Of course not! Who would I marry, anyway?"

"There is that widower—"

Alessia smacked her playfully on the arm. "Oh, stop it. You're as bad as Mama."

Liliana's face grew somber. "What does Mama say about it? She believes this vision is going to come true?"

Alessia shrugged her shoulders. "She hasn't said anything of it since. I'm not worried about it."

Liliana's eyes narrowed at her. "That's why you're out here. Alone. Not thinking about your future groom?"

"What? I'm not going to marry, Liliana. I'm much too old for that, and besides, what would you all do without me here to nag you? To take care of everything?"

"Please. I think we deserve some credit. We're not completely hopeless, you know," Liliana said with a snort. "Well, at least, I'm not."

Alessia nudged Liliana with her shoulder and looked up at the night sky. "I know. But I couldn't leave you. Not for anything."

Liliana grew quiet. A gentle touch on her hand startled Alessia. She turned to face her younger sister. The seriousness written on Liliana's face made her heart twist.

"As much as I love your nagging, Alessia, this decision shouldn't be made on our account. You know that, right?"

Alessia waved off her words. "Of course. It's not. It's my decision. I know that."

Liliana looked like she was about to say something more, but stopped herself. She frowned and raised her finger into the air.

"What?" Alessia asked.

Liliana motioned for her to be quiet. A strange crashing sound came, followed by a loud ripping sound.

"What is that?"

Liliana jumped to her feet and pulled Alessia up with her. They leapt back just in time as a patch of the roof tiles caved in, the coffee mug falling in.

Someone screamed inside. They exchanged a look. Alessia fought back a groan. There would be no more putting off repairs now.

* * *

Morning came too early for Alessia, bringing with it a flurry of worries and activity. She'd been awake most of the night tossing and turning, but one quick cup of Pamina's magical caffé and she'd be ready to face the day.

Mama was already in the kitchen when Alessia arrived. She paused mid-stir and looked up at Alessia.

"You're feeling better, Mama?" Alessia asked.

"Much. The girls told me about our new count," she said innocently, returning to stirring the batter in her bowl.

Alessia was saved from having to answer by her sisters bursting into the kitchen.

"Ooh! Are you making crespelle, Mama?" Fiorella clapped, hurrying over to look.

"I'll start the caffé!" Pamina announced.

Bruno, waiting at the table, scowled at all the movement around him. He didn't like mornings, and he liked them even less when they were noisy.

"Alessia, are you sure those boards will hold up on the roof?" Liliana asked above the chatter.

"For now. It'll be fine," Alessia answered as she set out plates.

Outside, the cats and Gio went wild, alerting them to a visitor.

"I'll get the gate!" Fiorella offered, disappearing outside. Serafina trailed behind her.

Alessia stood in the doorway and watched as a wagon drove in. It was Angelo Rossi. Liliana, who was standing behind her to look, met her gaze.

"Angelo? I wonder what he's doing here so early," Pamina said, peering around Alessia, spoke their question aloud.

The cats and Gio swarmed Angelo's horse, causing a raucous. Bruno pulled his little red hat down over his ears and shook his head.

"I better go help him before Serafina causes trouble," Alessia muttered, straightening her skirt as she left. Liliana followed.

"Invite him in for breakfast," Mama called after them.

"Good morning, signoras," Angelo said with a polite nod, trying to be heard over the noisy cats and Gio.

"Good morning," Alessia and Liliana returned.

Out of the corner of her eye, Alessia saw Fabrizio, the goats, and some of the chickens starting toward them. She shot Serafina a warning look.

"What do you want, Angelo?" Serafina asked sharply, ignoring Alessia.

Alessia frowned at her. There was no need to be so rude to him. Annoyed or not, Serafina needed to mind her manners.

"I—. The goats—" Angelo could hardly get a word out over the noisy animals.

"Fina, get the animals out of here. Now," Alessia commanded.

Serafina huffed but did as she was told. With a discreet nod, she silenced them and sent them away. Angelo's eyes widened on her as the animals dispersed.

"Well?" Serafina demanded.

He raked his fingers through his wavy, dark hair and

blinked at her. "I'm sorry for coming unannounced like this, but I didn't know what else to do."

Angelo's eyes met Alessia's. "It's about the seeds. Now, I have to admit, I don't know much about planting and harvesting. As you know, we're goat and horse breeders," he said with a proud look, chest out.

Serafina snorted but kept her words to herself. Thankfully.

Unfazed by her, he continued. "I didn't expect the seeds to take so... quickly."

"So, they grew fast. What of it?" Serafina asked with a huff of impatience.

Alessia nudged her shoulder. Pranks aside, Angelo had done them a great service buying all the seeds.

Liliana exchanged a worried look with Alessia. Fiorella looked on the verge of tears.

Angelo glanced behind them and dipped his head. "Signora Silveri. Sorry to disturb you."

Mama and Pamina had come out to see what was going on.

Mama smiled warmly at him. "It's good to see you, Angelo. Won't you come in and join us for breakfast? How is your family?"

"Oh. They're well. Thank you for your offer, signora, but I don't want to trouble you all."

Mama waved his words away. "Nonsense. Serafina will see to your horse. You come inside and tell us what all this is about."

"But, Mama. I—"

Mama's stern look cut Seraphina's protest short. She waited for Angelo to hop down before leading his horse to the stables, mulishly ignoring Angelo's hesitant smile.

"I told you it was a mistake," Liliana hissed with a shake of her head as they followed Mama and Angelo into the kitchen.

Alessia glanced back to see Fiorella run off toward the

woods. She stopped, torn between wanting to chase after her and wanting to hear what Angelo had to say.

"I'll check on her," Pamina offered, wiping her hands off on her apron and going after her.

Alessia turned to Liliana. "Do you have to be so harsh? You know how sensitive she is."

Liliana gaped at her. "All I said was it was a mistake. You all coddle her too much. Her magic isn't something to trifle with. It's—never mind. You wouldn't understand."

Alessia's gut clenched. Her face heated at her sister's words.

Liliana met her eyes. "No. I didn't mean it like that, Alessia. It's just that she's growing up, and we have to prepare her for the reality she'll face. You can't shelter her forever."

"Of course I can. It's not for you to decide, Liliana. I'm the oldest. I—"

"That doesn't mean you can control our lives."

"What? I'm not trying to."

Liliana shook her head and continued walking, clearly done with the discussion. Alessia watched her go, wrapping her arms around herself. Liliana's words echoed in her mind.

Chapter 10

The Goat Farm

Massimo finished the caffé and toast they'd brought up to his room. He'd opened the jar of strawberry jam Alessia had given him the day before and though he wasn't usually fond of that flavor, he had to admit it was the best jam he'd ever eaten.

It left him feeling much fuller than it should have and much more energetic. He felt as if he could run up and down the mountain. Of course, he wasn't going to do that, but there was definitely something special about the jam.

"It was made by witches, after all," he muttered to a lounging Lucia.

She lifted her head to look at him before turning away.

Now that the Strawberry Festival was over, everyone seemed to have forgotten about him and moved on. Back to whatever it was they normally did. Massimo preferred it that way.

Zamerra was a breath of fresh air. A nice break after all the meetings and greetings he'd endured at the palazzo. If only he could extend his stay. The mountain air was doing him good.

Massimo glanced at the jar of jam, wondering what Alessia was doing now that the festival was over. Making his wine, probably. Did she enjoy making wine? What other things did she enjoy? He'd been up most of the night with these nagging, nonsensical questions.

He'd tried to read the novel he'd been currently working through, but thoughts of the beautiful witch kept pulling him out of the story. He couldn't stop puzzling over her. She'd become the latest mystery to solve. The story he was most interested in discovering.

Massimo snorted. This really was getting quite ridiculous. He needed to do something. *Yes, a walk.* That would help him clear his mind.

He stood and brushed off the crumbs from his trousers before turning to his cat. "Would you like to take a walk with me, Lucia?"

She opened one eye to give him a baleful look before promptly shutting it again and ignoring him. Massimo took that as a no and went for his hat, before stopping himself. No one in Zamerra seemed to be concerned with covering their heads. Even at the festival during the hottest part of the afternoon, no one put on a hat.

Massimo rather liked this custom. Hats had never been comfortable to him, and hat-wearing was one of the reasons he preferred to stay indoors. Here, though, he could enjoy nature without worrying if his head was covered.

"Alright then. I shall be back... well, I don't know exactly when, but I won't be gone for too long. I don't imagine," he told Lucia.

She stared blankly back at him. Making sure she had fresh water and a sandbox to relieve herself, he buckled up his boots and made his way downstairs and out of the inn.

It was a bright, sunny Spring day and Massimo paused for a

moment to take it all in. The fresh mountain air filled his lungs and the scent of honeysuckles and freshly baked bread wafted around him.

Everyone seemed to still be sleeping, though the sound of a wagon echoed from somewhere in the distance. That was another thing Massimo admired about Zamerra. Everything moved at a slower, more relaxed pace.

A horse neighed from the stables near the inn. Massimo considered finding the stable hand and requesting a horse-drawn cart, but he'd never actually driven one and he didn't want to bother anyone.

"Walking will do me good," he spoke aloud as he headed toward the giant fountain.

He returned greetings to the few townspeople who were out and about. It wasn't long before he'd made it to the edge of town. Curious to see where the dirt road led, he kept going. The rushing river sounded nearby as he went, Zamerra growing farther and farther.

Eventually, Massimo's legs grew tired, and the town had long disappeared behind him. Should he keep going? He still wanted to see where the road led, but who knew how long it stretched. He could walk for days and still see nothing.

Making up his mind, he decided to keep going for a little more, then he would turn around. Maybe he would take a break by the river and get a drink. His throat was getting parched, and the sun was beginning to make his head pound.

"Should have brought my hat after all," he muttered to himself.

He was ready to turn back when a loud braying noise came from ahead. Squinting, Massimo could just make out the outline of something in the distance. A farm, perhaps?

Whatever it was, it was much closer to him than the town

was. Maybe they'd invite him in for a glass of water and a rest. With that thought in mind, he pushed himself on.

Wildflowers and tall grass lined the dirt road leading up to the farm. The buildings grew clearer as he approached and voices echoed from them. A warm breeze blew a pungent smell his way. Definitely a farm.

Thankful, as the smell drifted away, Massimo walked toward the stone villa. He glanced around and listened as voices came from around the stables. Feminine voices mixed with masculine and there was something distinctly familiar about them.

Turning away from the villa, he made his way around the stables instead. Massimo hoped they wouldn't find his unexpected arrival rude or presumptuous.

He walked past the horse stables and stopped short. Alessia was there. She looked up at his approach, eyes widening in surprise.

Then everyone turned to look at him, with equally surprised looks.

"Good day," Massimo greeted them, suddenly feeling quite foolish.

"Count Gallo! Hello," one of the young men stepped forward to shake his hand. "I'm Angelo. Angelo Rossi. This is Rafaelo and Marco."

Massimo took his hand with a polite smile. "Oh, are you any relation to Signor Salvatore Rossi?"

Angelo beamed. "Yes. He's our oldest brother."

"Ah. How nice. I apologize for dropping in like this. I was out for a walk and curious to see your farm."

"You mean you walked all the way here? From town? Why didn't you take a wagon?" Alessia's sister asked incredulously.

Alessia elbowed her gently.

Massimo's face heated. "Well, I like walking, and truth be told, I don't know how to drive a wagon."

"You don't? How old are you?" the girl asked.

"Fina!" Alessia shook her head at her sister. She turned to Massimo, cheeks reddening. "I'm sorry, Count. My sister is... curious."

"I could teach you how to drive one if you like," the girl continued, unfazed by her older sister's glare.

Before Massimo could answer, a loud bleat sounded beside him, making him jump. He turned to see the largest goats he'd ever seen. Some of them were nearly the size of ponies. One butted its massive head against the wooden pen, shaking the entire structure.

"My, what large goats you have!" The words slipped out.

Everyone followed his gaze to the enormous creatures.

"Er... yes. Thank you," Angelo said, darting a look at Alessia and her sisters.

Massimo squinted at the animals. Something was strange about them. One bleated loudly in his face.

"Why, you must be exhausted from the walk, Count. Would you care for some water or something?" Alessia asked, drawing his attention away from the goats.

She gave Angelo and his brothers a questioning look.

Angelo's face reddened. "Oh, yes. Of course. We have water or limonata if you prefer, Count."

"Limonata sounds perfect. Thank you, Signor Rossi."

"Marco, go bring the pitcher and glasses for everyone. Let Papa know the count is here too," Angelo said, pushing his younger brother toward the villa.

Marco looked less than pleased by this but went, anyway. The youngest Silveri sister followed to help him, giving Massimo a shy look over her shoulder as she left.

"I think the count would prefer to take his refreshment

inside. Out of the sun," Alessia spoke up, eyes darting away from Massimo.

Was she trying to get rid of him? Massimo frowned.

"Oh, no. I'm fine. Thank you," he answered.

She glanced at her auburn-haired sister, who had lowered herself next to the goat pen. Her hand stretched toward one of the goats.

"Serafina?" Alessia asked quietly.

The younger Silveri was staring hard at one of the brown goats. Angelo and his brother watched with curious looks.

Massimo's skin prickled. *Magic.*

Alessia stepped in front of Serafina, blocking her from their view, and smiled. "Count, have you heard the good news? Signora Rossi's sister in Merona has just welcomed her first baby. She'll be sorry to miss your visit, seeing as she left to go help her sister."

Massimo glanced at the Rossi boys. "Oh? Congratulations on your newest addition to the family."

Rafaelo and Angelo nodded politely in return.

Alessia met Massimo's eyes, a pleading look on her face. Was she trying to hide her sister's magic from the Rossis? Didn't everyone already know they were witches?

"I'd love to see your horses. I've heard they are the best stallions in Zamerra," Massimo said, turning to the young men.

"Oh, yes. Of course," Angelo answered, motioning him toward the stables.

Massimo followed them, throwing a look back at Alessia. A look of understanding passed between them.

True to the rumors, the horses were beautiful. Though Massimo tried to listen to Angelo, his thoughts kept straying back to Alessia. Marco and the youngest Silveri sister returned with the limonata just as they left the stables to rejoin Alessia and Serafina.

Massimo glanced up at the sky. Clouds had started to gather. That was worrisome. The last thing he wanted was to get stuck in the rain.

"Here you go, Count," the young Silveri said, smiling shyly at him as she handed him a glass of limonata.

Massimo smiled back as he took it. "Thank you, signorina."

She flushed. "You can call me Fiorella."

"That's a lovely name," he replied before taking his first sip. It was refreshingly cold, but terribly tart.

Alessia sighed and stood with her hands on her hips, giving the goats another inspection. Massimo's mind raced with questions, but he held his tongue, not wanting to bother her. He knew nothing about goats or farming, but he was fairly certain that something was amiss with the massive creatures.

Though he was fae, the only knowledge he had of magic came from the books he read and from his friend, Dante. Perhaps he should write to his warlock friend and inquire about it. That was if they asked for his help or opinion, which, so far they had not.

Alessia turned to Angelo. "And the tomatoes?"

"We dug up the plants and burned them. Just in case..." Angelo's eyes darted to him and away.

Not wanting to intrude, Massimo hung back, listening to the odd conversation. From what he could gather, the Silveri sisters had sold the Rossis some tomato seeds which had produced tomatoes that had been eaten by some of the goats. The goats were now double, and in some cases, triple the size of the others.

He took a sip of his limonata and watched as Alessia and her sisters huddled together, whispering while the brothers exchanged concerned glances. Massimo, having an advantage with his hearing, couldn't help but listen.

"What are they saying, Serafina?" Alessia whispered.

Massimo paused, the glass at his lips. Were they talking about the goats? The creatures were bleating loudly, the larger ones nearly stampeding the smaller ones.

He glanced over at Angelo and his brothers, but they didn't seem to have heard what Alessia was saying. Serafina merely shook her head and threw a cautious look over her shoulder at them.

Massimo averted his gaze and took another gulp of the drink.

"Fiorella? Did you check for any more seeds?" Alessia asked the youngest sister, her voice barely audible to the others.

The young girl nodded. "I couldn't find any more."

"Well?" Angelo finally broke the quiet tension.

Alessia turned to the Rossis with a brilliant smile, though Massimo could read the worry behind her eyes. Her deep, brown, mesmerizing eyes. She met his gaze briefly before addressing Angelo.

"Just let us know if anything should change, please," Alessia said with a tight smile.

The boys exchanged wary looks with each other. Alessia motioned for her sisters to walk back to their wagon.

"We should be going. Don't want to get caught in any rain," she added, chin lifted toward the cloudy sky.

"Oh!" Massimo said aloud.

They all turned to look at him. He hadn't thought about how he would get back to town, and the thought of walking in the rain all the way back made him weary.

"You can ride back with us if you like, Count Gallo," Serafina offered.

Massimo glanced at Alessia. She smiled and nodded in agreement, though he couldn't help but sense she didn't look very pleased. That reaction stung. He didn't know what he'd done or said to displease her so, but hopefully, they'd have the whole ride back for him to make amends.

"Yes, thank you. I should have thought things through before walking all the way out here."

"Yes, well, we're happy to help," Alessia added with a polite smile.

Massimo followed her to their wagon and horse. He was about to offer his assistance, but Rafaelo and Angelo had the cart hitched before he had the chance. Not that he would have known how to do it properly anyway.

He inclined his head toward Angelo and his brothers. "Thank you again for your hospitality."

They returned the gesture and watched as Massimo offered the young Silveri girls an arm into the wagon. When it was Alessia's turn, she flinched at the contact, making him frown. Did she really dislike him so?

He climbed up after her and sat beside her as she took the reins. The younger two rode in the cart, leaving him with the seat on the bench with Alessia. It was a small bench, which meant their thighs and shoulders were nearly touching.

Warmth radiated from her, as well as the smell of lilac. Massimo didn't know what the custom was like in Zamerra, but where he was from, maintaining a proper distance was expected. Did his proximity make her uncomfortable? Should he offer to sit in the back instead?

"Are you well, Count?" she asked, giving him a curious sideways glance.

He nodded. "You smell nice. I mean clean. I mean..." The words came out in a rush before he could stop them.

Giggles sounded from behind them as the cart started moving. Alessia stiffened beside him, her face growing red. Massimo bit back a groan, shaking his head at himself.

"Thank you," she finally answered, her eyes not meeting his.

Massimo looked forward at the dirt road stretched before them. Perhaps riding with them had been a mistake, after all.

"Are you staying in Zamerra for long?" Fiorella's question startled Massimo out of his thoughts.

"Ella, I'm sure he has much more important business elsewhere," Alessia answered for him.

"Are you coming to dinner tonight? At Signor Rossi's home?" Serafina asked.

"Fina!" Alessia admonished her, blushing at Massimo.

He turned his head to smile at the girl. "Why, yes. I was invited for dinner."

The girls squealed in delight. "Mama will be so thrilled to meet you!"

Massimo glanced at Alessia. "Will you be joining as well?"

Her eyes widened before turning away to face the road once more. "Yes. We've been invited too."

Massimo couldn't hide his grin. "That sounds marvelous."

Chapter 11

The Dinner Invitation

Alessia's heart skipped at the sight of their new count standing at the front entrance of their neighbor's villa.

His gold-brown hair was tied back loosely, revealing his pointed ears, high cheekbones, and sharp jawline. He was dressed in a fine dark blue dinner suit, which complemented his golden skin. There was a fluffy gray cat tucked into the crook of his arm. The cat glanced moodily around the room and stared at Alessia.

"Count Gallo! Welcome," Salvatore said, stepping forward to offer his hand. The cat hissed.

He withdrew his hand. "Ah. I see you brought your cat."

"Yes. Thank you. This is Lucia," the count replied as he held the cat aloft.

"Oh, she's lovely! May I?" Serafina asked, rushing forward to take her from his arms.

"Oh, wait! Hmm. Well, she seems to like you," the count replied, blinking in surprise.

Serafina cooed at the cat, setting her down to explore.

Alessia watched, heart pounding, as the count turned to greet Adriano and her sisters, saving her for last.

His amber eyes snapped to Alessia. Heat rushed through her at his stare. There was a slightly flushed look to his golden skin, and his lips parted in a gentle smile.

"Signora Silveri," he said as he took her hand and kissed it.

His lips were warm and soft, the sensation making her skin tingle with awareness.

His eyes met Alessia's again. She looked away, unable to hold his piercing gaze. What was it about this fae man that made her so... unsteady?

"Good evening, Count Gallo," she finally managed.

"Did you walk up the mountain?" Serafina asked, breaking the tension. She sat on the ground, dressed spread out, as she stroked the cat's furry head. Fiorella joined her.

The count nodded. "Yes. It's a beautiful walk."

"Yes, well, why don't we all move to the parlor? My family should be arriving shortly," Salvatore said with a clap of his hands.

"You mean Angelo?" Serafina asked.

Mama, who'd been helping their cook, appeared in the room and threw Seraphina a warning look.

Her dark eyes landed on the count. Stepping forward, she clasped hands with him. "Count Gallo! I'm Signora Silveri. I'm so pleased to meet the handsome new count everyone's been talking about."

Alessia watched, horrified, as her mother gushed, still holding onto the count's hand. Liliana exchanged a sharp look with her.

The count smiled graciously at Mama. "It's a pleasure to meet you as well, Signora Silveri."

"Come, you must tell us all about yourself," Mama continued, leading him to the parlor.

Pamina, Serafina, and Fiorella followed along with Lucia, leaving Alessia and Liliana with Adriano and Salvatore.

Salvatore stood by the front door, staring out the window.

"You know your father never leaves the farm and perhaps your mother is still in Merona with your aunt," Adriano said, placing an arm around his husband.

Salvatore nodded. "Yes, well. Their loss."

He turned to Alessia and Liliana and smiled brightly. "Can you believe we're having dinner with a count?"

Adriano motioned for him to be quiet.

"What?" Salvatore asked with a furrowed brow.

"He'll hear you," Adriano replied, waving for Salvatore to lead the way.

Alessia followed, her chest tight. Worry gnawed at her. What if Mama thought the count was the answer to her vision? What if the townsfolk heard about this intimate dinner?

Do you really think to snare yourself a count? The woman's words echoed in her mind.

"What's wrong?" Liliana asked quietly beside her.

"Nothing."

Liliana frowned at her. "Don't lie to me."

Alessia shook her head and forced a smile. "I'm not. Everything's fine, Liliana. Now be quiet before you draw everyone's attention."

Before her sister could respond, Alessia hurried into the parlor after the men.

Unlike the Silveris' villa, the Rossis' villa was stylish and new. Oil paintings depicting different areas of Zamerra, done by Adriano himself, covered nearly every inch of the walls. Fire blazed in the fireplace, filling the room with a cozy glow.

The count's cat was lounging on the couch between Serafina and Fiorella, looking right at home. Her master, on the other hand, was sitting next to their mother and looking red-faced and flustered.

Liliana nodded in their direction and snorted. "Still nothing wrong?"

Alessia ignored her and joined them. "Mama, are you sure Signora Sanchez doesn't need more help in the kitchen?"

Pamina stood immediately. "Oh, I'll go check."

Mama smiled. "Alessia, the count was just telling me about his friend. A warlock."

She turned back to the count. "You simply must invite him on your next visit. Do you know when that will be?"

Count Gallo flushed. "Well, I'm not sure, signora. It depends on what other tasks await me back home."

"Oh. Such a pity you have to leave so soon. Just as we are getting to know you," Mama continued, eyes snapping to Alessia.

A knock at the door sounded, saving Alessia from further embarrassment. Salvatore stood and headed for the entrance, Adriano close on his heels.

"Santos, I hope that's not Signora Rossi," Serafina muttered aloud.

Mama frowned and stood up, her chin lifted high.

Liliana exchanged a worried look with Alessia. Ever since the snakes and Serafina's expulsion from school, there had been bad blood between the mothers.

Pamina reappeared with a smile. "Dinner is ready!"

Lucia, the count's cat, meowed loudly and hopped down from the couch.

Serafina snickered. "I don't think we're having mackerel tonight. Sorr—" She stopped herself too late.

The count's head whipped toward her. "You can under-stand her?"

Serafina glanced guiltily at Alessia and Mama. Liliana

shook her head at her, and Fiorella watched from the couch, green eyes wide and lower lip trembling.

Voices sounded from the entrance, coming closer. Any second and they'd be joined by the rest of the Rossis. The Rossis, who didn't like them and would eagerly out them to the rest of the town.

Alessia launched herself at the count, linking arms quickly with him and pulling him toward the back of the room.

His eyes widened. Warmth spread from the contact, making Alessia's pulse race. She sucked in a breath, trying to calm herself. The smell of cedar and spice enveloped her.

"Count, I know you don't know me or my sisters well, but you have your warlock friend. You understand, don't you? And well, you're... I mean. People don't trust magic. That's why..."

He gave her an understanding smile. "You don't want them to know."

Alessia released her breath and nodded. He looked as if he wanted to say more, but glanced back at the now-crowded room, and fell silent.

His gaze drifted to their linked arms. Alessia withdrew her arm, face heating. Everyone was staring at them with curious looks. Even their newest guests, who turned out to be Rafaelo and Angelo.

"Well, shall we? Signora Sanchez has prepared the best braciola you've ever eaten." Salvatore said, motioning everyone out of the room.

Serafina made a face and opened her mouth to object, but Signora Silveri silenced her with a look.

"There's penne all'Arrabbiata as well," Adriano said kindly, knowing Serafina didn't eat meat.

Alessia hurried to follow everyone, her heart feeling as if it were going to burst out of her chest. She didn't like having to share their secrets with the count. She'd never felt so exposed before. What if they couldn't trust him?

She could feel his stare upon her back, but she refused to look back.

As she entered the dining room, she found her nameplate placed next to the count's. Her mother's doing? She looked around to find Mama. Signora Silveri had pulled Serafina aside and whispered something to her.

Thankfully, her sisters and the Rossis kept the count's attention as dinner was served. Despite her worry, Alessia found herself relaxing and enjoying herself. Even Liliana looked at ease and Serafina, who'd been seated next to Angelo, was uncharacteristically gracious to the boy. Though that didn't stop the two from teasing each other every now and then.

"Angelo, you wouldn't happen to know a handyman available, would you?" Alessia asked as the Rossis cook brought out dessert.

"Signor Delfino is the best—"

"No. Not him," Alessia cut him off with a shake of her head.

She didn't want to elaborate, but the last time the poor man had come to fix something, Bruno had given him quite a scare.

"Nico is looking for work," Rafaelo spoke so softly that at first Alessia wasn't sure he had even spoken.

Angelo nodded. "Yes. Our cousin. He's very skilled and is available right now."

"Perfect. Can you tell him to come by at his earliest convenience? We have some repairs that need to be made."

"Of course, signora," Angelo answered with a polite nod.

Once again, Alessia felt Count Gallo's heavy stare upon her. Heat rushed through her. The sooner he left Zamerra, the better it would be for them all.

* * *

It was late by the time Alessia arrived home with her family. Serafina and Fiorella chattered excitedly about the count as they headed for the stairs. Pamina and Liliana followed them.

"Alessia." Mama's voice was soft, but firm.

It was a tone that meant business. Alessia paused in the kitchen, gathering all her strength. There would be no more putting off this conversation.

She turned and gave her mother her full attention. Mama's dark eyes searched her face, her lips pressed into a thin line. Tension hung in the air between them. Alessia didn't like it. Why couldn't things go back to how they were supposed to be?

Mama smiled. "I hope you know how grateful I am for everything you do. All your hard work. Your leadership. You do so much for me and your sisters."

Alessia blinked in surprise. She'd been expecting another lecture about marriage. About change. Not these compliments. She didn't know what to say.

"Oh. Thank you, Mama. We all work hard," she said with a shrug.

"Have you thought any more about what I said? About the vision?"

Alessia frowned. "I thought we'd agreed to let things play out on their own. There's no certainty with visions, Mama."

"Hmm. What do you think of our new count?" Mama asked, watching her carefully.

"I don't... what do you mean? We hardly know him. I haven't given him much thought at all."

Mama's eyebrow arched. "Oh? Well, he seemed quite taken with you at dinner tonight."

A scoff escaped Alessia. "Mama, please. We both know that's an impossibility."

Her mother's eyes narrowed. "Impossible? Why?"

A suspicious creak sounded from the stairs, drawing

Alessia's attention. She glanced at the door and back to her mother. "He's the count. I'm... this isn't a fairytale."

Mama took her hands in hers. "What have I done to so dissuade you from love?"

Alessia pulled her hands away with a short laugh. "Love? Mama, please. This is nonsense. I'm going to bed."

Wiping her hands on her dress, Alessia looked around at the empty kitchen. Silence hung between them. Even the villa was quiet.

Mama sighed deeply and removed her shawl, setting it around the back of a chair. "Do we have enough to pay Angelo's cousin for the roof? I was thinking I could offer readings in town again."

Alessia stared at her mother in surprise. "What about your head? You shouldn't strain yourself. I'll handle the roof. Please, don't worry about it, Mama."

Her mother glanced at her, brow arched. "I'm the mama. I'm supposed to worry. Sometimes, I think you take on too much, Alessia."

She held up a hand at Alessia's protest. "Your life should be your own, amore."

Alessia frowned. "It is my own. When have I ever complained about the work? About the others?"

Mama gave her a sad smile. "How many times have you sacrificed what you want?"

"What? This is what I want!" Alessia's voice echoed around them.

She waited for her mother to argue, but to her surprise, her mother just shook her head sadly and kissed her forehead.

"Goodnight, Alessia."

Alessia watched her leave, her chest aching. The kitchen was quiet, and the flickering candles filled the room with a soft, warm glow. Bruno's tiny snore echoed from the pantry, making Alessia smile.

This villa held everything she loved most in the world. How could she ever leave? What would happen to her family if she did?

Before the dark thoughts could creep in, Alessia blew out all but one candle. She held the chamber stick aloft and made her way upstairs to the room she shared with Liliana. Serafina's voice came from the other room, followed by Pamina's laugh and Fiorella's gasp.

Light streamed from under her door. Guilt filled her. Was Liliana waiting up for her? She slowly opened the door and glanced around.

Liliana turned toward her, lying in her bed. "Is everything alright?"

"Yes. Just talking to Mama," Alessia answered, setting down her candle.

The light cast a shadow on the wall, making Alessia look gigantic. A slight breeze blew in from the open window, bringing in the scent of honeysuckles and lavender.

"Did you ask her if she's lost her mind?"

"What?"

"Oh, come on. Don't tell me you didn't notice how she was fawning over the count. Don't tell me you're worried about impressing him, too?" Liliana's tone was teasing.

Alessia scoffed. She ignored her sister's remark as she started undressing. Weariness filled her.

"Are we really not going to talk about it?" Liliana asked, a sharpness in her tone.

"Oh, Santos. Liliana, there's nothing to talk about! Go to sleep," Alessia answered, a sharpness in her voice.

"Well. Excuse me. You're the one who said there would never be secrets between us."

"I'm not keeping secrets," Alessia said with a deep sigh.

Liliana met her eyes. "I saw how you looked at him. Everyone did."

Alessia's face flamed. "What are you talking about? The count? Now you sound like Serafina."

"Deny it all you want, Alessia. If that's how you want to be. Just know you're not fooling anyone," Liliana said, turning her back to her.

Alessia frowned. Ignoring the thoughts buzzing in her head, she pulled down her covers and slid in.

The count's burning eyes flashed in her mind, making her stomach flutter. Her skin warmed at the memory of his touch. His kind smile. She tried to push the images away. The last thing Alessia needed was to fall for a count.

Chapter 12

The Dance

Zamerra really was one of the most beautiful places Massimo had seen. Though most of the homes and shops were old and modest, they were well-kept and cozy looking. The cobblestoned streets were made of a mixture of colorful stones that shone brightly in the sunshine.

Massimo stopped to wave to a little girl who was staring down at him from her open window. She smiled and waved back, her hand raised above the pink carnations growing in the window planter.

"Count?" Patrizio Foncello stopped and waited for Massimo to catch up.

Massimo joined him near the fountain. "Yes?"

"Should I get the cart, Count Gallo? Perhaps you're not used to so much walking?" the older man asked with a look of concern.

Massimo shook his head. "Oh, no. Thank you, Patrizio Foncello. I'm fine. Just want to stop and get a good look at... everything."

The man smiled broadly, chest out. "Yes, of course. The

architecture of Zamerra is definitely something to be admired. You probably don't see this cut of stone in Via Delle Rose."

"Well, actually—"

"It was imported by my ancestors. Cut by dwarves in the Pertosa Mines. After the war, of course, but..."

Massimo tuned out the rest of the words as Patrizio Foncello went into lengthy detail about the stone-laying technique. The buildings didn't seem much different from what Massimo was used to, though they were clustered closer together than the ones at home.

Zamerra was much smaller than the city he was from, and everyone seemed to know each other. It was a close community, but what really set the little town apart was the breathtaking mountains surrounding it.

That and a certain alluring witch.

Alessia's face flashed in his mind. Massimo quickly shook the image away. He was there to see to the town's needs, and Alessia clearly didn't need him. The more he tried not to think of her, the more her face haunted him. The memory of her closeness made his skin heat.

"Count Gallo?" Patrizio Foncello's voice boomed over the noise of the crowd.

Massimo's head whipped back toward him. He flushed, feeling guilty for missing most of the conversation.

People moved out of their way as they walked. Massimo returned their smiles and waves, feeling strangely welcomed. He'd only been there for such a short time, but they seemed to have accepted him as one of their own.

Not used to so much attention, Massimo didn't know what to make of it. A part of him wondered what it would have been like to grow up in the little mountain town. Would they have accepted him and his mother?

Massimo shook the thoughts away and turned his attention back to Signor Foncello.

"Everyone is sad to see you leave so soon, Count Gallo. But of course, they are looking forward to the dance tonight," Patrizio Foncello said, leading him past the crowd.

"Yes. I hate to leave as well. Perhaps—oh, Signor Rossi!"

Salvatore looked up at the sound of his name and Massimo waved him over. He walked up and bowed and nodded at the patrizio.

"Good day, Count Gallo. Patrizio," he greeted.

"Good day," Massimo returned with a smile.

"I would love to stay and chat, but I'm afraid I must get back home. Adriano gets upset when I'm late for our caffé time."

Massimo nodded. "Of course. I'll see you tonight, then?"

Salvatore frowned and glanced between Massimo and Signor Foncello. "Tonight?"

"Yes. The dance." Massimo turned to the patrizio. "You did invite the whole town, didn't you?"

Signor Foncello nodded emphatically. "Of course. Everyone is invited. To say goodbye to our dear count. Perhaps the news didn't reach up the mountain."

Salvatore bowed. "Ah. Well then, of course, we'll be there." His dark eyes met the patrizio's briefly before he turned to Massimo. "I'll make sure the news reaches everyone. Up the mountain."

"Thank you."

"Wonderful." Massimo and the patrizio spoke at the same time.

With another bow to Massimo, Salvatore took his leave.

Forcing a polite smile, Massimo turned to the patrizio. "You will make sure everyone is included, won't you, signor?"

The man's face flushed red. "Of course! It was probably just an oversight. What with such last-minute planning. I'm sure the patrizia intended for everyone to hear the news."

"Good. I would be very upset if anyone was left out," Massimo added.

Especially Alessia and her family.

By lunchtime, Massimo was ready to return to the inn for some peace and quiet. Signor Foncello was nearly as long-winded as himself, which had given Massimo a nice reprieve from having to come up with conversation. Though his head ached with all the information the patrizio had bestowed upon him.

Once back at the Blossom Inn, Massimo hurried to his room before Signora Giordano could appear with her daughter to attend to him. As lovely as the young woman was, Massimo had no interest in her.

Besides, the king had made clear that he expected Massimo to choose a *proper* match. Someone from the nobility. There was no such eligible person in Zamerra.

"Hello, Lucia. Napping again, are you?" Massimo asked as he entered his room.

Lucia continued to snooze, not bothering to look up. The memory of the previous dinner replayed in Massimo's mind. Serafina could understand Lucia. So, the rumors were true. Alessia and her sisters were witches.

People don't trust magic. Alessia's words came back to him.

What kind of magic did she have? Had she spent her whole life trying to hide it from the town? Massimo frowned. He didn't know what he could do for her, but he felt obligated to help her in some way. Perhaps Dante would know what to do.

A knock on his door startled him out of his thoughts.

"Pardon me, Count Gallo. Are you coming down for lunch?" Lena Giordano's voice came from the other side of his door.

Kissing sounds erupted, followed by a fit of childish giggles.

"Hush!" Lena hissed.

Massimo stiffened. "Thank you, but I'm feeling a little tired. Could you have it brought to my room instead, please?"

"I'll bring it up shortly!" Lena exclaimed, footsteps fading away.

Massimo sat on the bed beside Lucia and stroked her head. "I'm afraid I won't be able to get out of dancing tonight. I better get some rest beforehand. Do you think the people will be expecting a speech?"

Lucia didn't stir.

Massimo sighed. "It's our last night here, Lucia. Tomorrow, we go home."

At this, her eyes opened, and she sat up to look at him. '*Meow?*'

He continued petting her. "I don't know what that means, but I'm guessing you're going to miss it here?" He turned to look at the open window. "I think I'm going to miss it too."

* * *

The plaza was filled with people. There were tall people, short people, large people, small people. All kinds of people.

Vendors moved along the streets, selling their wares. The air was warm and filled with the smell of salted pork fat and sugary pastries. Bodies pressed in all around Massimo, everyone clamoring around him with excitement. It seemed the whole town had turned out to wish him goodbye. All except the Silveris.

Where was Alessia? Was she coming?

The sky was darkening above them. Massimo followed Signora and Signor Foncello as they led him through the crowd, ordering everyone to make room.

Music started, and the townsfolk spread out, readying themselves for the first dance. Not wanting to be rude, Massimo danced with everyone who came up to him. Young girls and wizened signoras alike. Even Lena Giordano eagerly claimed two dances and told him he had the most handsome jaw.

As the day wore on, Massimo was beginning to worry that Alessia wasn't coming at all. He wouldn't get to dance with the beautiful witch or tell her goodbye.

Trying to push his disappointment aside, he took a seat next to the patrizio and nodded politely as he droned on about Zamerra traditions.

"Look who's come now!" a woman's voice caught his ear. Whispers echoed around Massimo.

"The witches have come."

"Well, why shouldn't they? They are a part of our town."

He jumped to his feet and watched as Alessia and her sisters made their way through the crowd. Her dark eyes met his.

Heat surged through Massimo. Her curls were pulled back into a loose braid, decorated with little white flowers. She stood there in her forest green skirt and a white blouse, somehow looking otherworldly, though she fit in with the other townsfolk. Massimo couldn't tear his eyes from her.

She was mesmerizing.

Before he realized it, he was moving toward her as if pulled by invisible strings. Murmurs erupted around him, but Massimo paid them no mind.

"Signora Silveri, I'm so glad you came," he greeted her, taking her hand in his.

The warmth of her touch spread across his skin. Her eyes snapped to his as she curtsied.

"We wanted to say goodbye, Count." Her voice was gentle.

"Goodbye. Right." Massimo frowned.

Reality crashed in around him. This was goodbye. The

words of the townsfolk echoed in his mind. He was a count. He had his duty to the king, to them all. As alluring as she was, he knew it was foolish to hope for any affection from her.

As if reading his mind, she withdrew her hand and moved away with a polite nod. Massimo watched, chest tight, as she led her sisters past him. Cold spread through him in her absence.

"Another song!" Patrizio Foncello commanded the musicians, who had stopped playing, to watch the awkward scene.

Everyone was watching and whispering. A lively song started, encouraging everyone back to their dancing. Massimo, not feeling as cheery as before, returned to his seat beside the patrizia and sipped his wine.

He listened half-heartedly to the conversation, offering a nod and answer here and there. The air grew cooler as night set in. How long was he expected to stay?

A flurry of skirts twirled before him, a dark green one catching his eye. Massimo turned to see Alessia joining in the slow dance. His breath caught in his throat at the sight. Time seemed to stop as Alessia danced. There was something about her that kept drawing him in. Despite his best intentions, he couldn't stop watching her. When a young man moved in to claim a dance from her, Massimo's jaw clenched.

He turned to his host and hostess. "It's getting late, and I have an early day of travel tomorrow. I think I'll retire now."

"Oh, but not before you address everyone. I think everyone would love to hear from our count," Patrizio Foncello said, rising to his feet.

He motioned for the musicians to stop. Massimo couldn't help but feel a touch of satisfaction as Alessia and her partner's dance was halted.

Patrizio Foncello glanced at Massimo and waved for everyone to listen. Put on the spot, Massimo reached into his pocket for the notes he'd written just in case. The letters were smudged. He squinted at the notes and tried his best to make out the words.

Something about Lucia and a mention of a library. Massimo couldn't remember what he'd written. And why bring up his cat?

"Well, this is no help," he muttered aloud and shoved the paper back into his pocket.

He gave everyone a tight smile, his throat suddenly growing very dry. His mind had drawn a blank and a nervous gurgle escaped him. How funny that he'd been afraid of rambling and yet here he was frozen instead.

A wave of nausea hit Massimo as he stared out at their expectant faces. His eyes roamed the crowd, snagging on a familiar face. *Alessia Silveri.* She gave him an encouraging smile.

"Thank you, Patrizio Foncello," Massimo finally found his voice.

He scanned the crowd again before meeting Alessia's gaze once more. Though he couldn't quite read the strange look she gave him, he found focusing on her helped him regain his train of thought.

Instead of addressing the whole town, he could address her. For some reason, that seemed much more doable.

"And thank you all for coming to say goodbye. Everyone has been very hospitable and Zamerra is truly one of the most beautiful places I've had the pleasure of visiting. I know you have all worked so hard to make the festival and this dance a great success. I have enjoyed myself immensely. So, thank you," Massimo finished, pausing a moment to catch his breath.

"Oh, and one more thing. I don't know when I will be able to return but knowing that everyone is accepted and well-cared for here will put my mind at ease. Should anyone, anyone at all, ever be in need of anything, speak to Patrizio Foncello, and he will communicate with me. I won't forget you. Any of you."

His eyes met Alessia's.

The crowd clapped and cheered. A rush of relief filled Massimo. The speech was over. People rushed him from all sides, reaching out hands and leaning in to plant air kisses on his cheeks. He looked for Alessia, but she had disappeared.

Perhaps it was for the best.

Music started up again, the sound of the stringed instruments filling the air. Everything moved in a blur as people began dancing and cheering. Massimo took the seat the patrizio offered, grateful for a chance to clear his mind.

Patrizio Foncello and his wife sat beside him, introducing everyone who came up to say goodbye. Massimo's head spun, trying to keep track of all the names before he finally gave up.

When the lively song ended, the musicians played a ballad, the last of the night. The sun had set, and the streetlights were lit. Massimo took the mug of caffé offered to him and sighed contentedly.

By the time the song was finished, the streets were lit with the golden glow of the lanterns. People began packing up their carts and belongings. Patrizia Foncello bid him goodnight before kissing her husband goodbye.

Massimo hopped into the wagon and glanced around the town. The sooner he left Zamerra behind, the sooner he'd feel more like himself again. *Hopefully.*

Chapter 13

The Roof Incident

"I don't think I've ever danced so much in one night," Alessia said with a groan as she trudged up the mountain.

Pain shot through her feet as she tried to take light steps. She didn't know what time it was, but she was ready to drop into bed. A breeze blew past them, bringing with it the various scents she'd picked up from town. *Perhaps a bath first. Then bed.*

"We should have brought the cart," Pamina said beside her.

"And have Fabrizio run off again?" Liliana muttered on her other side.

Alessia stumbled in the dark, caught by her sister's arms. There were no streetlamps up the mountain to light their way. The moon and the stars were the only reliable source of light because the lanterns Serafina and Fiorella held kept bobbing around. They looked like giant fireflies zagging drunkenly in the sky.

"Stop your bouncing! You're moving the lanterns all over

the place," Liliana snapped, seeming to have finally reached the end of her rope.

She stomped beside Alessia, grumbling under her breath about lengthy parties and foolish girls. Pamina chuckled, not seeming tired in the least. The youngest two laughed and chattered away, ignoring them. They appeared to be even more awake now than they had been in the morning.

Alessia smiled. Their excitement would eventually wear off. Tomorrow, it would be back to business as usual. The count was leaving, and things would settle back down.

The image of Count Gallo leapt to her mind. His dark trousers and freshly pressed white shirt that showed off his tanned, muscular arms. Warm amber eyes flashed in her mind. No one had ever looked at her so frankly before. As if by one mere look, he could uncover all her secrets. Heat flooded her at the memory. She stumbled into Liliana with a grunt.

"What's wrong with you?" Liliana asked, shoving her off.

"Too much wine?" Pamina asked innocently.

"No. I just lost my footing," Alessia replied hastily.

What was wrong with her? Why couldn't she get the count off her mind?

Before her thoughts wandered too far into dangerous territory again, she pushed them aside and looked around at the darkness that surrounded them.

The starry, cloudless sky stretched above them. Up ahead, the shadowy structure of their villa appeared. A light was on in Mama's room, shining like a beacon against the dark mountainside.

A nagging thought tugged at the back of her mind, but Alessia refused to acknowledge it. Mama's vision could wait.

Welcome home, the villa seemed to say, in its special, sleepy voice.

Alessia waved back, too tired to respond properly. She let

her sisters go first and followed after them. They were greeted by the bevy of cats and little Gio as they made their way to the back door of the kitchen.

Alessia waited for Serafina to shoo her entourage out of the way before shutting the door. Pamina was unbraiding Fiorella's hair in the kitchen, taking out the little daisies she'd weaved in. Bruno stood tiptoed on the table, snooping into the bag Fiorella had brought home.

"Here, Bruno," Fiorella said, handing a wrapped tart out to the little elf.

He took it and sniffed it. Then he broke it in half and stuffed half in his mouth, wrapper and all. Alessia shook her head at him as he struggled with the enormous bite before running to his room in the pantry.

"I wish Mama could have come to the dance. She'll be sorry that she missed the count," Fiorella said, her chestnut hair now hanging loose around her shoulders.

Liliana sighed. "I don't understand why she's still getting these headaches. I've tried all the tonics, but nothing seems to be helping much."

Pamina patted her on the back. "Don't worry, Liliana. I'm sure she just needs more rest."

Liliana's eyes met Alessia's. They hadn't told the others about Mama's vision and Alessia planned to keep it that way. She could only imagine what her sisters would do if they found out.

"I'm going to miss Count Gallo," Fiorella added with a sad little sigh.

Liliana snorted. "Miss him? You hardly know him."

Serafina frowned at her. "Even you can't dislike him, Liliana. He's wonderful. So is his cat. I'm going to miss her."

Alessia cleared her throat and addressed them. "Yes, well, it's late. We should get some rest so we can start on the chores in the morning. I want to check on the strawberries, Fiorella. For the wine. Liliana, can you go check on Mama?"

Her sisters left, groaning about work. Only Liliana stayed behind. Alessia tried to ignore the imploring look on her sister's face.

"When is Angelo's cousin coming to see about the roof?" Liliana broke the silence.

"Hopefully soon."

Liliana's dark eyebrow arched. She looked so annoyingly like Mama when she did it that it was hard for Alessia to face her.

"Well, hopefully with the count gone, we'll be able to focus on what needs to be done," Liliana added.

Heat rushed across Alessia's face. "What are you trying to say, Liliana?"

Her sister gave her a long, silent look before finally answering, "Only that you seem distracted lately. I know you said you could never marry, but..." She trailed off.

With a sigh, Liliana pulled out the last of the lilies tied in her hair and walked toward Alessia. "Do you like him?"

"The count? Don't be silly. I have no chance with a count."

Liliana frowned. "That's not what I asked."

"He's handsome, I admit, but there's nothing there. I said I won't marry, and I won't. Forget Mama's vision. I'm not going anywhere."

Liliana nodded, but the troubled look in her eye made Alessia's heart twist. What could she do to convince them all that she was happy with how things were?

* * *

By some luck, the rain hadn't begun, though the morning was gray and foggy. Such a dreary start that seemed to have put the villa in a somber mood. Despite the lack of Spring sunshine and the long list of to-dos, Alessia felt light and cheery. An odd feeling that she couldn't attribute to anything in particular.

The memory of the night before replayed in her mind. The music. The dancing. The count standing so close beside her. She flushed at the memory of his warm body and burning gaze. The smell of forest on his skin. Cedar with a hint of vanilla and spices.

"Here, try one." Fiorella's voice interrupted Alessia's thoughts.

She held up a juicy, plump strawberry to her.

Alessa took it and nodded her thanks. She bit into the fruit and nearly choked. Fiorella's face fell, her cheeks reddening in embarrassment.

Unable to stomach it, Alessia spat the strawberry onto the grass. "What happened? It tastes like—"

"Onions," Fiorella finished miserably.

She waved her hand over the row of bright red strawberry plants. "I was hoping it was just me. I've eaten more than a dozen and they all taste like that. I don't understand. I didn't do anything different with these ones."

"Santos," Alessia muttered.

Fiorella sniffled, the noise snapping Alessia to attention. Her heart twisted at the sight of her youngest sister growing teary-eyed. Poor Fiorella. No one had worked harder on the strawberries than she had.

Alessia pulled her into a hug and squeezed. "It's alright, Ella. We'll figure something out. We should still have enough, even without this row."

Fiorella wrapped her arms around Alessia and buried her face in her blouse. "What if I mess up the other strawberries?"

"We can fix them. We still have time to fulfill the wine

orders. If worse comes to worst, we can trade for the rest of the strawberries we need with one of the farmers in town."

Fiorella looked up at her, aghast. "Oh, no. We can't do that. What would they think?"

"Who cares what they think? You are the most talented gardener in the history of Zamerra."

Fiorella rolled her eyes at her but smiled. She pulled away from Alessia's embrace and wiped her face with her arm. She turned to look at the strawberries and sighed. "They looked so good, too."

Alessia nodded in agreement.

"Alessia! Ella!" Pamina's voice called from the kitchen.

"Come on, let's take a break," Alessia said, urging her sister away from the strawberries.

The enticing aroma of caffé enveloped them as they entered the kitchen. Everyone sat at the table, digging into Pamina's pastries.

"How is your head this morning, Mama?" Fiorella asked, going to the sink to wash her hands.

Mama gave her a brilliant smile. "It's fine, amore." She turned to Liliana. "I haven't felt this well and whole in a while. Thank you"—her gaze roamed over them—"all of you. You are the best daughters a mother could ask for."

"And you're the best Mama anyone could ask for," Fiorella replied, crossing the room to give Mama a kiss on the cheek.

Everyone echoed her sentiment.

A troubled look passed across their mother's face but was gone quickly, replaced with a smile.

She shook her head, her dark curls bouncing with the movement. "How are the strawberries coming along? The ones for the wine for our new count?"

Fiorella's face crumpled. Mama took her hand and pulled her into a tight embrace.

"They'll be along soon. We can ask the patrizio for the count's address when it's time," Alessia said.

Before she could say more, the sound of wagon wheels came from outside. Everyone jumped to their feet and poured out of the kitchen to see who had come.

"I hope that's Angelo's cousin," Liliana muttered.

Alessia turned to Serafina. "Find Bruno. I don't want him scaring Nico away. Give him some sweets and limonata in his pantry and close him in."

Serafina gaped at her. "How am I supposed to find him?"

Alessia sighed and waved her away. "Set out the sweets in his room. He'll come. Just hurry!"

They opened their gate to allow their visitor in and moved out of the way. Angelo arrived along with a taller, scrawnier young man who, aside from the same strong curved nose, looked nothing like him.

"Greetings, signoras!" Angelo called as they drove in.

His eyes swept over them, a look of disappointment crossing his features. They returned his greeting and walked alongside the wagon.

A chorus of meows followed by the high-pitched bark of Gio filled the air as the group of felines (and the dog) descended upon them. Alessia and her sisters shooed them out of the way, letting their guests pass through.

Liliana and Fiorella tended to Angelo's golden mare and cart as Alessia led their visitors into the kitchen. Serafina was there, a startled look on her face when she saw Angelo.

He gave her a dimpled smile, which she pretended to ignore. Alessia frowned at her rudeness. Mama and Pamina offered the young men caffè and the leftover pastries, which they ate leisurely at the table. Alessia forced a smile and listened to the small talk. Why couldn't they hurry up and get started on the roof? It would be nice not to have a gaping hole when it started raining.

Pushing down the wave of impatience, she tried to be a courteous hostess. They were making the repairs for quite a discount, after all. Once the pastries were gone and the carafe was drained, they fetched their tools and headed for the roof.

Soon, the pounding sound of hammers filled the air. Alessia turned to watch Angelo and his cousin working. She glanced at the darkening sky. It was nearly afternoon, but thankfully it seemed they were almost finished with their work.

Mama and Pamina tended to Fabrizio and their other animals while Alessia and the others took care of the yard and gardens. The housework could wait until the boys were done.

A startled cry broke the pounding hammers. Another pained shout followed and Alessia could see Angelo's arms flailing, his body dangerously close to the edge.

Her heart leapt into her throat. He was going to fall. Without wasting another second, she ran for the villa, her sisters close behind her.

Serafina outran Alessia, reaching it first. "Steady, you fool!" she shouted up to him.

Angelo regained his footing and glanced down at them with a panicked look, quickly disappearing from the edge. From the ground, they couldn't see what had happened. Another shout came, followed by a lot of clanging and scrambling sounds.

"I'm going up!" Alessia announced, running inside and into her bedroom.

She could hear her sister's footsteps pounding behind her, but she didn't wait. Climbing out the window, she stepped out onto the roof.

Angelo was kneeling beside his cousin, their tools scattered all over the roof. His cousin held up his hand—his bleeding hand—with a pained look.

"What happened?" Alessia found her voice as she carefully made her way over to them.

She glanced back and motioned her sisters to stay back. They watched from the open window with worried expressions.

"I don't know. Something attacked us," Angelo answered.

"Something small and fast," his cousin added.

"Maybe a squirrel?" Angelo said with a frown.

His cousin shot him an incredulous look. "A squirrel with a hat?"

Angelo shrugged, meeting Alessia's eyes. "It was too fast to get a good look."

Alessia tore off a piece of her skirt and reached for the poor boy's hand. There was a distinct bite mark on his palm.

Bruno.

She wrapped up his injury gently and helped Angelo lead him back into the house. She stayed behind to scan the roof for the troublesome elf. There was no sign of him, but her gaze snagged on the hole. The boards they'd been putting down were ripped off now, and somehow the hole had become even bigger.

Thunder crackled above. *Fantastic.* The boys, now in her sisters' care, she hurried back inside to find a covering strong enough to keep out the rain. Liliana, who had stayed behind, hurried to help her.

Together they covered the hole just as the first raindrops splattered down.

"I don't think they're going to finish the job now," Liliana muttered as they crawled back in through the window.

"I'll go into town tomorrow to get supplies. We'll have to fix it ourselves. Can you find a bucket? Just in case?" Alessia sighed.

Liliana nodded. "What are you going to tell them about Bruno? The first time, people took it as a rumor, but now...," she shook her head, "Angelo is no fool, despite Serafina's opinion. If he tells people..."

Alessia frowned. "He said they couldn't get a good look. Let's not press the issue." She sighed. "I told Serafina to shut him in the pantry with sweets."

"She did. I checked it myself. He must have squeezed under the door."

Alessia felt her mouth drop. "What? How?"

Liliana shrugged. "I don't know, but when you find him, we should ask."

Alessia groaned. She should have known better than to let the little elf have too many sweets. That, in addition to the loud hammers, had probably put him in a frenzied state. It was her fault, not anyone else's, that he'd acted out.

When she found him, she'd make sure he was okay before scolding him. Thankfully, the bite wasn't very deep. Following Liliana, she rejoined the others in the kitchen.

Angelo and his cousin were seated, drinking limonata and eating Pamina's lemon cookies. Alessia nodded approvingly. The cookies had a calming effect and would help soothe the poor young man's nerves.

"Here are your tools," Alessia said, breaking the silence.

She set the box on the table between them. They exchanged a silent look.

"Perhaps tomorrow if the rain lets up, we can come back and finish?" Angelo offered with a sheepish grin.

His cousin's head whipped toward him, an incredulous look on his face. Clearly, he didn't want to return to the Silveris' villa. Alessia couldn't blame him.

She waved away Angelo's offer. "That's alright. We've put up something for now, and I'll go into town to get more supplies tomorrow. We'll still pay you for your time and work, of course." She motioned for Fiorella to go and retrieve the coins.

Fiorella stood and left the kitchen.

"But we haven't finished the job," Angelo protested.

His blue eyes searched Serafina's stony face. He didn't seem to hear when Alessia assured him not to worry about it.

Serafina had become unnaturally quiet since the incident. Alessia had never seen her sister in such a state of panic as she'd been seeing Angelo teetering on the roof. It had given them all a scare.

Alessia shuddered to think what could have happened. Angelo had proven his loyalty to their family more than enough times now. She couldn't ask more of him.

Confident she was making the right decision, she stood to get herself a cup of caffé. The rain pounded harder; the sound echoing through the kitchen.

Please hurry, the poor villa seemed to say.

Chapter 14

A Hasty Offer

"A pity your trip was delayed yesterday," Signora Giordano said as she poured Massimo more caffé.

"Yes. Well. I'm sure the king will understand. Lucky for me, I have such a lovely place to stay."

She beamed at him and nudged her daughter toward him before scurrying back to the kitchen. Massimo glanced to see the younger children peering around the corner, watching them in the dining room.

"The rain is coming any day now, and I'm afraid travel is quite impossible when the road muddies," Lena explained, fidgeting nervously as she stood before him.

"Well, Lucia is grateful for that. She's not a fan of carriages, but she has been enjoying being spoiled here by you and your siblings."

Lena smiled brightly. "If you like, Count, I can show you around the town today."

Giggles came from around the corner.

"Thank you, but I don't want to be a nuisance. I think I'll just take to my room and read," Massimo answered politely.

Before she could object, Massimo bowed and took his leave.

When he entered his room, Lucia looked up at him and cocked her head.

Turning to the side table, Massimo picked up the book he'd been struggling to read and sighed in frustration. Alessia's dark eyes and full flips flickered in his mind. He closed the book and set it back down. Try as he might, he couldn't get the beautiful witch out of his mind. Was she thinking of him as well?

"Nonsense. I'm sure she has better things to do than think of me." His words startled Lucia out of her nap.

She gave him a long-suffering look, clearly unimpressed by his troubling thoughts.

Massimo drummed his fingers on the side table and decided it was time to leave the room. The sky was gray, but the rain hadn't begun yet. Better to get out before the storm moved in.

"I'll be back shortly, Lucia," Massimo called, grabbing his hooded cloak from the hook.

He buckled up his boots and waved goodbye from the doorway. Lucia turned her head to blink at him before returning to licking her front paws.

Outside, Massimo found the town changed from the first day he'd arrived. Puddles of murky water dotted the cobblestoned streets and the banners from the festival were now faded and drooping. All the shutters were closed tightly, making the buildings look as if they were asleep.

The only sign of life was the fresh smell of caffé and wood burning that came from the buildings. With no plan or direction, Massimo walked along, stopping only when he heard a bell chime overhead.

He looked up to find Alessia. His heart hammered loudly in his ears. *Imagine that.* Just the woman he'd been trying to get out of his thoughts.

She returned his startled look, her dark eyes widening and her mouth gaping.

"Count Gallo! Hello." Alessia finally spoke.

"Hello," Massimo returned.

"I thought you left," she said, glancing around the empty street.

"My ride was delayed. and then well, the rain came," Massimo explained.

They stood staring at each other, and Massimo wondered if she was as affected by him as he was by her.

"Fine weather we're having, no?" his words left of their own will.

Alessia glanced at the dark sky and gave him a confused look. "Yes?"

Massimo's face flamed. *Fine weather?*

Trying to recover, he inclined his head toward her. "I look forward to tasting your strawberry wine."

Her smile tightened. "Yes. Well, a proper harvest can take some time. I'm afraid it won't be ready before you leave, but we can send the bottle to you wherever you like, Count."

"Massimo," he replied without thinking.

She lifted an eyebrow in question.

"You can just call me Massimo."

Alessia gaped at him, making him flush harder. What was he thinking? It was highly improper to give her his first name as if they were...

"Then I suppose you can call me Alessia, if you like." She smiled with a curtsy.

Warmth filled him. It was the first time she'd given him her first name.

"Alessia." The word slipped out soft and reverent.

Her dark eyes snapped to his. Massimo's heart skipped. There was something there between them; he was sure of it now. It felt as if the air was charged around them. A strange energy that made him want to move closer to her. Touch her. His gaze snagged on her full lips.

"Well, I should be on my way," Alessia said, breaking the spell.

Alarm filled him. He noticed now that she had a basket full of what looked like building supplies.

"Where are you going with that?" he asked, cursing himself for his impertinence.

Alessia glanced down at the basket before meeting his gaze. "My roof needs fixing," she said with a shrug.

"I can do it." Once again, the words left him too quickly to stop.

She looked just as surprised as he felt. Never mind that he knew absolutely nothing about home repairs. What was this spell she had him under? After giving it more thought, Massimo was even more determined to help her. How hard could fixing a roof be?

A look of uncertainty flashed across her features. "Oh, thank you for the offer, Count—"

"Massimo, please," he interjected softly.

She shook her head slightly. "I couldn't impose on you."

"You're not. In fact, you'd be doing me a favor."

"Oh?"

Massimo nodded and swept his hand toward the sky. "Truth be told, I'm growing a little restless inside the inn all day. Some light manual labor sounds like a delightful break."

Alessia gave him a disbelieving look. Whether she doubted his enthusiasm or his ability, she didn't say. Instead, she only nodded in acceptance and gave him a hesitant smile.

Together, they walked through the empty town, stopping at her wagon. Her horse looked up with tired eyes, glancing from her to Massimo.

He snorted and threw his head to the side as if to say, *"Oh, the strange fae. Wonderful."*

That thought reminded Massimo of the day at the Rossis' dinner. He'd learned Serafina's secret. What kind of secrets did Alessia have of her own?

He hopped into the wagon beside Alessia. Her warm body was pressed against him, turning his thoughts toward her. An alarming one filled his mind. What if Alessia possessed similar magic to her sister? What if she could read *his* thoughts? What if she was reading them right now?

She turned toward him with a worried expression. "Are you well, Co—Massimo?"

His heart lurched. Hearing his name on her lips made heat rush through him. *I hope you can't read my mind now.*

Somehow Massimo managed to keep himself from rambling too much as they made their way up the mountain. Instead, he listened intently as Alessia told him about how they had come to Zamerra.

Thunder rumbled in the distance, and gray clouds moved across the sky. The king couldn't expect him to travel in such poor weather conditions. He'd have to stay in Zamerra longer than planned. A smile spread on his lips at that thought.

"Oh, I should warn you. The animals tend to get a little excited when we have visitors," Alessia said as they pulled up to a large wooden gate.

As if on cue, a series of yowling and yapping came from the other side. Massimo watched as Fiorella and Serafina appeared, opening the gate for them with surprised looks.

Alessia led them in and gave Massimo an apologetic smile as a swarm of cats descended upon them. One little, scrappy-looking dog followed, barking loudly.

"Count!" Fiorella exclaimed with an excited clap.

"Shoo! Go!" Serafina waved the animals out of their path.

She smiled up at them and squinted. "Did you bring Lucia?"

"I'm afraid not," Massimo answered as he stood to hop down.

Alessia, not waiting for his help, hopped down on the other side and motioned for Serafina to help with Fabrizio.

Pamina and Liliana stood in the doorway, eyes widening in surprise. Signora Silveri was nowhere to be found. Fiorella ran past them all and disappeared into the back door.

Massimo looked around at the large yard and lush gardens. The woods surrounded the villa, trees pressing in and nearly swallowing up the building entirely.

"This is lovely," Massimo said, staring up at the tanned stone face of the villa.

Thank you. Welcome, a sleepy-sounding voice echoed back.

His head whipped to Alessia, jaw-dropping.

Her dark eyes met his, surprise flickering across her features. "Did you hear it?"

Massimo shook his head. "I don't know what I heard exactly, but... there's something special about your villa."

Alessia smiled and nodded, making his pulse race. She had the most beautiful smile.

"Count Gallo, what a nice surprise! Just in time for caffé," Pamina called, waving them over.

Liliana stood beside her, arms folded over her chest and eyes narrowed at him. She gave him no greeting.

Alessia noticed his hesitant smile and shot her sister a sharp look.

"And to what do we owe this pleasure?" Liliana asked, dark eyes still fixed on Massimo.

"The count has been nice enough to offer his assistance with our roof," Alessia answered for him, giving him an encouraging smile.

Massimo felt himself nodding along.

"I thought you'd left Zamerra, Count," Liliana added with a frown.

"Well, I was going to, but my trip was delayed," he answered, shifting uncomfortably under their heavy stares.

"Oh, that's wonderful!" Serafina said with a grin.

She turned to Liliana and made a sour face. "Why don't you go back to making your smelly potions?"

"Fina," Alessia said with a warning tone.

Ignoring Alessia, Serafina turned to him and smiled. "Liliana makes potions and Pamina can make magical food and drink. And Fiorella—"

"Serafina!" Alessia cut her off.

The girl frowned. "What? He already knows about my magic. Do you have magic too, Count?"

"No. Sadly, I don't, but I do have excellent hearing."

Serafina's eyes gleamed. "Oh! Alessia doesn't have magic either."

"Santos," Alessia muttered, shaking her head at her sister.

Massimo smiled. "Well, I think you are all very exceptional. Magic aside." His eyes met Alessia's.

"Count Gallo!" Signora Silveri appeared with Fiorella by her side.

She greeted him affectionately, ushering everyone inside. Massimo let her lead him as the others followed.

"Please sit, Count. Pamina, caffé, please," Signora Silveri waved Massimo to one of the chairs.

"Thank you," he said as he sat down in the wooden chair.

He glanced around their cozy kitchen. It was much smaller than his kitchen back home, but there was something special about it. The candles were lit, casting a glow along the wooden cabinets and the large window above the sink was open, cool air blowing in. Garlic hung from the rafters near the hearth, filling the room with its smell, a sharp distinction from the sweet-smelling caffé Pamina poured into his mug.

Massimo nodded in thanks as he took a sip. The warm, smooth liquid filled his mouth with a sweet and nutty taste.

His eyes widened. "This is the best caffé I've ever had."

Pamina beamed and the others laughed.

"Magic!" Serafina exclaimed, earning herself a scowl from Liliana.

Alessia sat beside him and pushed a plate of delicious-looking pastries toward him. Massimo met her eyes, a wave of desire washing over him. She glanced away first.

Turning to Signora Silveri, Massimo tried to calm his racing heart. "I was sorry to miss you at the dance the other night, signora. But glad I have this opportunity to give you a proper farewell."

The older woman smiled. "Yes, what a nice surprise. I'm afraid I wasn't feeling up to dancing. Not as young as I used to be, you know."

"I'm sorry to hear you were unwell. I hope you're feeling better now."

Her smile widened. "Much better now, thank you." Her eyes darted to Alessia, and a mysterious look passed between them that Massimo didn't know what to make of.

"Count, do you like music?" Fiorella asked shyly.

Massimo turned to her. "Of course."

She glanced at her sisters and brushed back a wavy strand of hair from her face. "Would you like to hear my song?"

"I thought the count was here to fix our roof," Liliana muttered behind her.

Signora Silveri shot her a dark look. She rose to her feet and smiled at Massimo. "How very kind of you, Count Gallo. You simply must hear Fiorella's song first, though. She has the loveliest voice," she said, smiling proudly.

Massimo stood and nodded. "Of course. I'd love to hear it."

He moved to follow her at the same time as Alessia moved, nearly bumping into her. She inhaled sharply at the near contact and stepped back.

"After you," Massimo said, the words coming out low and deep.

She curtsied and hurried out, her sisters following out of the room. Liliana was the last to move. She gave Massimo a long, hard look, blocking his path.

"You seem like a decent person, Count," she said, dark eyes piercing him.

"Uh... Thank you?"

"I don't know what your goal is here today, but you should know. We look out for each other. If you think we are somehow incapable of protecting ourselves or vulnerable in any way, let me assure you, we are not."

"No! I don't think that at all, signora. I have the utmost respect for you. For all of you. I only want to help. I promise," Massimo said quickly, face warm.

Liliana stared at him. "Why?"

Her question startled Massimo. He blinked before answering. "Well, maybe because I wish someone had helped me and my mother."

Liliana frowned. "You grew up in the upper class. Didn't you have all the help you needed?"

Massimo flushed. "We were lucky, yes. Privileged. But I do understand what it's like to be an outsider."

"Count! Are you coming?" Signora Silveri interrupted, eyes darting between him and Liliana.

"Yes, of course," Massimo answered, nodding at Liliana before following her mother out of the room.

Chapter 15

Entertaining a Fae Count

The count—or Massimo as he insisted she call him—
was in her family's sitting room, drinking caffé with
her mother and sisters as they listened to Fiorella's
song. As if he'd always belonged there with them.

Fiorella finished with a blush and a quick curtsy.

Massimo stood and applauded. "That was amazing!" He
smiled.

"Thank you," Fiorella said, beaming.

Something stirred inside Alessia, and a lump grew in her
throat. Massimo was nothing like she had imagined a count
would be. Born and raised in high society, his manners were
impeccable, but he didn't seem offended in the slightest at her
family's lack of decorum.

He looked oddly comfortable as he sat back down on their
lumpy couch and answered their questions. Not once did he
seem annoyed or appalled at her nosy sisters' probing.

"Did you really go to the Palazzo delle Stelle?" Serafina
asked.

"Yes. Lucia and I both went," Massimo answered with a nod.

Alessia listened as he told them about his time at the grand palazzo. His voice was soft and melodic, and his eyes gleamed with affection as he talked about his cat and the king's massive library.

"Do you have any brothers or sisters?" Serafina asked, taking the lead in drilling their poor guest.

"No. Unfortunately, I don't. I have to admit I'm a little jealous seeing how close you all are," he answered with a small smile.

"What about your parents? Where are they?" Fiorella asked, green eyes filled with pity.

Massimo's smile faded. "They've passed on."

"Oh, I'm sorry to hear that, Count," Pamina answered first, brow furrowed.

"Do you miss them terribly?" Fiorella asked softly.

Alessia shook her head at her. "Ella."

Massimo only smiled. "I do. Especially my mama. I know she would have loved to meet you all."

"Was she fae like you?" Serafina asked.

He nodded. "Yes. She was the kindest soul you'd ever meet. Always saw the best in everyone. Even when they didn't deserve it."

"She sounds lovely, Count," Mama said kindly. "Seems like you've inherited her kindness. I'm sure she is so proud of you."

"Thank you, signora."

"Does that mean you live all alone?" Fiorella asked with a frown.

"Well, I have Lucia. And my housekeeper, cook, coachman, and the maids. They all come often."

"But those are all servants. Don't you want a family of your own?"

"Ella!" Alessia admonished her sister.

Massimo's eyes met hers. "Yes. I think I do. Someday."

Heat spread across Alessia's skin at his burning gaze. The memory of his muscular arm brushing against hers as they rode in the wagon made her pulse race.

There was a thought, a question, she'd been trying to squash since he'd arrived. What if he was the answer to Mama's vision? Her wed to a count? *Impossible.*

Her place was here, in Zamerra, and his was not.

"Well, I think I should get to work on your roof. I'm sure you... do you have a house elf?" Massimo's abrupt question made Alessia turn to follow his gaze.

They all turned to look. Bruno scurried in and hopped up onto the couch beside the count. Alessia frowned. She hadn't been able to find the little elf since the incident with Angelo's cousin. Where had he been hiding all day?

Bruno shot her a miserable look. Then, to all of their amazement, he took off his hat and bowed before Massimo.

"His name is Bruno," Fiorella said, breaking the silence.

"*Grava fla!*" Bruno stretched out his little hand toward the count.

Massimo smiled at him and offered him a finger in return. "It's a pleasure to meet you, Bruno. I'm Massimo."

Alessia sucked in a breath, relieved to see the little elf wasn't going to bite their guest. Instead, he rattled off in his elvish tongue, his eyes growing wide with fear.

Massimo nodded and gave him a sympathetic smile as if he could understand him.

"Do you know what he is saying?" Alessia couldn't hide the surprise in her tone.

Bruno finished his rant, giving Alessia a guilty look. He put his hat back on and sat down on the side table beside Massimo's mug.

The count met Alessia's gaze. "He says he is very sorry for what happened yesterday. Something about biting someone's hand. It seems he thought they were hurting the villa, and he didn't realize you invited them in."

A troubled look crossed Massimo's face as he continued. "He's worried you are going to send him away. He very much wants to stay, and he says he'll be a good elf."

A chorus of dismay echoed in the room. No one would let her kick him out, even if she wanted to.

Alessia smiled and held out her hand toward Bruno. "All is forgiven, Bruno. We could never send you away. You're family. Family is forever."

The little elf stood on the table and kissed her hand, wiping tears from his eyes. Pamina handed him a piece of pastry, which he gobbled up heartily.

"*Grava fla!*" He held out his hand for more.

"How did you learn to speak Elvish?" Serafina asked Massimo.

Alessia turned to look at the count, curious of his answer as well.

He shrugged. "I guess it just comes with having fae blood. We used to have a house elf when I was young. Ruella." A smile spread on his face at the memory. "She and I used to have such fun together."

"What happened to her?" Fiorella asked.

Massimo frowned, his forehead creased. Alessia had the inexplicable urge to smooth out the wrinkles.

"She grew old. When she passed, Mama and I couldn't bear to find a replacement. She was like family to us. You can't replace family."

Everyone murmured and nodded their agreement. The sorrow written on Massimo's face twisted Alessia's heart.

"Besides, you can't hire house elves like that, anyway. They go where they're needed. They find you." He turned to Alessia. "You have something very special. It's not every home or family that is blessed so."

His words made Alessia's eyes grow hot. How had he, a stranger, wormed his way so quickly and so sincerely into her life? It had only been a few days since his arrival, and he had turned her world around so suddenly. Would it right itself when he left?

The thought of him leaving left a strange ache inside her.

"Thank you for your kind words, Count. We are blessed to have you join us. You are welcome here for as long and as often as you like," Mama answered for them all.

Massimo met Alessia's gaze, his amber eyes sharp and burning. He gave her a sad smile. "Thank you. Unfortunately, I must see to more business as soon as the roads have dried up enough to travel. Now then, should we see about getting your roof fixed?"

Alessia nodded, trying to ignore the well of emotion rising inside her. Standing and brushing down her skirt, she motioned for him to follow her.

"I'll bring the tools!" Serafina and Fiorella spoke in unison.

They scurried out of the room.

Alessia led Massimo outside and pointed out the ladder. "Thank you for your help again. I was going to try to fix it myself with Bruno, but I'm afraid this repair is much beyond us."

He nodded. "Well, he's still a young elf. His skills will probably improve over time."

Mama and the other girls had stayed inside, leaving Alessia alone with the count. They stood together in silence, looking up at the old villa.

"Thank you for your hospitality. Your family is lovely," the count said softly.

Alessia met his sincere gaze. "Thank you. We've enjoyed your visit as well."

"Here you go!" Serafina called as she and Fiorella carried the large toolbox together.

They set it down at Massimo's feet and glanced between him and Alessia with conspiring looks.

"Thank you," the count said, nodding to them.

"Here are the supplies," Alessia said, pointing to the pile of wooden boards she'd bought.

Massimo picked up the toolbox and stared at the wood.

"We can hand the boards up to you," Serafina offered.

"Ah. Yes. Thank you," Massimo answered as he walked toward the ladder. A look of uncertainty crossed his features.

Alessia followed him. "Do you need help?"

Massimo stared at the toolbox in his hand. "Oh, no. Thank you. I think I can manage."

Mama, Pamina, and Liliana had come out to join them. They stood together and watched as he started climbing the ladder, toolbox in one hand.

"No one else thinks this is a bad idea?" Liliana asked.

Alessia turned to her. "What do you mean?"

She scoffed. "Do you think he's ever fixed a roof before? He's a count!"

Alessia motioned for her to be quiet. What if he heard them? Count or not, they couldn't turn down his offer.

"I'm sure he knows what he's doing. Why would he have offered if he didn't?" Pamina whispered back.

"Could you hand the boards up now, please?" he called from the rooftop.

Serafina and Fiorella rushed to help him.

"If he falls off our roof, the town is going to be furious with us," Liliana muttered with a shake of her head.

"Liliana!" Alessia hissed.

Worry filled her at her sister's words.

The pounding of the hammer filled the silence, followed by a loud cracking and popping sound.

"Oh dear." Massimo's voice rang out over the noise.

Not wasting any time, Alessia climbed the ladder up to him.

He turned to her, wide-eyed. A horrible splintering sound filled the air.

"Oh!" Alessia exclaimed, pulling him back from the hole by his arm.

They watched, horrified, as more of the roof caved in, pushing them back toward the edge. What had been a decent size hole was now rapidly becoming a gigantic one. They watched, helpless, as pieces of the roof disappeared down into the house.

Finally, and thankfully, the cracking stopped. The villa seemed to moan in anguish.

Massimo turned to face Alessia with a stricken look. "I'm so dreadfully sorry. I promise I will send someone to fix this straight away. Someone more skilled than I, obviously. I apologize, I should have... oh, perhaps I could try—"

Alessia gripped his arm, cutting him off. "Thank you, but I think you've done enough for today. I..." Her gaze drifted to the gaping roof.

"What happened?" Mama called from the ground.

Alessia looked down to see her family staring up at them. Even Bruno had come out to see what was going on. Her stomach churned.

"At least everyone is safe. That's the most important thing," she found herself saying, trying to force a smile for the count.

"Alessia, please. Let me make this right. I'll get someone to come out today."

She shook her head. "I... I don't think anyone will come out on such short notice, and we can't afford to pay them much, anyway. I... I'll think of something. Thank you, though."

Massimo frowned. "No. This is my fault. I will fix this."

He took her hand in his and squeezed it. Warmth flooded her at the contact, his eyes meeting hers. "It's the least I can do. I can't leave you like this."

"Okay. Thank you."

She looked at their clasped hands, face heating.

"Alessia? Is everything alright?" Mama's voice broke the tension.

"Yes. We're fine. Coming down now," Alessia answered, turning away from the count.

"What happened to the roof? The hole is much bigger now!" Serafina said, her voice coming from inside.

"Fina, get out of there before the roof collapses!" Liliana shouted.

Alessia didn't hear her reply as she climbed down the ladder and waited for Massimo. He followed her down, shaking his head glumly.

"Santos! What happened?" Pamina asked as they rejoined everyone.

The count flushed. "I'm sorry. I've made things much worse. But I will fix it. Right away."

He turned to Alessia. "Could you drive me back to town? I'll speak to the patrizio. Find someone to come out now and fix your roof."

"Does this mean we can't go back inside?" Serafina asked, eyes wide.

"Let's wait and see when it's safe," Mama replied evenly.

Massimo sighed. "I'm so sorry. Why don't you all come back to the Inn with me, and I'll ask Signor Giordano to provide rooms for you."

"What about Bruno?" Fiorella asked, picking up the little elf.

"There is plenty of room for him as well."

Alessia turned to face the villa. *Are you alright?*

Yes, it answered, making her sigh in relief.

Feeling better, she met Massimo's gaze. "Thank you."

Pamina glanced at the sky overhead. "At least the rain is holding off."

"Oh, but that means the roads will be dried," Fiorella said with a sad look.

Alessia's eyes met Massimo's. He was leaving and he probably wouldn't be returning. Maybe not ever. That thought made her chest tighten. Why was she having such a hard time with his departure? The sooner he left, the sooner she could forget him.

Chapter 16

The King's Letter

"When will you be back?" Alessia asked, her dark eyes capturing his attention. A dark curl had fallen from her bun. It bounced as they moved in the cart, taunting him.

Massimo felt the sudden urge to touch it but refrained. "I don't know. Patrizio Foncello mentioned hosting a festival at the end of the season. Perhaps I'll be able to return then."

She nodded and turned away, falling silent once more. Despite Massimo's insistence, the others had opted to walk into town, leaving him alone with Alessia.

His throat turned dry. Her nearness made his stomach feel queasy. Hopefully, he wasn't getting sick. Though he wouldn't mind an excuse to stay longer.

Behind them, Serafina's laugh echoed. Massimo smiled. He would miss all the Silveris. Especially a certain dark-haired witch.

"If you leave your address, we can have the wine sent to you once it's ready. If you like, that is," Alessia spoke, interrupting his wayward thoughts.

Massimo swallowed hard and nodded. "Yes. Thank you. I'd like that very much. Perhaps I could write you?"

Alessia flushed. "I... I don't know if that would be proper."

"Why not?"

She bit her lip, eyes focused on the road. "Well, you're a count. I'm sure there are many eligible suitors with noble blood. I'm flattered, of course, Count, but—"

"Massimo," he interjected softly.

Alessia glanced at him. "Massimo, I'm a witch. A nobody from nowhere."

He frowned. "Is that how you feel?"

She shrugged. "It doesn't matter what I feel. It is what's true. I'm happy here. My family needs me, and I could never leave them. Your life... that's not what I want. Forgive me if I'm speaking too boldly."

"Ah. I see. Forgive me for being too forward, then."

With that, they fell quiet the rest of the way. Feeling dejected and even more the fool, Massimo apologized once more to Alessia and her family as they arrived at the Blossom Inn. After securing them the necessary accommodations, he went out to call on Patrizio Foncello.

"Ah! Count Gallo, I went to the inn to call on you earlier, but they said you'd gone out." The older man smiled warmly at him.

"Yes. I had a lovely visit with the Silveris," Massimo replied as the doorman waved him further inside.

Patrizio Foncello's eyebrows rose. "Oh? How is Signora Silveri?"

"They all seem well to me, but there is a concern. Their roof is in desperate need of repair. Right away. Can you send someone out there?"

The man blinked in surprise at him. "Send someone right now?"

Massimo nodded. "As soon as possible. I want it fixed before the rain starts. Tell them I'll pay double for them to work as quickly as they can."

"Oh, well. That's very gracious of you. I will have them go straight away."

"Thank you."

"I was coming to call on you earlier to let you know I can take you to Port de Bella first thing in the morning if you like. Now that the road is dry. From there, you should be able to find transportation or lodging if you wish it... unless of course, you wanted to extend your stay."

Massimo sighed. "I'm afraid I've extended as long as I can, Patrizio. Thank you for your offer. Lucia and I will be ready in the morning."

"Yes, of course. I understand. I hope you enjoyed your visit, Count."

"I did. Funny as it is, I've come to see Zamerra as somewhat of... a home. I'll miss it. Along with its inhabitants."

"Well, you'll have to frequent trips back. You are welcome anytime."

Massimo nodded to him in thanks and took a sip of the caffè offered to him. It tasted nothing like Pamina's magical brew. Alessia's smiling face flashed in his mind. He would miss her most of all. But would she miss him?

* * *

"Would you care for more caffè, Count?" Santino's voice pulled Massimo out of the story he was reading. Or had been trying to read.

He looked up at him and blinked. "Oh, Santino. I'd nearly forgotten you were there."

The older man hesitated. "Forgive me for the interruption. I just noticed you finished your cup. Would you like me to have the maid pour you some more, Count?"

Massimo glanced at the steaming carafe on the tray. "Thank you, signor. But I'm quite capable of pouring my own cup."

"Of course, your Countship. Forgive me for interrupting your reading," Santino said hurriedly, with a quick bow.

Setting the book down on the side table, Massimo shrugged off his apology. "It's alright. I was having a hard time getting into the story, anyway."

He'd been having a hard time getting into any book lately.

"Would you like me to pull you down another one?" Santino asked, hurrying over to the crowded bookshelf.

Massimo fought off a wave of irritation. Santino was just doing his job. He knew this, but still. He wasn't used to or comfortable with the man's constant hovering and assistance. Though he would never say so, Massimo suspected that Santino also found his role irritating. It was clear the valletto was used to keeping busy and since Massimo had returned home, he had hardly left his library.

To escape all the fervent would-be brides, Massimo stayed indoors. It was safe at home. Thankfully, he wouldn't need to be traveling as much now that everything was properly organized. Things were finally beginning to slow down.

"Count?" Santino asked again, uncertainty written on his face.

"Yes. Count Gallo. Back to your usual spot, I see," Dante's warm voice interrupted.

Massimo turned and stood to greet his friend. Even Lucia glanced at him.

"Santino, can you go ask the cook for some honey cakes, please?" Massimo asked, waving the valletto out.

"Yes! Right away, Count," Santino answered with a quick bow.

Massimo sighed deeply.

Dante's eyebrow arched at him. "What's wrong? Don't you like your valletto?"

"Nothing is wrong. Santino is wonderful. He was a valletto in the royal court, you know. Very efficient and responsible."

"And a complete nuisance?" Dante asked with a smirk.

"I didn't say that."

Dante shrugged as he sank down in the seat beside Massimo. "Why don't you just pay him a severance and let him retire?"

"I would if I didn't need a valletto."

"Why do you need one?"

Massimo sighed. "Because everyone expects me to. It's what's proper, Dante."

His friend laughed and gave him a strange look. "So is accepting invitations from the upper class. Instead of hiding like a hermit in your library. Speaking of invitations, I would love one to Signora Petrelli's party. Do you think you could tear yourself away from your busy schedule for one night?"

Massimo frowned.

Dante leaned toward him. "Please? I heard she was in the market for a new potion maker."

"So, this is about her ailing health and nothing to do with her daughter?"

A wicked grin spread across his friend's face. "I didn't even know she had a daughter."

"I find that hard to believe." Massimo shook his head. "I'm not going to help you with your rakish intentions."

"I assure you, my intentions are pure. As tempting as her daughter is, I would never mix business with pleasure. Signora Petrelli holds a lot of sway with the upper class, Massimo. One sale and endorsement from her... I could really use it."

"Is business that bad? Dante, I've offered before, but you know I can help you."

The warlock stiffened. "I'm not a charity case, Massimo."

"No. I know that. But I'm not going to let my friend struggle when I have the means to help."

Dante shrugged. "Everyone has struggles. Mine are my own. Besides, don't you have enough to worry about what with all the towns you've inherited? Those are the people you should be turning your attention to."

"Pardon me, Count, the honey cakes will be ready shortly," Santino interrupted, reappearing in the doorway.

"Thank you," Massimo answered absentmindedly.

Dante's words echoed in his thoughts. *Everyone has struggles.*

His mind turned back to Alessia and her family. The patrizio had confirmed all the repairs had been completed and that he would personally see to it that the women had everything they needed.

Would Alessia appreciate his help? An ache filled him at the thought of her. What was she doing now?

"Massimo?" Dante asked, waving a hand in front of his face.

"Yes. I will accept Signora Petrelli's invitation. I'll make sure she extends an invitation to you as well," he answered, nodding at his friend.

Surprise flickered on Dante's face. "Oh. Well, thank you. I promise I'll stay by your side and help you fend off all the mamas and their eligible daughters. How is the search for a Contessa going, anyway?"

A groan escaped Massimo. "The king sent me a letter. It seems he already has someone in mind, though he didn't tell me who. Only that I should expect to meet them soon."

"Hmm. How mysterious. It's probably wise that he hasn't

named them. Imagine the public outcry if he did. The jealousy."

"Jealousy? What do you mean?" Massimo asked.

He caught Santino rearranging the books on his shelf behind them, pretending not to listen.

Dante stretched out his long legs and leaned his head back against the cushion. "Why, everyone wants to marry a count, naturally."

"Not everyone." The words slipped from Massimo.

His friend's dark eyes snapped to him. "Oh. There's a story behind that, I think. Let's hear it."

Massimo thrummed his fingers on the side table and frowned. "There's no story. It's just... I recently got to see what it was like for those... not in the upper class. I mean, you don't really talk about your... struggles, but—"

Dante snorted. "I may not be upper class, but I'm not exactly a pauper, Massimo."

Massimo flinched. "I know. I know. That's not what I mean. It's just... it seems there's a lot I've missed. Hiding in my library, as you like to put it."

The warlock gave him a sympathetic look. "You're a good man, Massimo. You can't blame yourself for the world's struggles."

"I know, but I'm a count now. I have the opportunity to do something about those struggles. I can't just go back to"—he waved a hand across the books—"this."

Dante nodded and opened his mouth to say something but was cut off by a loud rapping sound on the window.

"Oh, Santos! What is that?" Santino's sharp tone caught their attention.

Massimo and Dante stood and walked toward the window.

"Oh, it's just Ometta," Dante said with a laugh. He opened the latch to let her in.

"What are you doing, signor?" Santino asked with alarm, stepping back.

The large, black owl flew in, throwing a curious look at the valletto. She landed on the back of the couch and hooted at Dante.

"I thought owls were nocturnal!" Santino exclaimed, giving Ometta a wary look.

"They are," Dante answered with an amused smile.

He stroked the dark owl's feathery, large head and turned to the startled man. "If you're going to work here, Santino, you're going to need to get a hold of yourself."

The older man straightened, face reddening as he looked from Massimo to Dante.

"You're valletto to a fae count, Santino. Warlocks and their familiars are something you'll have to get used to."

"Familiars?" Santino's voice became strained, his face blanching.

Massimo shook his head at Dante's amused smile and turned to his valletto. "Yes. Ometta is Signor Lazaro's familiar. They are both my welcomed guests and will be treated as such."

"Of course, Count."

Dante snorted. "Be grateful she appeared in this form. This is her cuddliest form."

"Cuddly?" Santino asked, nearly choking, as he stared at the massive dark owl.

Ometta let out a shrill cry and flapped her wings. Santino jumped back, bumping into Massimo's bookshelf.

"Careful of my books!" Massimo exclaimed, watching to make sure none of them fell.

"Here are the honey cakes, Count. Signor." The maid's voice interrupted them.

She set down the tray on the coffee table and glanced at

Ometta. "I'll have the cook prepare something for your... owl as well," she said with a curtsy.

Dante waved a hand as she left. "See. Even Bianca knows the protocol here."

"Yes. I see," Santino answered, still not moving from his spot.

Dante shrugged and turned back to Massimo. "Now, should we discuss what we're going to wear to Signora Petrelli's party?"

Massimo sighed heavily. "Yes, I suppose we should. But I think I'm going to need some more caffé first."

He sat back down and poured himself another cup before offering some to Dante. "Does Ometta want some?"

Dante glanced at the owl and held out his cup to her. She made a shrill hissing sound that made Santino shrink back.

"No. I don't think she does, but thank you," Dante answered, drinking the caffé himself.

Massimo took a long drink, trying to clear his thoughts. The king was expecting him to receive this mysterious match. It was time to put away all wishful fantasies of Alessia once and for all.

Chapter 17

The Letter

A lessia wiped the sweat from her forehead and stood to survey their work. It was a daily battle to keep their garden from growing too wild. Even with all their efforts, the abnormal sizes, shapes, colors, and fragrances made it clear it was no ordinary garden.

It was a witches' garden, after all. All the stray cats and farm animals roaming the yard as they pleased only added to the eclectic aesthetic.

"What do you think? Another couple of days, perhaps?" Alessia asked Fiorella.

They stared at the green-white strawberries in their garden. The berries were full now, but still unripe with a bitter taste. Not ready to be made into wine.

Fiorella sighed. "I don't know. These ones are... different. They don't want to listen to me."

"Maybe we should start another row? Try it again?" Liliana asked, frowning at the plants.

Poor Fiorella looked like she was near tears. Alessia wished she could help, but she didn't know the first thing about plant magic. Only that it was tricky.

Serafina wrapped an arm around Fiorella and rested her head against her little sister's. "They'll ripen when they're ready. Don't worry."

Alessia's heart warmed at their exchange. Serafina, for all her fieriness, was fiercely protective of and gentle with their youngest sister.

"Not long now and they'll be ready to be pressed into wine for the count," Pamina added with a reassuring smile.

Alessia's heart lurched at the thought of him. *Perhaps I could write to you...*

A crackle of thunder sounded, startling her out of her memories.

Pamina sighed. "Good thing the count fixed our roof when he did. It's been raining almost every day!"

Liliana snorted. "You mean good thing he sent people to fix it. Do you remember his help?"

Alessia frowned at her. "He tried his best. Regardless, it's fixed now."

"It looks even better now," Serafina added.

"I miss the count," Fiorella said.

Alessia found herself nodding in agreement. It had been nearly two weeks since Massimo had left Zamerra, but the memory of him was still fresh. His burning gaze. Soft smile.

She wiped the dirt from her hands onto her trousers and turned toward the villa, pushing away such thoughts. It was over. She needed to move on.

"Now that we're finished, how about I make us some fresh limonata?" Pamina offered, wiping her hands on her dress.

"Oh, I'll get the basil!" Fiorella said with a squeal.

Not waiting for an answer, she took off to the herb garden. Pamina headed inside to the kitchen and Serafina followed.

Alessia started walking but stopped at Liliana's gentle touch.

"I'm worried about Mama."

"The headaches?"

Liliana nodded, wrapping her arms around herself. "I don't understand it. I've changed the formula so many times, but nothing seems to work."

Dark clouds gathered overhead, and birds squawked noisily, heading for the forest behind their villa. A warm wind rustled the leaves.

"What does Mama say?" Alessia asked, chewing on her bottom lip.

"She won't say! Just that she knows I'll figure it out. It's infuriating."

Alessia gave her sister a sympathetic look. She wished she could help, but if Liliana couldn't get the tonic to work, there was little chance she could. Maybe what they needed was some outside help.

They started walking back to the villa together.

"She was doing so well, but ever since Ma—the count left she seems to have worsened. Do you think we should ask him for help?"

Liliana shot her an incredulous look. "Help? He doesn't have magic. How can he help?"

Alessia shrugged. "He mentioned his friend was a healer. Might be worth asking?"

"No. I can figure it out. We don't need his help. Are you sure that's the reason you want to reach out to him?"

"Oh, don't start with that again. I told you, I'm not interested in the count," Alessia replied.

Liliana didn't look convinced, but before she could respond, Fiorella caught up to them.

The strong smell of the basil in Fiorella's hand filled the air.

Alessia smiled at the sight of her little sister. Her hair hung loose and wild, dress crumpled and dirty.

She swiped her hand across a smudge of dirt on her chin, making it even dirtier. "What?"

Alessia squeezed her shoulder. "Let's get you cleaned up, Ella."

"Are you coming? The limonata is almost ready," Pamina's voice called from the kitchen.

Alessia swallowed the lump in her throat and motioned for the others to lead the way. She followed after them, glancing back out at their expansive yard and gardens.

Sunlight streamed in from the open window by the stone sink, casting a golden glow in the cozy little kitchen. Garlic mixed with dried herbs filled Alessia's lungs as she sat at the kitchen table. Soon it would be time to start the fire and get supper ready.

Pamina brought the pitcher over to them and set out the ceramic cups. Fiorella handed her the fresh basil leaves, which she took to the sink to wash, dry, and chop.

"How are the strawberries?" Mama's raspy voice broke the silence.

They all turned to her as she entered the kitchen. Her dark eyes sought Alessia's. Her bushy brows knitted together, and her lips pursed.

"Mama! You should be resting," Alessia answered, rising to her feet.

"Would you like some limonata, Mama?" Pamina offered, scraping the crushed basil off the wooden board and into the pitcher.

"Yes, thank you, Pamina," Mama answered, sliding into the chair at the head of the table.

Alessia watched the little green pieces and ice swirl in the liquid as her sister stirred. Mama's eyes darted between them all, shrewd and calculating.

"Are you feeling better?" Liliana asked her with a frown.

Mamma nodded. "Yes. Thank you. How is the wine coming along for our count?"

Fiorella blew out her breath. "The strawberries aren't ready still."

"They'll be ready any day now. I'm sure the count has better things to do than worry about the wine. We—" Alessia paused as Pamina poured limonata into her cup.

She took a sip, savoring the tart citrus and fresh basil flavor. The drink was refreshing and cooling in the warm, stuffy kitchen.

They fell quiet again, their sips and slurping filling the silence.

"*Grava fla!*" a little voice called from the rafters.

Alessia looked up to see Bruno, launching himself at the table. He dropped with a 'thud', nearly knocking over the pitcher.

"Bruno!" Serafina scolded him.

He made a face at her before peering into the pitcher, his little hands pressed against the ceramic.

Pamina chuckled. "Do you want some limonata, Bruno?"

His head swiveled to her. "*Grava fla!*"

"Please," Alessia added for him.

He ignored her and pointed to the pitcher. Alessia shook her head and shrugged helplessly.

"Too bad the count isn't here to translate for us," Fiorella said.

"Oh, he said he would lend me a book on Elvish so I could learn," Serafina said, eyes flashing with excitement.

"He did? That was nice," Alessia said with a smile.

"Here you go, Bruno," Pamina said, handing him his own little cup.

He gulped down the liquid noisily and belched even louder.

Fiorella giggled, making the little elf smile. His face was smudged with dirt and limonata dribbled into his beard. Though he was a house elf, he spent a lot of his time outside and refused to bathe.

It took a lot of bribes and effort to get him cleaned up and afterwards, he would disappear for a few days, only to return even messier than before. If it weren't for the smell and dirty tracks he left, Alessia would have given up on trying to wash him.

"Hungry?" Pamina asked, placing a plate in the middle of the table.

She grabbed her cup and took her chair beside Liliana with a tired sigh.

"Thank you, Pamina. These look delicious," Mama said with an approving smile.

Everyone murmured their agreement. Alessia helped herself to a sandwich, savoring the bite of fresh mozzarella, basil, and juicy tomato. Bruno turned his nose up to the sandwiches and scurried to the cookie jar instead.

"Not too many, Bruno," Alessia reprimanded him.

She turned her attention to the others. "Mama, I was thinking of writing the count about your headaches. He has that warlock friend, remember?"

Serafina's eyes widened in excitement. Pamina and Mama exchanged a look that made Alessia frown.

"If your headaches are getting worse, we should do something. Maybe his friend knows of a tonic or something to help," she said this, watching Liliana's reaction carefully.

Her sister scowled. "I don't see how he could help. I've tried every tonic and salve."

Serafina and Fiorella were smiling. "Oh! Imagine a real warlock coming here," Fiorella squealed.

An alarmed look crossed on Mama's face. "Oh, no. I don't think we need to go to all that trouble. But perhaps a visit from the count? He—"

"The count? He doesn't even have magic! How would he help?" Liliana demanded.

Alessia gave Liliana a gentle pat on her hand. "His friend then. You've done all you can. Maybe it wouldn't hurt to get someone else's opinion?"

Liliana withdrew her hand and shook her head, a look of hurt flashing across her features. She could be almost as stubborn as Serafina at times. Alessia knew it was eating at her sister, not being able to make the tonic work. She also knew Liliana would see reason.

"That doesn't mean you have to stop trying. But we have to do whatever we can to help Mama," Alessia added.

Liliana sighed heavily and nodded. "Yes, of course. I know. Perhaps another opinion wouldn't hurt."

Serafina squealed, earning herself a glare from Liliana.

"Oh, you girls... I'm sure I'll be fine. There's no need to go to all that trouble," Mama said, eyes darting to Pamina and Serafina.

"Nonsense. I'm sure he'll be happy to help. Now that's settled. I'll post the letter in the morning," Alessia said, hoping the matter was indeed closed.

Serafina clapped her hands over her mouth, eyes darting to Fiorella. Fiorella shuffled her feet, face red.

"What? What is going on?" Liliana demanded.

Fiorella met Alessia's eyes. "We've already sent a letter."

"What?" Alessia and Liliana asked at the same time.

Serafina gave her a guilty smile. "I found a note with his address on your desk."

"You wrote him about Mama's headaches?"

Serafina's eyes danced away. "Um. No. Not exactly."

"Then what did you write him about?" Alessia asked, more confused than ever.

Fiorella rushed to Serafina's side, arms spread in a desperate gesture. "It's not her fault! It was my idea" She turned to Alessia with a worried look.

Liliana groaned. "Not you too."

Alessia was losing her patience. She leaned forward in her chair and held Serafina's eyes. "What did you write?"

"Only that you missed him and wished for his return."

"You wrote him about me?" Alessia couldn't hide the surprise in her voice.

Serafina shrugged. "Well... I wrote him... as you."

Alessia gaped at her, horrified.

Her eyes snapped to her mother. "Was this your doing?"

Signora Silveri frowned. "Of course not, Alessia." She turned to Serafina. "You shouldn't have done that, Fina."

Liliana scoffed. "That's it? She lied to our count! That is serious."

"We didn't mean to hurt anyone. We just wanted to see him again!" Fiorella said, growing teary-eyed.

Liliana threw her hands in the air. "Oh, don't start crying, Ella."

"I'm not!"

Serafina turned to Liliana with a savage look. "I don't know why you're so upset. It has nothing to do with you!"

Liliana made a disgusted sound. "Nothing to do with me? Don't be an idiot. Everything you do reflects on me. On all of us. Isn't it bad enough that everyone in this town hates us? And now you've played this nasty trick on the count. Did you ever stop to think of how it will affect Alessia? How is she going to explain this to him?"

"That's enough, Liliana," Mama said, rising to her feet.

Liliana's dark eyes snapped to her. "You told them, didn't you?"

Alessia's head whipped to her mother. "No. Mama, you didn't, did you?"

Pamina cleared her throat. "I think everyone should take a minute to calm down. We—"

"Did you? Tell them about your vision?" Alessia cut her off, staring at their mother.

Mama sighed. "I did. I realize now, I probably shouldn't have. I'm sorry."

Serafina scowled. "It's not Mama's fault. I'm the one who sent the letter. I'll write another one. Explain everything."

"No!" Alessia said with a shake of her head. "I'll write the letter. I can fix this. No more letters, Fina. And I'll tell you all right now, I am not interested in marriage. Not to the count. Not to anyone. That is the end of that."

"But you two are a perfect match!" Serafina argued.

Alessia shot her a glare. "Enough, Serafina."

"But—"

Mama cut her off with a squeeze on the shoulder and a shake of her head. Alessia took a deep breath, trying to clear her mind. How was she going to undo what her sister had done?

Chapter 18

The Letter

"Don't you look dashing!" Dante greeted as Massimo stepped off his carriage.

Massimo turned to nod to his coachman before facing his friend. "Come, let's get this over with."

Dante chuckled. "It's a party, Massimo. Do try to have some fun."

"These parties have never been fun for me, Dante. I can't imagine they'll be any better now that I'm count."

The warlock gave him a sympathetic look. "I know. I'm sorry. Thank you for coming. Just a few dances, then."

Massimo sighed and motioned for his friend to lead the way. They walked up the marble stairs together to Signora Petrelli's mansion, Santino falling in step behind them. Forcing a polite smile, Massimo waved and greeted everyone who approached them.

By the time they made it to the inner courtyard, he was already ready to go home. Instead, he made the rounds with Dante by his side, introducing the warlock and answering everyone's incessant questions.

Yes, he enjoyed his new title.

Yes, the lands he'd inherited were prosperous.

No, he wasn't engaged yet.

At least Dante seemed to be enjoying himself. He seemed to fit in naturally, charming men and women alike, despite his warlock-ness.

Massimo found himself missing the slow pace of Zamerra and their casualness. The parties there had been much more enjoyable. There wasn't so much pressure to do things properly. To impress everyone.

"May I join you out here?" A feminine voice broke his thoughts.

Massimo turned to see a young blonde woman approach. She smiled as he bowed, motioning her forward.

Her gown swept across the stones, crystals sparkling under the lanterns' glow. Massimo forced a polite smile, glancing at Santino, who stood silently in the corner of the balcony, pretending not to watch them.

"You must be the new count everyone is raving about," she said with amusement.

"Yes. Count Gallo. Forgive me, you are?"

Her smile widened. "You don't know how refreshing it is to hear that question."

She joined him at the balcony and peered over, before turning to him. "I suppose I should give you my proper title. Duchessa Francesca D'Almerita."

A wry look spread on her face. "A mouthful, I know."

The king's niece.

Massimo bowed quickly, feeling stupid for not recognizing her right away. "Of course, forgive me. The lighting is so dim out here, I didn't realize..." He cut himself off before he could sound even more foolish.

She turned and gave him her full attention. "No need to

apologize, Count. I take it by your flustered appearance, you received my uncle's letter"—she moved closer, voice lowering —"about our match?"

"Match?" Massimo said, voice heightening.

Was this the mysterious suitor the king had written him about? His niece? She could have anyone she wanted. Why would the king want to match her with him, a lowly count?

The duchessa laughed. "Am I that repulsive?"

"No! No, of course not, Duchessa. You are very... lovely."

"But?" she teased, blue eyes staring up at him with amusement.

Massimo flushed. She was lovely. Yet he couldn't help but picture a curly-haired witch in her place. He forced the thoughts away. Alessia didn't want him. He needed to let it go.

"No buts. I'm sure you're a lovely person, inside and out."

She laughed again, placing her hand atop his. "Well, I should warn you. I'm a hopeless romantic and speak freely everything on my mind."

"Those are... good traits," Massimo answered, not sure how to respond to her openness and frankness.

"Oh, Count Gallo, I think we're off to a good start. At least for a budding friendship, yes? I should also warn you, I'm not easy to pin down. I may be a romantic at heart, but commitment. Marriage. That's something I simply won't agree to. Unless I'm completely, undoubtedly sure."

Massimo's head spun as she talked. The cool night air suddenly felt stuffy.

Undoubtedly sure? Massimo didn't feel sure of anything anymore.

Realizing she was still waiting for his response, he forced a smile. "A friendship I can definitely agree to. Whatever happens from there, I suppose we will just... leave to fate?"

The duchessa smiled and withdrew her hand. "Spoken like a true romantic."

Her compliment startled him. A romantic? Massimo had never considered himself as such, but after meeting Alessia, he found himself longing for such things.

The memory of her touch made his heart race. Her soft voice. The way her eyes lit up when she smiled.

"Should we join the rest of them and do some dancing?" the duchessa's voice pulled him back to the present.

"If you wish, Duchessa," Massimo said, trying to put aside all thoughts of Alessia from his mind.

She smiled up at him, blue eyes sparkling. "Has anyone told you that you have a very handsome jaw?"

Massimo shuffled awkwardly. "Er. Yes, actually. Though I don't see why."

"I think it's fae-like. Very attractive," she added with a smirk.

"You do speak very freely," Massimo murmured.

The duchessa laughed. "I did warn you."

Slipping her arm into his, she turned to him. "I dance freely too. Just follow my lead, and I promise I won't make you look a fool."

Massimo nodded politely, his mind drifting to a different time. A different dance. Alessia's green skirt billowing out, her dark curls bouncing with the movement.

I should have danced with her when I had the chance. He pushed the thought away. It was too late now.

* * *

The smooth, rich caffé warmed Massimo right through. It had a nutty, sweet taste, and had always been his favorite, but after having Pamina Silveri's caffé, he couldn't help but compare it and find it lacking.

Of course, it was hard to compete with magically brewed beans.

He could use the surge of energy after the busy week he'd had. Dinner after dinner. So many parties and so many people. The duchessa had been a welcome relief from the swarm of eager suitors, but despite her cheery presence, Massimo found himself missing something.

Sighing, he glanced over at the giant pile of letters on the side table. Most of the correspondence he'd received had been congratulations and invitations.

"What's this? Oh, yes. Villa de sole," Massimo murmured, holding up the letter from the late count's estate. Like the land, he'd inherited the large villa as well. But he was in no hurry to move. Villa de Sole was much grander and bigger than his home.

Probably lonelier too.

Pushing that thought away, Massimo pulled another letter out of the stack and began reading. Another congratulations with an invitation and not-so-subtle mention of their eligible daughter.

He placed it in the other pile of the letters he'd opened. Footsteps echoed, making him look up.

Santino bowed in the doorway. "Count, would you like me to ask the servants for more caffé?"

"No. Thank you. I'm finished."

The older man nodded. "Very good, Count. I'll let them know."

He disappeared back down the hall as the doorman arrived. "Pardon me, Count. Signor Lazaro is here. Should I show him in?"

"Yes. Thank you. Show him in," Massimo replied.

Though he'd grown up with servants, he'd found on his travels, he liked doing things for himself. Having Santino as his valletto had been a challenge. The man was excellent at his job, but Massimo felt funny having someone constantly hovering around him, rushing to assist him with every little task. It was... tiresome.

He picked up another letter to open as Dante walked in, wearing a deep rich blue suit and a feathered felt hat that on anyone else would look ridiculous.

The warlock tipped his hat toward Massimo in greeting. "Good day."

"Good day," Massimo replied as he moved the letter to the 'opened' pile.

"Ah. The life of a count, eh? More letters?" Dante smiled as he sank down into the armchair.

"Yes. This is my life now."

Dante's dark eyebrow arched. "You don't sound like your usual cheerful self."

Massimo shrugged and grabbed another letter to open.

Dante let out a low whistle. "I've never seen you like this. So quiet. What's wrong? I thought you were getting along with the duchessa."

Massimo frowned, turning his friend's question over in his mind. What was wrong with him? He had lost interest in many of the things he'd once loved, and he found himself more and more unsettled.

As lovely as the king's niece was, there was something Massimo couldn't put his finger on.

"Have you ever thought of marriage?" Massimo asked his old friend.

Dante gave him an odd look and cocked his head. "What of it?"

Massimo discarded the letter and leaned forward in his

chair. "Have you ever met someone that you... wanted to marry?"

Dante snorted. "My dear friend, I've yet to meet a suit that I've wanted to keep for more than a year."

"What?"

What did a suit have to do with marriage?

Dante spread his arms out and sighed. "No. To answer your question. I've never met someone that I could see myself bonded to. Have you? Is that what your sour mood is all about? The king's command?"

Alessia's face flashed in Massimo's mind, making his chest tighten. She'd been haunting his thoughts no matter how hard he tried to forget her. They hadn't had enough time for him to really know her and the not knowing was tearing him up. The 'what ifs' were many.

"So, you don't like the duchessa? Is there someone else?" Dante interrupted his thoughts.

Massimo couldn't help but smile at the memory of the dark-haired witch. He shook away the image and pulled another letter out of the pile.

"I don't know. I've met a lot of people in my short time as a count. Though I have to admit, I haven't been able to get someone in particular out of my mind. This..." His words trailed off.

The address on the letter. It came from Zamerra. *Signora Alessia Silveri.* Massimo's heart lurched.

"What is it? What's wrong?" Dante asked, worry in his voice.

Santino returned at that moment, motioning one of the servant girls forward to clear the dishes.

"Oh, I'll take some honey cakes and caffé, please," Dante said with a flirtatious smile.

The servant girl nodded, turning scarlet, as she hurried out with the tray.

Santino sniffed, pressing down his shirt as he came to stand beside Massimo. "Your countship, would you like me to dispose of the opened letters?"

Massimo didn't answer. His eyes were glued to the letter, his heart speeding up. Alessia had written him a letter. She missed him. Wanted him to return. A warmth spread through him, making his skin flush.

She missed him.

"Are you going to share what's in that letter that has you so worked up? I'm beginning to worry, friend," Dante said, interrupting Massimo's thoughts.

He looked up from the letter, holding it tightly. "She wants me to return."

"Return? She? The duchessa?" Dante pressed.

Massimo smiled, suddenly feeling much lighter. He could only nod in response, his cheeks burning.

"Santos. Santino, have you ever seen him stunned into silence like this? What do you suppose we should do? Call the doctor?"

"Uh. I don't know, signor. What do you suggest?" Santino asked, his eyes darting between Dante and Massimo.

The poor valletto didn't seem to understand, nor appreciate, Dante's sarcasm and teasing.

"I could suggest a tonic, but I think that would be unnecessary." Dante turned to Massimo. "Come back to us, friend. Whatever witch has bespelled you, shall I banish her from your thoughts?"

Massimo shook his head, still gripping the letter. He turned to Santino. "Ready my carriage, please."

He looked over at Lucia. "We're going back to Zamerra."

Santino gave Dante a startled look, which the warlock just

shrugged off. Seeing that his master was not jesting, the valletto hurried out.

Dante folded his arms behind his head and sighed. "Can't I at least have my caffé and cakes before you leave?"

Massimo didn't answer. He was too busy envisioning his return to Zamerra. To Alessia.

Chapter 19

Massimo returns

After a few weeks, Alessia's shock and anger had worn off, leaving only dread and anticipation. When would Massimo write her back? Would he? She'd written a second letter, herself this time, to explain her sisters' misdeed and ask him about her mother's headaches. So far, he hadn't responded to either letter.

"Good day, signora!" Salvatore's rich voice called from the gate.

Immediately the herd of cats and Gio rushed toward it in a chorus of meows and barks. Alessia pushed her way through them, shooing them off the path.

"Good day, signor," Alessia returned as she reached the gate.

She opened it and motioned him in. He gave her a dazzling smile as he walked in, doing his best to not step on any of the cats underfoot. Gio ran in circles, yapping with a wag of his little tail.

"Would you like to come in for caffé?" Alessia asked, practically shouting over the noise.

Salvatore shook his head. "No, no. There's no time. He's on his way up."

Alessia frowned. "He?"

"Yes. The count. He's returned. I don't know how long he's been here, but this morning at the bakery, I saw him myself. He was getting ready to come up the mountain."

Alessia's heart leapt at this news. Massimo had come back? Why hadn't he written her? A new worry filled her. What did he have to say that he couldn't put it in the letter?

Salvatore glanced around at the yard, running his fingers through his dark waves. "I thought you would want to know. In case you needed time to... prepare." His eyes darted to her dirt-stained trousers.

"Oh, yes! Thank you. If you'll excuse me, I need to go tell the others," Alessia said, her hand flying to her messy bun.

Salvatore nodded and showed himself out, the animals all following him to the gate. Alessia raced back toward the villa, her heart pounding.

Liliana looked up as she burst through the kitchen, nearly dropping her glass vial.

She threw Alessia an irritated look. "What is it?"

"He's coming! The count. He's coming here."

Liliana's nose wrinkled in confusion. "The count? Coming here? When?"

Alessia poured herself a glass of water and guzzled it down before she could answer. "Now. He's coming right now. I have to go change. Can you tell the others? Oh, and maybe put away the..." She looked pointedly at the pile of fish bones laying on the table.

The whole kitchen smelled like fish now.

Liliana frowned. "I'm in the middle of a brew."

Alessia didn't take the time to argue. Instead, she scurried out of the kitchen and up to their room to ready herself. She passed Fiorella in the hall and told her the news, confident her sister would make sure everyone else knew.

By some magic, they were all cleaned, dressed, and ready to greet him in a mere matter of minutes. The villa, having sensed Alessia's anxiety, had taken it upon itself to help them with the cleaning. Floors were swept, windows opened, and the fish bones hidden. Though there was still a faint odor left behind.

Pamina strung together some herbs to wave around the room and Fiorella lit one of Liliana's lavender candles. Even Serafina, who looked more nervous than Alessia, did her share to help them ready.

"How is Mama?" Alessia asked Liliana as they all waited in the kitchen.

Her sister sighed and groaned in frustration. "She's the same. I've tried everything, and it should be working. I don't understand."

Everyone fell quiet. Alessia wrapped her hands around her mug and stared into the dark, steaming liquid. Worry gnawed at her. What if Mama was getting worse? Could Massimo help them? What would they do if he couldn't?

The sound of wagon wheels broke the silence and set the cats and Gio into a frenzy. Alessia's chest tightened. Her palms were sweaty. She frowned, wiping them on her clean skirt.

"I'll go get the animals," Serafina offered, rushing out of the kitchen.

"Is he here to help Mama?" Fiorella asked.

Alessia looked at her little sister. "I don't know."

There was a knock at the front door, startling them all. Serafina reappeared from the yard. "He must have gone around."

"Probably to avoid the cats," Liliana muttered.

Alessia stood and headed for the entrance, her sisters following suit. She stopped short, heart jumping to her throat.

The door stood open, revealing Massimo standing in the frame with a perplexed look on his handsome face.

He gave them a hesitant smile. "My apologies. The door... it just opened for me."

Surprised murmurs from her sisters followed.

Alessia glanced toward the ceiling. *Your doing, I suppose?*

You're welcome, the villa seemed to say.

Its voice didn't sound as sleepy in her mind as it usually did. No. Instead, it sounded much more awake and alive. Excited, even.

"How did you get here? Why didn't you come through the gate?" Serafina asked, her curiosity snapping her out of her guilty reservation.

"Please, come in," Alessia said, motioning him forward.

The door slammed shut behind him, making his eyes widen. Alessia's sisters gasped, whispering to themselves. Alessia couldn't help but smile. Maybe now they would believe her that their villa was alive.

"Oh, thank you. But I should probably stable my horse?" Massimo shook his head. "I meant to come through the gate, but... well, driving a cart is much harder than it looks."

"You mean you drove yourself up here?" Alessia asked, her voice heightening with surprise.

Massimo gave her an embarrassed smile that made her stomach flutter.

"Yes. I do apologize for the unannounced arrival. It's just... when I got your letter, I didn't want to waste any time. At first, I found it a friendly greeting, but then you wrote for me to hurry. I was afraid something was wrong. An emergency of some sort. Is everyone well?" His eyes danced around the room, stopping to land on her.

Alessia felt that familiar stirring. Burning. She could hardly speak.

"Yes, we are well, Count. Thank you. Serafina and Fiorella, tend to the count's horse, please." Liliana spoke up for her.

Serafina's mouth opened to protest, but the glare Liliana shot her made her snap it close. She glanced back at Alessia and Massimo with a pleased look on her face as she led Fiorella out the front door.

A snort escaped Alessia. Serafina didn't seem sorry in the least.

"Alessia?" Massimo asked, bringing her attention back.

She met his burning gaze and took a steady breath. "Did you get... both letters?"

The handsome fae frowned. "There were two letters?"

Alessia's heart sank. So, he hadn't heard the explanation. That meant he'd come because of Serafina's letter. He'd come for her. To see her. That thought both surprised and flattered her.

Only now she would have to set him straight.

"Would you like some caffé?" Alessia asked, trying to plan out her words carefully.

"Yes. Thank you."

"I'll get it!" Pamina offered, turning to leave.

Alessia motioned him further into the room to a sofa where Regina, a very plump tabby, lay curled on the cushion. She glanced up at Massimo with a disgruntled look. Alessia tried to shoo her away, but the cat ignored her.

"Come along, Regina. Your subjects await," Serafina said, returning with Fiorella. She picked up the large feline and took her away.

The cat looked back at Massimo with a murderous glare.

"I'm sorry. We don't entertain much." Alessia shook her head, brushing cat hair off the sofa.

"We don't entertain at all!" Fiorella added.

Alessia gave her an irritated look. Liliana only nodded in agreement.

Massimo smiled and turned his attention back to Alessia. "Oh, I'm the one who should apologize. I should have written first."

He took a seat on the large sofa by the fireplace. Pamina and Liliana returned with trays. The rich smell of caffé filled the room, along with the chocolate pastries.

"Thank you," Massimo said as they poured him a cup and handed him a little plate of assorted pastries.

Everyone was quiet, looking from him to Alessia. Massimo took a sip of the warm liquid and waited for her to speak.

"I'm afraid there's been a... misunderstanding," Alessia started, her eyes darting to Serafina.

Massimo paused mid-bite. He gave her a puzzled look.

Alessia sat down in the armchair beside him, wringing her hands in her lap. "You see, Count. "Oh, I had everything written in that letter." She shook her head. "Well, you see. The letter you received wasn't from me."

"It wasn't?"

Alessia gave him a nervous glance. "No. It's silly really, but..."

"I wrote the letter. Pretending to be my sister," Serafina announced.

Massimo gaped at her. She held his gaze, a slight waver in her stance.

"Oh, but it was my idea in the first place! It was only supposed to be for fun," Fiorella said, jumping to her sister's defense.

All the Silveri sisters were watching him now. Massimo took the napkin and wiped the crumbs from his face. Alessia squared her shoulders, waiting for his anger.

"Ah. I see. It was... a prank?" he directed his question to the youngest.

They exchanged hesitant looks and nodded, their eyes downcast.

"Of which they are very sorry for. Right?" Alessia gave them pointed looks.

"Yes! We're so sorry, Count Gallo," the replied in unison.

"I'll never write another letter for the rest of my life," Fiorella added dramatically.

Massimo gave her a sympathetic smile. "Now, there's no need for that. I'm glad you sent the letter. It gave me an excuse to return to Zamerra. Perhaps that strawberry wine is ready now?"

Fiorella's shoulders slumped even further, face looking crestfallen.

"Not quite. But it will be soon," Pamina answered cheerfully.

Massimo turned toward Alessia. "No worries. Something so precious and rare is worth the wait."

Her eyes snapped to his. Her heart pounded against her chest as if it would burst right out. Could he hear it?

"You mentioned a second letter?" his question came out so softly.

Alessia's gaze darted to Liliana and back to him. "Yes. I did write you to let you know about the... their letter. But I also wanted to request your help."

"My help?"

She nodded, dark curls falling out of her bun as she did. "Yes. It's Mama. Her headaches have returned, and we haven't been able to come up with a remedy that works. We were hoping you, or perhaps your warlock friend, might have a suggestion?"

Liliana snorted beside her; arms folded across her chest.

"Oh, yes. She's been laid in bed for the past few weeks, wracked with the pain," Serafina added.

Massimo frowned. "Pain from the headaches? I'm so sorry to hear that. Of course, I'll help. I will send for Dante right away. I'm sure he'll have something to help her."

"Oh, thank you!" Fiorella exclaimed, throwing her arms around his neck.

"Ella!" Alessia admonished, trying to pull her sister off.

"It's alright," Massimo said as Fiorella let him go with a sniffle.

Massimo turned to Alessia. "It should take a few days for the letter to be posted, received, and a reply sent back. Is there anything I can do for Signora Silveri in the meantime?"

"You can stay for supper!" a cheerful voice called from the steps.

They all looked up to find the matriarch of the family standing on the landing, looking very much in good health.

The rest of the day's work was abandoned in favor of spending time with their guest. Alessia watched as Massimo made her sisters laugh with his latest adventures in avoiding the scheming mothers who hunted him. Mama, who had made a miraculous recovery, joined them and listened enraptured to Massimo's tales.

"But don't you want to marry, Count?" Serafina asked bluntly, ignoring the sharp glare Alessia shot her.

Alessia looked at her mother, but she was no help. She looked just as curious as Serafina.

Massimo shifted uncomfortably in his chair at the table. "Well, yes. I suppose. Some day. If I meet someone who feels the same."

His eyes met Alessia's. The force in his gaze left her shaken. She'd hardly known him for very long, but he was already beginning to feel as though he were part of the family. That thought scared her.

"Seeing as you're much better, Mama, I don't think we'll need to send for the warlock after all," Liliana spoke, breaking the tension.

Serafina made a disgruntled noise. "But we've never met a warlock."

Alessia looked at her mother, who was watching her and Massimo with rapt interest. She didn't seem to hear her daughter's words.

"Yes, well, I'm glad to see your health has improved, Signora Silveri," Massimo said with a genuine smile.

Bruno, who'd been politely eating his supper with them, interrupted the moment with a loud juicy-sounding belch. Fiorella tried to smother her giggling, making the little elf laugh too. Alessia's face burned in embarrassment.

To her surprise, Massimo laughed along.

After eating, Alessia led the handsome fae so he could see for himself how the strawberries were coming. The sun was beginning to set, streaking the sky with gold and orange. No sooner had Massimo stepped out, than all the animals descended upon him. Alessia did her best to shoo them off, but he promised her they were no bother.

In fact, he seemed delighted to pet all the noisy, pestering cats. Even little Gio allowed him to scratch behind his ears, his little tail wagging so happily. Alessia couldn't help but smile at the scene.

The air grew cooler as they walked toward the strawberry plants. Alessia rubbed her arms, trying to ward off the chill.

"Are you cold?" Massimo asked.

He frowned and shook his head. "Of course, you are. Silly question. I wish I had a jacket to offer you. I'd give you my shirt, but that would leave me shirtless and, um, indecent."

Alessia flushed. The image of a shirtless Massimo made her face warm.

"Alessia, forgive me. I spoke out of turn. I didn't mean to offend... your sensibilities," Massimo said, a worried look on his face.

Alessia snorted. It was a good thing he couldn't read her mind and see just what her 'sensibilities' had conjured.

He looked so concerned. Before she realized it, Alessia reached out to touch his cheek. The contact sent a shiver up her back. His eyes widened, the sharp inhale of his breath sounding so loud in the quiet.

He was so close now. His scent of cedar and spice enveloped her, making it difficult to breathe. She was lost in his burning gaze. Those amber eyes held her captive.

"Alessia." His voice had become gravelly. As if he was becoming unraveled too.

She started to withdraw her hand, but he held it there with his hand, his eyes darkening. "I know you didn't send the letter. The first letter, but... did you miss me?"

His cheek felt warm against her hand. Hot. Flushed. His question held so much longing. Desperation. She wanted to tell him yes. Tell him that she hadn't stopped thinking of him since the moment that he'd left. But where would that lead them?

He was still a count. She couldn't be a part of his world. Alessia glanced back at the villa, a sorrow filling her. She couldn't leave. This was her home, and her family was here. This was where she belonged.

Blinking back the tears that had gathered, she shook her head and pulled her hand away. The fallen look on his face pained her. But it was better to tell him now. Before it became impossible.

"Count—"

"Massimo," he interrupted, his brow furrowed.

Alessia nodded. "Yes, Massimo. I'm very flattered, but... I... I'm afraid I can't give you what it is you're seeking?"

"What am I seeking?" he asked, his voice soft and low. He had a faraway look in his eye as if he was not asking her but himself this question.

"Oh, I didn't mean to assume anything. It's just... I think very highly of you. As our count. As... a friend."

Alessia watched as pain flickered across his face. It was the most difficult thing she had ever had to say to anyone. Her stomach churned and her chest ached.

"I see. I think very highly of you as well." He smiled sadly. "You can always count me as your friend."

His words only left her broken. A friend? It felt wrong.

"Alessia! Massimo! Hurry, come quick. It's Mama!" Serafina's shout cut through the air.

Chapter 20

A Final Goodbye

Massimo stood in the doorway, watching as Alessia and her sisters hovered around their mother. His throat went dry. Memories of the last days with his own mother flooded him and he hoped with all of his being that Signora Silveri would make a quick recovery. He couldn't bear the thought of Alessia going through the same heartache that he had been through.

The villa seemed to be holding its breath as well. Outside, the sun had almost disappeared completely. Candles lit the room in a soft glow and though Massimo knew he should bid them goodnight and return to town before nightfall, he couldn't bring himself to leave now.

"Should we fetch the doctor?" Alessia asked her mother, holding her hand.

Signora Silveri shook her head against the cushion. She was sitting up in bed, sipping the pungent tea Liliana had brewed for her. It was such an intimate moment, and Massimo felt he was intruding on their time. Yet, he couldn't seem to tear himself away. Not until he knew for sure, everything was okay.

"I'm feeling much better now. I just need some rest." She glanced at Massimo. "I hate that you should see me in such a state, Count. It is getting late. Alessia will make up a room for you. I won't have you driving down the mountain in the dark."

Alessia whipped toward him, a startled look on her face as if she had just remembered he was still there. Massimo didn't blame her for forgetting. Her mother was her only concern at the moment, which was how it should be.

Remembering his manners, he gave Signora Silveri an appreciative smile. "Thank you for your warm welcome, signora, but I can't impose on you."

The older woman handed her mug to Pamina and sat up higher on the bed. "Nonsense! I won't accept no for an answer. You may be the count, but I'm the lady of the house. You wouldn't want to cause me worry, would you? You could drive your cart right off the mountain and dash your handsome face against the rocks."

"Mama," Alessia hissed.

Massimo felt as if he had no choice but to accept her offer, though he hated to put Alessia in a difficult situation. She'd made it clear how she felt—or didn't—feel about him. He didn't want to make more work for the sisters either, but neither did he want to drive off the mountain.

"Liliana, go and help your sister prepare the guest room," Signora Silveri motioned them out.

"Oh! We've never had anyone stay in the spare room," Fiorella said excitedly.

She exchanged a sharp look with Serafina before they both scampered out. Massimo started to follow them but was stopped by Signora Silveri's loud grunt.

Pamina, who was the only one left in the room with the two, started picking up the cups and plates to load back onto the tray.

"Count Gallo, I understand the king has requested you to find a bride. Is that right?" Signora Silveri asked.

Massimo nodded, unsure of where the conversation was going. If the woman was about to offer up one of her daughters as all the other mothers had done, he wasn't sure what he would tell her.

The only woman he'd ever felt anything close to romantic feelings for was Alessia, and she'd just told him she wanted to remain friends. Massimo frowned at the memory. At least he hadn't spoken his feelings aloud and made a complete fool of himself.

"I'm sure you'll find what you're looking for," the matriarch said kindly, a gleam in her eye.

Before Massimo could respond, Alessia and the others returned. He followed them to the guest room and thanked them again for their hospitality before bidding them good night.

The room was small and cozy, and the bed made up nice and tidy. A cool breeze swept in from the open window, bringing the scent of honeysuckle along with it. Against the back wall stood a desk that was covered with an assortment of potted plants in various growth stages.

Alessia cleared her throat, making Massimo turn around.

She stood in the doorway with a look of uncertainty. Her sisters had disappeared, leaving just the two of them.

"There's an oil lamp there if you need it. I can bring some candles as well." She nodded toward the burning lamp on the bedside table. It bathed the room in a warm glow, making it look quite inviting.

"Thank you. I think I'll manage with just the lamp."

Alessia nodded in response, wringing her hands together. She looked as if she wanted to say more, but shook her head instead. Massimo tried not to feel disappointed. There was more he wanted to say as well, but he didn't want to make her more uncomfortable than she already was.

He wished they could go back to how they'd been before the garden. Had his question messed everything up? Or was she thinking of her poor mother?

Pushing the questions aside, he walked toward her. "I'll write my friend Dante as soon as I return to town tomorrow. I'll leave first thing in the morning."

Alessia gave him a grateful smile that made his heart lurch.

"Thank you. For everything." Her voice was small, and her eyes darted away.

Massimo's heart sank. Why did it feel as if she was saying goodbye? He found that thought quite distressing, but what had he expected? They'd been welcoming and friendly to him, but he had the suspicion they would have shown anyone the same kindness.

He was still the count in their eyes.

"Good night... Massimo," Alessia finally spoke, her dark eyes darting back up to meet his.

"Good night, Alessia," he heard himself answer.

She flinched and turned away quickly, closing the door behind her as she did. Massimo listened as her footsteps faded away.

Sleep eluded him that night. All he could think about was Alessia and how she had looked standing in the garden. The setting sun behind her gave her an otherworldly glow.

When dawn broke, Massimo blinked the weariness from his eyes and readied himself to leave. He needed to return to the inn where Lucia would no doubt be furious with him for leaving her overnight. Poor thing would probably be hungry too. Unless one of Signor Giordano's children had fed her. Surely, they had another set of keys.

Massimo made his way downstairs and found Alessia alone

in the kitchen. She jumped when he entered, nearly dropping her cup.

"Good morning. I was just on my way out," Massimo said.

Alessia poured him a cup of caffé and pushed a plate of sliced lemon cake toward him. He thanked her and sat down to eat it quickly. Bruno looked up from his spot on the table, his beard full of crumbs. Massimo returned his little wave.

"Massimo, I—"

"Alessia!" Serafina's voice cut in.

Alessia sighed and gave him an apologetic look. Massimo only smiled, motioning for her to go. He watched her walk away with a sinking feeling that whatever chance he had to win her affection was gone.

* * *

"Oh, Count! We were so worried when you didn't return last night. Signor Giordano nearly sent for the patrizio to send out a search party," Signora Giordano greeted him, eyes wide.

"Forgive me, signora. I didn't mean to cause you worry. Is Lucia well?"

She nodded. "Lena took care of your cat, Count. Would you like breakfast in your room?"

Massimo shook his head. "No. Thank you. I've already eaten."

"Oh. My. I see," Signora Giordano replied, hand on her chest.

She wrung her hands together and bit her lip.

"Is something wrong, signora?" Massimo asked, confused.

She shook her mass of curls and hesitated. "Oh, no, Count. It's none of my business."

"What?"

"Favia, the count has re—Count! There you are. Are you well?" Signor Giordano interrupted, barreling into the inn.

Massimo frowned. "I'm fine. Are you all alright?"

The innkeeper bowed. "Fine. Better now that we know nothing nefarious has fallen upon you."

"I didn't mean to make you worry," Massimo said with a shake of his head.

Lena and her siblings had joined them at the reception desk, eyes wide with interest. Signora Giordano shooed them to the back room and gave her husband a pointed look.

Signor Giordano cleared his throat and drew himself up to face Massimo. "Uh... Count, may I have a frank word with you?"

"Of course. What is it, signor?" Massimo asked, perplexed at their odd behavior.

The innkeeper stood barely at his waist, but the fierce look he fixed on Massimo made him look intimidating. "I know it's none of my business where you've been, but as a father... No, as a good citizen, I must say, whatever conduct happens else-where... such a thing cannot happen here. We run a business of repute, you understand. Furthermore, the Silveri girls may not have a father to look after their... well, their reputations, but this town will not stand for such... a—"

"Hold on. Are you accusing me of... being disreputable?" Massimo asked, stunned.

Signor Giordano's face reddened. "No, Count. I would never accuse you of such a thing! I know things might seem backward here in our little town, but those girls have seen enough hardship and many in this town would judge them unfairly. I... oh, Santos. I'm making a mess of this, aren't I?"

Massimo couldn't help but smile. "I believe I know what you are trying to say, signor. I take no offense. I'm afraid to admit that I hadn't been concerned about all the ramifications of my... choice, but I assure you, there was nothing untoward. Signora Silveri has fallen ill, and with my lack of driving skills, they asked me to stay. So that I didn't drive off the mountain in the dark."

The innkeeper's eyes widened. "Oh. I see. Well, it's none of my business. But you know, the town will talk..."

Massimo frowned. "And I'm sure you will assure them of the truth. Should I hear anything slanderous about Signora Silveri or any of her daughters, I will take great offense."

"Of course, Count! I would never speak ill of them. Of anyone. Nor will my family. It's the others that like to spread gossip."

"Hmm. Perhaps I should address everyone before I leave then."

Signor Giordano glanced back at the door, cracked open. "You're leaving, Count?"

Massimo sighed. "As soon as I know that the signora is well. I need to post a letter today. Once she's settled, I must return home right away."

"Of course, Count. I'll get the letter out. I'm sure you have much to return to."

Massimo smiled sadly. "Yes. Thank you. Can you bring some caffé to my room?"

"Yes. It will be right up," the innkeeper replied as Massimo headed for the stairs.

Tiredness filled Massimo. He hoped the town didn't give Alessia or her family any grief. He hadn't meant to bring any more trouble to her doorstep.

Her words echoed in his mind. *I think very highly of you. As our count. As... a friend.*

The memory of it still stung. Opening his door, he tried to push them away. Soon, he would return home to his books. To the duchessa.

"*Meow.*" Lucia greeted him with a deadly stare.

"I know. I'm sorry, Lucia. It was an emergency. I'll make it up to you."

As if sensing his sour mood, the cat jumped from the bed and came to rub herself against his ankles. She purred softly, looking up at him with curious eyes.

"Thank you, Lucia. I needed that."

Massimo bent to pick her up. He sat down in the chair with her in his lap, stroking her fur before she hopped down.

"Well, I guess I should write that letter now."

He picked up his pen and pulled out a fresh piece of paper to address to Dante. The sooner the warlock arrived and helped the Silveris, the sooner Massimo could leave. This time, it would be for good.

Chapter 21

A Warlock Comes to Call

It had been nearly three days since Massimo had left and no matter how busy she made herself, Alessia couldn't stop thinking about him. About their moment in the garden. Her skin warmed at the memory of it. He'd been so close.

For a moment, she had thought he was going to kiss her. The thought flustered her. She'd been kissed before when she was young, but somehow she imagined a kiss from Massimo would be much different. Much better.

Would she have let him? Yes. She knew there was no denying her attraction.

A wave of regret washed over followed by the cold realization that this was for the best. It had been like that since he'd gone. Regret. Resolution. Acceptance. Over and over in an emotional cycle. One Alessia was desperate to be rid of.

"The strawberries are ready!" Fiorella's voice startled Alessia, making her hit her head on the top of the bathroom cabinet she'd been cleaning out.

Pulling her head out, she rubbed the sore spot and turned to find all of her sisters there, all smiles and good cheer. Even Liliana looked pleased.

"Well, aren't you all in a good mood," Alessia grumbled, standing up and brushing off her skirt.

"Well, aren't you happy about it, too? Now we can invite the count back for supper and give him the bottle he's been waiting for!" Fiorella said with a clap of her hands.

Alessia's stomach churned at the thought of facing Massimo again. The truth was, she did want to see him, but that would only make it all the harder to say goodbye again.

"I'm sure the count won't be staying in Zamerra much longer. The only reason he's still here is to wait for his friend's arrival," Alessia explained.

At this, Fiorella's smile vanished. "The warlock. Do you think he'll really be able to help Mama?"

Liliana grunted. Alessia nodded and tugged one of Fiorella's braids gently. "Of course. He's a powerful warlock. I'm sure it will be easy for him."

Liliana grunted again.

"I guess we should start picking," Alessia said, changing the subject.

She followed the others to the garden, glancing back at the stairs leading up to the bedrooms. Mama had been doing so well for a while; they'd thought the worst was over. Alessia hoped Massimo's friend could indeed help. After all the things they'd tried, she didn't know what else to do.

It was a bright spring day. The warm sunshine and slight breeze soothed Alessia's nerves. She breathed in the fresh mountain air and sighed.

They'd only filled half the basket when the sound of wagon wheels broke the silence. The cats and Gio went wild, rushing at the gate. Alessia wiped her hands on her skirt and followed her sisters.

Serafina managed to herd the animals far enough to the sides to let the wagon through. Alessia's breath hitched as two men drove in. Massimo and a handsome man sat beside him.

Massimo's eyes met hers. Alessia fought the urge to shudder, the weight of his gaze making her feel light-headed and off-balance. He looked rather dashing in his linen shirt and trousers. His long, golden hair was tied back, revealing his pointed ears and high cheekbones.

"Good day!" His friend cheered as the wagon came to a stop.

"Good day," Alessia and her sisters replied.

He removed his straw hat and jumped off the wagon. Massimo followed after. The two men stood side by side, nearly the same tall height, but where Massimo was athletically built, his friend was slender and his skin darker.

"You don't look like a warlock," Serafina announced, eyes narrowed on their visitor.

Alessia threw her a sharp look.

The man smiled. "And what is a warlock supposed to look like, signorina?"

"Ugly. Red eyes and hairy. Covered in warts," Serafina replied evenly.

Alessia grabbed her sister by the wrist, trying to shush her. Massimo's friend was there to help them not be insulted by her unruly tongue.

"My. Well, I'm sorry to disappoint you," he said, placing his hat back on his mass of dark curls.

He gave them an amused smile, his dark eyes scanning their faces. When his gaze landed on Liliana, a startled look flashed across his features, but he recovered quickly, giving her a dazzling smile. Liliana glared in return.

Massimo cleared his throat, commanding their attention. "Signoras, this is my dearest friend, Signor Lazaro. He—"

"I'm your only friend. And please, signoras, call me Dante. I should hope that we will all become good friends," the handsome warlock interrupted, his eyes locking with Liliana's.

She scoffed.

Alessia groaned inwardly. Her sisters seemed determined to offend their guest. It would be up to her to keep the peace and ensure everything went smoothly.

"Serafina, keep the animals back, please," Alessia addressed her sister, who was still scrutinizing Dante.

He watched her with interest as she waved the cats back. Only Gio wouldn't listen. The little dog crept forward, ears and tail tucked, and sniffed the warlock's boot.

After giving it a good sniff, he decided the stranger was alright and ran to join the cats. Alessia watched nervously as Dante took this all in.

Their many animals, the nearly overgrown gardens, and their towering villa. Could he sense the magic? Massimo had told them how Dante had studied many of the magical arts in one of the few schools that taught such things. Would he have an answer for them about Mama's headaches?

Pamina and Fiorella ran ahead to prepare caffé and a tray for their guests while the others followed.

"Massimo tells me your mother is a seer?" Dante asked her as they walked.

"Yes. That's right. The visions sometimes give her headaches, but this... this is different. She's been laid up in bed because of the pain."

Dante frowned. "When was the last vision?"

"Nearly a month ago."

Alessia's gaze snapped to Massimo. The warlock wasn't going to ask her what the vision was about, was he?

"Hmm. That is strange that the pain should last that long.

Unless the vision was very upsetting. May I see the tonics you've been giving her?"

Alessia turned to Liliana, who was walking beside them, listening. Her sister nodded.

"They're all in the bedroom. Would you like me to bring up a tray of caffé and sweets?" Alessia offered.

Dante smiled. "Yes. Thank you. Honey cakes, if you have them, please."

Alessia watched as Massimo's friend inspected all the vials and bowls of various mixtures. Everyone watched quietly as he touched and sniffed them.

Liliana stood beside him, scowling.

"So, kind of you to come and aid us, Signor Lazaro," Signora Silveri said from her bed.

The warlock glanced up at her and gave her a dashing smile. "Not a trouble at all, signora. It is my pleasure to help a damsel in distress."

Liliana snorted. Dante's eyes snapped to her, an amused smirk on his lips.

"Was it you who made all these?" The warlock swept a hand across the concoctions.

Liliana lifted her chin. "Yes. Why?"

Alessia exchanged a look with Massimo. He looked away quickly, making her flinch. The memory of their last encounter still hung between them.

"You've done well enough with the limited ingredients on hand," Dante added with an impressed look.

Liliana's eyes narrowed. "What is that supposed to mean?"

Alessia sucked in a breath and gave her sister a warning look, but Liliana wasn't paying attention. She had moved to stand in front of the vials, holding the warlock's gaze.

He towered over her, head bent to meet her glare.

The room fell silent at their stare off. Alessia watched with growing apprehensions. Should she step in? What was happening?

Dante flashed Liliana a wide smile. Liliana's glare only deepened.

"I only mean that you've done very well with what you have on hand. This, for example, you used rose petals, no? While that's a good substitute for toccasana, it's not as effective."

"Toccasana doesn't grow here," Liliana said with a wave of her hand, "and that's not the problem, Signor Lazaro. W—"

"Dante, if you please. We are friends, aren't we?" the warlock grinned impishly.

Liliana's nostrils flared. "No. We are not."

"Liliana!" Alessia said with a hiss, her face flushed.

"Would anyone care for some more caffè?" Pamina spoke up quickly, grabbing the tray.

A rustling sound came from the bed, making them all turn. Signora Silveri stood, brushing lint off her cotton dress.

She gave them all a stern look. "I think we should all go down for a break."

"Mama, your head! You should lie back down," Alessia rushed toward their mother.

Serafina and Pamina exchanged sharp glances. Massimo stood by Alessia and gave her a questioning look. She blinked rapidly, feeling just as perplexed as he was.

Dante and Liliana were still staring at each other, seemingly unaware of everyone else.

Signora Silveri sighed deeply and held her head high. "I'm afraid I owe you gentlemen an apology. I owe all of you an apology."

"Mama, what are you talking about?" Alessia asked, dread coiling inside her.

Her mother waved off her concern and turned to address Massimo and Dante. "This wasn't supposed to go on for so long, nor did I mean for anyone else to become involved," she directed this at Dante.

"Mama?" Alessia's voice softened to a near whisper.

Liliana tore her gaze away from Dante to stare at her mother as well. A remorseful look flashed on Signora Silveri's face.

"I'm afraid I've taken this too far."

"Taken what too far?" Liliana demanded.

"The headaches. I've been... exaggerating them a bit." Her dark eyes snapped to Dante, "I didn't mean for them to write to you. I thought my ailment would force Alessia to..." She trailed off, her gaze darting to her eldest daughter.

"Mama!" Alessia cut her off, feeling as if the ground had dropped beneath her.

She couldn't tell them about her vision. Not now. They all stood in that uncomfortable silence for what seemed like an eternity.

"You mean, you're okay?" Fiorella's question broke the silence.

Liliana moved forward, fists clenched by her side. "You mean you've been lying to us this whole time? Do you have any idea how many hours and worries I've spent going over formula after formula?" Her voice was low and full of anger.

Serafina marched over to her mother and faced her older sister. "We told you not to worry so much over your potions! We couldn't tell you because you'd tell Alessia and give it away."

"You knew about this?" Alessia and Liliana asked at the same time.

Pamina, still holding the tray, moved toward them as well. "We didn't want to lie. We didn't want to do any of this, but Mama's vision... Alessia..." Her voice wavered.

"Pamina! You knew this too?" Alessia asked, unable to hide the hurt in her voice.

Liliana scoffed and pointed an accusatory finger at Serafina. "And I'm sure *you* had no problem lying to our faces!"

"How could you?" Fiorella said, bursting into tears. She pushed Serafina out of her way and ran from the room. Serafina, looking distressed, chased after her.

Dante coughed. "Well, seeing as my expertise is no longer needed, I suppose we should be off, Massimo?" He gave Massimo a pleading look.

Alessia's face flamed. She didn't know what to say.

"Forgive me, signors. This is entirely my fault. My daughters were only trying to aid me," Signora Silver said, regret evident in her voice.

"Of course. I'm... I'm just glad you are well, signora," Massimo replied kindly.

Dante nodded in agreement. His eyes darted to Liliana, who was still glaring at their mother.

Pamina bowed to them. "I'm sorry, Count. Signor."

"And where is our apology?" Liliana demanded, her back to the men now.

"Uh... I think we'll take our leave now," Massimo said, motioning his friend out.

Alessia turned to watch him go, his eyes briefly meeting hers before he tore them away. She could only nod in reply, unable to speak.

What had they done?

Chapter 22

An Unexpected Visitor

Massimo sat in the dining room with Dante and Lucia as they finished their caffé. They were the only guests in the small dining room. In fact, they were the only guests in the whole inn.

How did the Giordanos make a living with no customers? Perhaps he could help come up with a plan to increase their business. When he returned home, he would look into what could be done.

"Well, are you going to explain what that was all about?" Dante asked, interrupting his thoughts.

Massimo set his mug down on the table and frowned at his friend. "You mean at the villa? With the Silveris?"

Dante gave him an exasperated look. "Yes! You must tell me what is going on. You know I love a good story."

"I don't know how 'good' of a story it is."

"I'll be the judge of that. Tell me everything."

Massimo took a sip of his drink and set it down again. Giving in to his friend's request, he spent nearly an hour going into great detail and explaining all that had happened between him and the Silveris since the Strawberry Festival. Dante, good friend that he was, listened carefully, interjecting here and there with his questions.

By the end, Massimo was nearly out of breath, but still as perplexed as ever. The scene in Signora Silveri's bedroom replayed in his mind.

The letter. The headaches. They'd mentioned something about a vision as well, but he didn't know what that had to do with him and Alessia.

"So, in short, you are in love with her," Dante said, slapping his hand down onto the table with a loud 'thwap'.

The silverware vibrated at the movement. Lucia, who was laying in the sunlight coming in from the open window, turned to give the warlock a disdainful look.

Massimo blinked at him, taking in his words. "Me? Love? Her?"

Dante nodded, grinning proudly at his own observation. "Oh, yes. It's very plain to see."

"It is?"

"Sure. And if my keen observations are correct, which they usually are, she loves you in turn."

Massimo nearly fell out of his chair. His friend's words rang in his ears and his throat turned dry. Alessia was in love with him? Was it true? His mind raced, analyzing every word and action of each encounter he'd had with her.

"How do you know?" he asked Dante.

The warlock sipped from his mug and shrugged his shoulders. "I'm good at telling these things."

Massimo frowned, unable to come to the same conclusion as his friend had. In fact, Alessia had quite pointedly told him that she wished to remain friends. That wasn't exactly a proclamation of love.

"Quite the opposite, actually," he murmured aloud.

Dante's dark eyebrow arched. "What's that?"

"You're wrong about this one, Dante. She told me herself that she thought of me as a friend."

His friend frowned. "Then she's lying."

"Really? But why?"

Dante shrugged. "You'll have to ask her that. You should tell her about how you feel, Massimo."

"How? I don't know if she ever wants to see me again. Even if that were to happen... what about the duchessa?"

"What about her?"

Massimo scoffed. "I can't just ignore the king's match, Dante. Besides, I don't even know if Alessia would want to talk to me."

"I wouldn't mind visiting their villa again. Once things settle down, that is."

"Oh?" Massimo couldn't hide his surprise.

Dante's smile widened. "Her sister."

Massimo huffed. "No, you don't. Don't even think about it... which sister?"

"Liliana," Dante said with a dramatic sigh.

A chuckle escaped Massimo. Between Pamina and Liliana, his friend had picked the harder of the two. The idea of Dante trying to woo Liliana made him smile. He could only imagine how quickly she would put the warlock in his place.

"Do you think I have a chance with her?" Dante asked, face suddenly growing serious.

Before Massimo could answer him, the innkeeper appeared in the doorway. He bowed quickly and stepped aside to reveal two finely dressed women.

It was the duchessa. An older and sour-faced woman, who was frowning at them, accompanied her.

"Pardon me, Count. We've new arrivals. Here to see you," the innkeeper announced.

Massimo rose to his feet, flabbergasted. Dante followed suit. Only Lucia remained where she was, giving the newcomers an unimpressed glance.

"There's a cat in your dining room," the older woman said with a haughty sniff.

"Oh, well... that's er..." Signor Giordano faltered.

"That's Lucia," Massimo said helpfully.

"Well," the woman returned, turning her scrutinizing eye on Massimo.

She gave a loud 'harrumph' which Massimo took to mean she didn't approve of having a cat in the eating area or she didn't approve of Massimo. Or perhaps it meant both.

"I am Signora Ricci, royally appointed chaperone. May I present La Duchessa Francesca D'Almerita," she said, gesturing proudly at the young woman.

Dante and Massimo bowed in unison.

"Duchessa, this is a surprise. I... I didn't expect to see you here in Zamerra," Massimo said, flustered.

She smiled. "I know. I got bored of waiting for you in Della Rosa. Did you receive my uncle's letter? He wants us back at the palazzo straight away."

Massimo gaped at her. Back to the palazzo? What did the king want that was so urgent for them both to go?

Realizing everyone was staring at him, he quickly recovered from his surprise. "No, I'm afraid I didn't receive the letter, Duchessa. I haven't been home... for some time."

Her lips quirked into an amused smile. "The letter was sent here, Count Gallo. Your valletto said he would forward it straight away."

"Signor Santino? Oh, I see. Well, I let him go. Perhaps he didn't have time to send it?" Massimo answered.

Dante glanced at him in surprise. "You decided to let your valletto go?"

"Yes, but I gave a good reference and a large severance pay," Massimo answered quickly.

Everyone was staring at him as if he'd lost his mind. It wasn't that Santino did poorly at his job. In fact, he was too good at it, but Massimo didn't need a valletto. He liked having his independence.

"Well," Signora Ricci said with another disapproving look.

She turned to the duchessa. "I don't think the king will approve of this match. Perhaps we should return home."

Duchessa Francesca just chuckled and waved off her chaperone's concern. "Oh, it's fine. I've been courted by much more scandalous men and women before."

The older woman inhaled sharply, giving her charge a scolding look.

Massimo and Dante exchanged surprised glances.

"Court?" Massimo's voice rose, echoing in the dining room.

Lucia, who had decided all the noise was too much for her, got up and sauntered past them through the doorway, giving them all a haughty look as she left.

"Besides, we've come all this way. I should at least like to have a look around," the duchessa continued, walking further into the room to inspect one of the paintings.

"Oh, yes. I would be happy to take you on a tour, Duchessa," the innkeeper said, hurrying to her side.

Signora Ricci didn't look very pleased with this decision, but she said nothing. Her sharp eyes landed on Massimo once more, studying him as the duchessa studied the art.

Her gaze shot to Dante, who winked rakishly at her, making her lip curl even further. She gave another loud 'harrumph' and turned to the innkeeper.

"We will need two rooms right away, then. Two *adjoining* rooms," she emphasized, giving Massimo a pointed look.

The man gave her a bow and motioned one of his sons,

who'd been peering in around the doorway to go and bring their luggage in.

Massimo, whose head was still spinning, approached the young duchessa and cleared his throat. How was he supposed to tell her of his situation? What had the letter from the king said? Did he promise his niece that Massimo would court her?

Dread unfurled in his gut.

She turned to him and smiled. "Don't worry, Count Gallo. I'm mostly here to escape my insufferable mother. My heart already belongs to another."

"Oh," Massimo said, unable to hide his surprise.

"Mine as well." The words escaped him.

A startling sentiment, but one he knew to be true. Dante was right. He was in love with Alessia. The question now was, did she love him too?

Chapter 23

The Duchessa

Alessia stood in Mama's bedroom, feeling as if the ground was swaying beneath her. Liliana's angry words echoed around her, but she couldn't make out what her sister was saying.

She was still shocked. Humiliated. She was sure the anger would come too, but she couldn't believe her mother and sisters had done such a thing. The letter sent by Serafina was bad enough, but this? Faking the severity of her pain just to have Massimo return?

It was wrong.

What would he think of her and her family now? Not that it should matter in the end. He would be leaving Zamerra soon enough and they probably wouldn't be seeing him again. Maybe not ever.

A lump grew in her throat at the thought. She would miss him. She shook away the dark thoughts and focused on the present. Liliana, having exhausted herself, was brooding with her arms folded tightly against her chest. Pamina was beside her, trying to console her.

Mama stretched out her arms to Alessia, but Alessia wasn't ready to embrace her. She was still reeling from her mother's confession.

"I hope in time you can forgive me, amore. I did it for your benefit."

"My benefit?" Alessia's words came out sharper than she'd meant.

Mama flinched, looking more vulnerable than Alessia had ever seen her. Deep down, Alessia knew her mother and sisters had only been trying to help with their meddling, but they could have at least included her! They hadn't even asked if she wanted to marry Massimo in the first place. Not that it was an option. Especially not now.

"You're the one who told us that visions are supposed to come true on their own. Not by force," Alessia said.

Mama nodded. "Yes, I know. Forgive me. I tried talking to you, but you didn't want to hear it. I just didn't want you to lose out."

"Lose out? Lose out on what? I told you, Mama. I'm happy here. I'm happy with my life. You had no right to try to force your vision into being. And with a count! Surely, it can't mean him?"

Mama frowned, dark eyes gleaming. "Why not? You can't tell me you feel nothing for him. It's plain for everyone to see."

Alessia felt her mouth drop. Pamina and Liliana nodded in agreement with their mother, leaving Alessia speechless. Did she feel something for him? There was attraction for sure, but that didn't mean anything. There were still the logistics to think about.

Marrying Massimo meant leaving Zamerra. Leaving her family. Being a countess. None of those things were what she wanted. An ache filled her. She'd never felt so torn before.

"If you let him go, Alessia, I'm afraid you'll regret it for the rest of your life." Mama's voice softened.

"But you never married," Alessia replied with a pointed look.

Mama shrugged. "That was my choice, and I have no regrets. You must make your own choice. For you."

A strangled sound escaped Alessia. That was just it. She didn't know what to do about her feelings. She'd never felt such things before, and though a part of her longed to explore those feelings, she was terrified of what it would ask of her in the end. What would she have to give up?

"But this is my home," she said, pain lacing her words.

Mama wrapped her in a warm hug. "It will always be your home, Alessia."

Yes, the villa agreed with its gentle, soothing voice.

"And we will always be family, amore," Mama added, squeezing her tighter.

Tears sprang into Alessia's eyes. Pamina and Liliana joined in the hug, pressing her in.

"What's going on?" Serafina demanded.

Alessia turned to see her and Fiorella with her red-rimmed eyes standing in the doorway. She was happy to see they'd made up.

Mama smiled at them. "Come here, girls."

They exchanged curious glances and joined the family hug. Alessia's chest tightened. As much as she loved her family, she couldn't help but feel as if someone was missing. Fear spread through her. What if it was too late to repair things with Massimo? What if the king forbade them to marry?

Alessia shook away the thoughts. She was getting too ahead of herself. Massimo had never admitted to feeling that way about her. Not outright. Not with words, anyway.

"Should I brew some caffé?" Pamina asked as they separated themselves.

Alessia sniffed and nodded. "Caffé sounds amazing right now."

"And honey cakes!" Serafina added.

"I'm afraid our warlock friend ate them all, but I can make some more," Pamina replied. She turned to Liliana. "Do we have any more honey?"

Liliana snorted. "Well, now that I don't need to make any more tonics for Mama, you can use whatever is left."

"Come and help me," Pamina said, motioning Serafina and Fiorella to follow her out.

Liliana looked at her vials and mixing bowls with a slight frown before taking her leave. Alessia turned to go too, but Mama stopped her with a gentle touch on her arm.

"What are we going to do about the count?" she asked carefully.

Alessia sighed. "There's nothing to do today. I think we should let things settle. We need to start on the wine, anyway. In the morning, I'll go into town and apologize for... all of this."

Mama nodded. "And then?"

"Well, I don't know. I don't even know how he feels about me. And I doubt the king would approve of him... with me."

Her mother only shrugged as if none of the things were problematic. Alessia wished she could feel just as confident, but even with the knowledge of the vision, she wasn't sure what her future held. Would Massimo be a part of it?

"Everything will work out in the end," Mama said cryptically, a gleam in her calculating eyes.

Alessia almost asked her about the vision but stopped herself. She wasn't sure she wanted to know. What if the vision didn't come true?

Pushing the worrying thoughts aside, she followed her

mother downstairs to join the others. Laughter echoed from the kitchen, making Alessia smile.

She couldn't be sure, but she imagined the villa was smiling too.

The next day, Alessia awoke to find her mother and sisters crowded around her bed. She gasped and bolted upright.

"What is it? What's happened? What's wrong?" she asked, her voice echoing in the room.

Mama smiled. "Shouldn't you be on your way into town to see a certain count?"

Even Bruno was there, standing atop her bed, eating a biscuit and spilling crumbs all over her quilt. He waggled his bushy eyebrows at her.

"A certain *handsome* count," Pamina added, handing Alessia a cup of caffé.

Alessia felt her face flush as she accepted the cup. She blew on it before taking her first sip. The warm liquid filled her with a sense of peace and determination. Now she was ready to face the day. Or she would be once she was dressed properly.

"I can do your hair!" Fiorella offered, holding up a basket full of strawberry blossoms and red ribbon.

"Here's your dress," Serafina added, stepping forward with a beautiful red sundress.

Alessia gasped. "Where did you get that?"

Pamina smiled. "We made it. Liliana and Fiorella used the strawberries that we couldn't use for the wine."

"You mean the... onion tasting ones?" Alessia asked.

Liliana snorted. "Well, you don't have to eat it. I took the smell away too. It smells like roses now because we added red petals for the dye."

Alessia set her cup down and stood, reaching a hand toward the dress. It did, indeed, smell like roses. "But when did you have time to do all this?"

Mama smiled. "They bought and dyed the fabric. Pamina and I sewed it up. While I was... sick."

Serafina huffed. "Fiorella and I helped with the design."

Mama gave her a placating pat and nodded.

"But... how? Why?" Alessia asked, still dumbfounded.

"If you're going to be courted by a count, you need a new dress, silly," Pamina said.

A wave of nausea hit Alessia. Their gesture was kind and thoughtful, but presumptuous. What if it was too late for her and Massimo? After her mother's stunt, she couldn't even be sure he wanted to see her or any of her family again.

"He won't be able to refuse you in this," Serafina said matter-of-factly.

Alessia rubbed her forehead as worry filled her. Before she could object, they were all embracing her, their joy contagious. Her heart warmed at their excitement. Though another dark thought crossed her mind. What if Massimo *did* have feelings for her? That was almost as frightening as if he no longer wished to see her.

If he proposed, she'd have to move far away and live in that giant villa the old count had lived in. A villa, she was sure, wasn't as alive nor welcoming as hers.

Change is good, the villa said in its old, familiar voice.

Despite their protests, Alessia walked into town by herself. She felt a little silly dressed up in her new dress with her hair braided and pinned up so intricately with the flowers and ribbon. Though she had to admit, her mother and sisters had outdone themselves.

Nerves filled her the closer and closer she got to Zamerra. Questions—so many questions—raced through her mind. Forcing the storm cloud of thoughts away, she tried to focus on the steps before her. It wasn't long until she arrived and headed straight for the Blossom Inn.

Alessia paused on the steps, the speech she'd rehearsed completely forgotten. Her mind was a blank. Her heart raced. What could she say to him? What if he didn't want to see her?

She didn't have to wonder for long because the door opened, and Massimo was there.

He stopped short. "Alessia?"

His amber eyes widened at her, taking in her dress and hair. Alessia's skin warmed under his hot gaze.

"Hello," she said rather weakly.

Massimo smiled, putting her at ease. "Hello," he said, his voice low and quiet.

"I came to apologize for yesterday. I had no idea of my mother and sisters' scheming, and I promise you I had no intention of deceiving you." The words came rushing out now.

As she spoke, Alessia realized they were not alone. Massimo's friend Dante appeared, along with two women she didn't know. Their fancy dresses made her new dress look quite plain. Snapping her mouth shut, Alessia gave them a curtsy.

Dread coiled in her gut. Who were these women?

Massimo followed her gaze to them. "Oh, Signora Ricci and Duchessa D'Almerita, may I present to you, Signora Silveri."

The older woman sniffed haughtily, but the young duchessa gave Alessia a polite smile. Alessia forced one in return. Her ears rang. A duchessa? In Zamerra? Had she come at Massimo's request?

She didn't remember him ever mentioning her and surely if he was courting someone already, he wouldn't have returned so quickly to Zamerra to see Alessia.

Suddenly feeling the fool, Alessia could only stand there and nod mutely. Her face warmed, and she wanted nothing more than to run back home and never leave the villa again, but she stood there instead.

"We were just about to take a walk around the plaza. Would you like to join us?" Massimo asked gently.

Alessia shook her head no. "I'm afraid I must get back home, Count Gallo."

Massimo's eyes snapped to hers. This time, he didn't correct her address.

Alessia's heart sank. She gave a quick curtsy to the others and excused herself. Heat rushed across her skin from the embarrassment. She could feel Massimo's eyes on her back, but she didn't pause to look back.

She didn't want him to see the tears welling in her eyes. It was too late, just as she feared. Perhaps it was for the best, though. He had found himself a proper bride and now she was free to stay in Zamerra. Forever. Alone.

No, not alone. She still had her mother and sisters. The villa. Bruno.

Alessia pushed the thoughts away as she climbed the mountain path home. Her attempts to cheer herself up were only making her feel worse.

Liliana greeted her first at the gate. "What is it? What's wrong?"

At this, the others came rushing out. The cats and Gio surrounded them with their usual noise. Mama motioned for Serafina to shoo them off as she walked up to Alessia.

Alessia met her eyes and burst into tears.

"What happened?" Serafina demanded as Mama pulled her into a tight embrace.

Alessia sniffed. "He's moved on. Found himself a duchessa."

"What? No! You two are meant to be," Fiorella exclaimed, words shaky.

"What happened, exactly, Alessia?" Liliana asked with a frown.

Mama let her go. She turned to face her sister and wiped her eyes.

"Did you tell him how you feel?" Pamina asked.

Alessia shook her head. "No... I saw him with the duchessa. It's too late."

"No!" Serafina howled, her face mottled with rage.

Liliana stepped forward. "You don't know that. He loves you. You know he does. You have to tell him. You—"

"Stop! Don't you understand? He's with a duchessa. She's a better match for him."

"Oh, Alessia," Mama said with a shake of her head. "That's not true."

"So, you're giving him up? Just like that? Like a coward?" Liliana asked, eyes narrowed on her.

Alessia's gaze snapped to her. "It's for the best. Isn't that what you wanted, anyway?"

Liliana looked as if she'd been struck. "No. Of course not."

Fiorella started crying. Pamina threw an arm around her and led her back inside. Serafina looked furious, glancing from Alessia to their mother.

Mama waved her away. "You girls go inside. We'll be there shortly."

Once alone with Alessia, she turned to her. "Are you sure about this, Alessia? Are you sure you can really let him go? It's not too late..."

Alessia blinked back the tears and met her mother's gaze. "Please. It's over, Mama. I just want to move on."

Before her mother could argue, she turned away and ran back into the house. Her mother and sisters' words echoed in the back of her mind.

Could she really let him go?

Chapter 24

Up the Mountain

"Count Gallo?" The duchessa's voice startled Massimo out of his thoughts.

He looked up to see her staring at him from across the table. What had he missed now? Massimo wasn't usually so poor at conversation, but seeing Alessia had thrown him into a spiral.

Why had she come to see him? Was it really just to apologize? He didn't completely understand the reason for her family's scheming, but he wasn't upset with them. He had a feeling she'd come for more than that and if it weren't for the guests he was entertaining, he would have chased after her. All the way up the mountain.

Why hadn't he stopped her from leaving?

"I said, it's a pity your lovely *friend* couldn't join us for caffé." The duchessa emphasized the word friend with a knowing smirk.

Signora Ricci paused mid-bite and frowned. "I do hope you're not suggesting anything untoward, Duchessa."

The young woman gave her an innocent smile. "Of course not, signora."

Dante coughed, hiding his smirk. It was a good thing his friend was there to entertain the women. All Massimo wanted to do was go after Alessia. He spent the day replaying the image of her in her beautiful dress as they toured the small town. What more did she have to say?

He had much to say to her, it turned out, and as soon as he could get away, he'd do it. Massimo would tell Alessia exactly how he felt. How she made him feel. Then he would wait for her answer. He hoped beyond anything that she truly did feel the same for him. And if not, he would return home, knowing he'd been brave enough to try.

"Well, gentlemen. As lovely as this town is, I think I've seen all there is to see. Tomorrow, I'll be leaving."

Signora Ricci nodded approvingly, returning to her dinner.

Dante shot him an expectant look.

"Oh, you're leaving? I'm sorry to hear that," Massimo replied.

She snickered and turned to Dante. "Would you care to join me, signor?"

Signora Ricci's eyes widened, and she nearly choked on her pasta.

Dante smiled. "Thank you for the tempting offer, Duchessa, but I believe my presence is needed here for a little longer."

The duchessa turned her attention back to Massimo. "Don't linger too long, Count. The king won't like to be kept waiting too long."

"Of course. Did he mention exactly what it was he wanted to discuss?"

"I imagine he wants to announce our courtship."

Massimo exchanged a worried look with Dante.

The duchessa laughed. "Don't worry. We can sort every-thing out."

After supper, the women retired, and Massimo was finally free to go. It was getting dark outside. Soon it would be too dark to travel by cart up the mountain. Alessia had walked to him. He could make the walk too. He'd walked all the way to the Rossis' farm after all. The Silveri villa was closer.

Dante, who seemed to have anticipated his move, handed him an oil lamp and asked if he wanted company.

Massimo declined the offer, wanting to speak privately to Alessia. Leaving Lucia in the room with a second helping of dinner, Massimo readied himself to go.

His mind raced and his nerves felt unraveled like a ball of yarn after Lucia was through with it. He took the lamp, making his way up the mountain. Below him, the town seemed to be sleeping as the sun set.

As he made his way up, the air grew cooler. Ahead, a figure appeared, making Massimo pause. It was Signora Silveri. She carried her own lamp and stopped when she spotted Massimo.

Worry filled Massimo. He ran forward, his heart racing. What if something had happened to Alessia?

Massimo's breath puffed out into the air as he hurried. Signora Silveri held up her lamp and met him on the dirt road.

"Signora? What is it?"

She pulled her shawl tighter around her shoulders before answering. "Count Gallo, forgive me, but I promise this is the last time I meddle. I hope my actions haven't dissuaded you from following your heart."

Her words surprised Massimo. If Alessia didn't return his feelings, surely her mother wouldn't have gone to such great lengths to bring them together. Signora Silveri was a seer. Did that mean she'd had a vision of Alessia and Massimo? Did Alessia know?

"Oh, Santos, not now," Signora Silveri whispered, a hand on her forehead.

Pain etched into her features, and she swayed forward, her lamp moving along with her. She clutched Massimo's outstretched arm and nearly fell to her knees.

"Signora! What is it?" he asked as he held her up.

Her dark eyes met his, but there was a glassy look in her eyes, as if she was looking right through Massimo. Was she having a vision?

A guttural moan came from her as she fell limp into his arms, her lamp falling to the road. Massimo dropped his lamp so he could hold on to her. The flames died as they hit the dirt, leaving him in near darkness. There was little light left from the waning sun as he turned Signora Silveri to the side so he could lift her.

"Help!" Massimo shouted, carrying her as fast as he could toward their villa.

When he reached the gate, Alessia was already there, along with her sisters and all their animals.

"What happened?" she asked, breathless.

"I don't know. She just fainted on the road."

"Bring her inside. Please. Liliana, get the tonic ready," Alessia ordered.

Massimo carried Signora Silveri into the villa and up the stairs to her room, where Pamina and the others were getting everything ready. A stillness hung in the air. As if the villa was holding its breath along with everybody else.

Liliana hurried to her mother's side, mixing up a pungent goo which she spooned into the poor woman's mouth. Massimo, heart in his throat, reached for Alessia's hand and squeezed it.

She turned to look at him, worry swimming in her dark eyes. "Thank you," she whispered.

Massimo squeezed her hand gently once more. "Of course."

There were still many things left to say, but he knew it wasn't the moment to speak them now. Not when her mother was in such a state, but he would tell her how he felt. When the time was right.

Signora Silveri started coughing the moment Liliana's potion went down her throat. Pamina hurried over with a glass of water and Fiorella followed with a mint leaf to get rid of the horrible taste.

"Thank you," Mama croaked after she sipped the water.

She looked at everyone and sat up higher. "I'm sorry for giving you all a scare. It was just an intense vision. I'm fine now. I promise."

"A vision! What did you see, Mama?" Fiorella asked, clasping her hand.

Her mother just shook her head and turned to Massimo. "Thank you, Count Gallo."

Massimo nodded. "I'm glad you're well, signora. Is there anything else I can do?"

An amused look passed across Mama's face, but she only shrugged and turned to Alessia. "Make the guest room up for him, please. Can you show him to the room?"

Alessia gaped at her. She glanced uncertainly at Masimo before disappearing down the hall.

Massimo started to protest but was cut off by Signora Silveri's hand. "You two need to talk. Without my meddling. Without any interference." She gave her daughters stern looks.

"Thank you." Massimo bowed and turned to follow Alessia.

"Are you really unwell this time, Mama?" he heard Fiorella ask as he left.

"I promised I wouldn't fake it again, amore. I really did have a vision, but this one was for Liliana, and I'll only share it with her."

Liliana groaned. "Not another vision."

"Are you coming?" Alessia stood in the hall, waiting for him.

Massimo nodded and joined her outside the guest room. He stood so close to her, he could smell the lilac scent of her soap on her skin and feel the warmth radiating from her body.

"Massimo," her voice sounded hoarse. Desperate.

His eyes locked onto her lips. What did they feel like? What did they taste like?

"Shouldn't you be with... your duchessa?" she asked, taking a step back.

Her closeness was making him feel light-headed. As if he'd drank too much wine.

Massimo frowned, her words finally registering. "Duchessa Francesca? She's leaving tomorrow."

"Oh. I'm sorry to hear that. Is she your... intended?"

A look of hurt flashed across her face, masked quickly by a forced smile. Is that what she had thought when she saw them together?

Massimo took her hand gently. "No."

Her eyes widened in surprise as she met his. "No? Why not?"

"Because I'm not in love with the duchessa. I'm in love with you" The words slipped easily from his lips.

Alessia inhaled sharply, the sound echoing in the hall around them.

"Are you sure?" Her question was a near whisper.

Massimo stepped back, worry filling him. "Do you not love me?"

Movement caught his eye, and he turned to see the edge of someone's skirt disappear around the corner.

Alessia took his hands in hers. "I do... but."

Massimo flinched. *But.*

"Is it... my fae blood?" he asked, preparing himself for her answer.

"What? No! Of course not. It's not that. It's just that... well, I'm not of noble blood, Massimo. And I'm a witch, well sort of. I don't have magic or anything like that, but people would talk..."

He shrugged. "Nothing that I'm not used to already."

"But... it wouldn't be proper, Massimo. They wouldn't accept us. And it's not just that..."

Alessia glanced around the dimly lit hall and sighed. "We'd have to move. Live far away from Zamerra. And the parties and politics. I didn't grow up in that world, Massimo. I don't know if I want that."

A coldness enveloped him. She loved him, but she didn't want to be with him.

"You love me, but you don't want to be Contessa? Is that it? And if I gave up being the count? Would you still feel the same?"

"Oh, I couldn't ask you to do that, Massimo! You can't give up your inheritance. Not after all your mother did... not after all you've done. You are a great count. We need you."

Massimo lifted her chin so she could meet his eyes. "I would give it up to have you, though."

"No, Massimo. Please. You can't do that."

His stomach churned. In truth, he didn't want to give up being count. He was thankful to be in a position to help those in need, but he couldn't let Alessia go.

Questions raced through his mind. He needed to figure everything out.

Clearing his throat, he turned to her. "I have to go. I have business to attend to with the king, but I'll be back for the end of the season. I'll figure this out. I promise. Don't give up on us just yet."

His gaze darted to her lips. "Oh, and Alessia, I'd like to leave you a parting gift, if I may."

Her dark eyes met his. She nodded, seeming to read his mind.

Massimo dipped his face to hers. She inhaled sharply, her warm breath enveloping him.

Then he kissed her.

Her lips were warm and soft against his. She returned the kiss, parting her lips for him. She tasted like caffè and sugar. Warmth filled Massimo from his head to his toes. He felt as if a fire had been lit inside him. Desire washed over him, and it was all he could do to not pull her into the room.

All too soon, she pulled away, leaving Massimo dazed. His eyes were smoldering. Massimo's sharp inhale echoed loudly in the silence.

"Good night, Alessia," he said, the words low and gravelly.

Alessia stood speechless, dark eyes burning, as he shut the door.

Chapter 25

A Second Chance

Alessia's heart leapt to her throat. She touched her lips, remembering Massimo's warm breath on her face. He tasted like caffé and smelled like the forest. Her skin still tingled from their embrace. A smile spread on her lips despite the turmoil running through her. He said he would figure everything out. What did that mean? She didn't want him to give up his title for her.

Putting the thoughts away, she walked to her room. There had never been a problem she couldn't figure out. For now, she knew he loved her, and she loved him. She would just have to trust everything else to work out the way it should. Even if that meant she would have to leave Zamerra.

For Massimo, she could do it.

Yes, you can, the villa echoed in her mind.

"Well?" Liliana demanded, sitting up on her bed.

Their door opened and Alessia turned to find all her sisters piling in, barely able to hide their smiles.

"Well, what? Don't think I didn't see you snooping in the hall," Alessia said teasingly.

Liliana gave her a flat look. "I wasn't snooping."

"We were!" Serafina said, unashamedly, outing Pamina and Fiorella as well.

Alessia couldn't stop smiling. She threw herself back onto her bed with a happy sigh. "He kissed me."

Pamina and Fiorella squealed, and Serafina gave her a smug look. Even Liliana was smiling.

"Was it the most perfect kiss in the world?" Fiorella asked dreamily, clapping her hands together.

"It was." Alessia smiled at her.

"Ooh! Does this mean you're going to marry him? You're going to marry a count!" Serafina said, jumping up and down with Fiorella.

"Alessia?" Liliana prompted, concern etched on her face.

Alessia sat up and met her gaze before looking at the others. "I don't know yet. Nobody says anything until... until he returns. Okay? There are still things... we have to work out."

"Is it about the duchessa? Do you want me to send snakes up her dress?" Serafina asked, wriggling her fingers in the air.

Alessia threw a pillow at her. "No!"

"No snakes!" she and Liliana replied in unison.

Mama stood in the doorway, smiling at them all. Alessia met her eyes and sighed. She didn't want to leave her family, but she knew if she did, they would be okay.

Yes. Everything will be okay, the villa answered.

Massimo left again, and it was even harder to endure this time. Days turned into weeks and aside from the two letters he'd sent, Alessia hadn't heard from him. He claimed he still loved her, and he was caught up in work but would be back as soon as he was able.

The memory of their kiss was still fresh in Alessia's mind, but she was growing worried. What if the king refused to approve their courtship? What if he was insisting Massimo court his niece?

"Well, did you hear the news about our count?" Signora Savelli's voice interrupted Alessia's thoughts.

She blinked, realizing the woman was addressing her. "The count?"

The matchmaker nodded. "He's found himself a bride!"

Alessia's breath hitched. She paused, still holding the basket she'd brought for supplies. Her sisters walked behind her.

"A beautiful duchessa! The king's niece. Can you believe it?" the woman prattled on.

The duchessa. Alessia couldn't breathe. She felt as if someone had stabbed her through the heart. Pamina and Liliana were by her side in an instant.

Serafina stepped up to Signora Savelli. "No, I don't believe it. You're lying! Spreading false rumors."

Others had gathered now, drawn by the noise. A buzzing sound rang in Alessia's ears. Massimo would have told her... he wouldn't do that to her.

Liliana squeezed her hand, bringing her out of her thoughts. "He said he'll be back. Stop your worrying."

"Signorina, you should take care with your words," Signora Savelli said with a loud huff.

Serafina pointed a finger at her. "You should take care with your words!"

"It isn't true! He's not marrying the duchessa. He's marrying Alessia," Fiorella said, shooting Alessia an uncertain look. "Right?"

Someone gasped. Murmurs and whispers erupted around the plaza. The matchmaker's head snapped to Alessia.

She clucked her tongue and shook her head at her. "Oh,

dear. Did you really think you had a chance? Didn't your Mama ever tell you... if you give the milk for free, then there's no reason for them to buy the cow."

Liliana shot her a glare. "Watch yourself, signora. You don't know what you're talking about."

Pamina frowned. "You should be ashamed of yourself, signora. Making such accusations with no foundation."

The older woman cackled. "We all saw how your sister threw herself at the count! Saw him go up the mountain. Twice, wasn't it?" She glanced around at the others for support.

Some people nodded along. Others shook their heads, frowning at the matchmaker.

"Signora, please. This is hardly the place," another woman said, giving Alessia a pitying look.

Alessia, who had gone silent, felt as if her skin had been lit on fire. Even with all the judging stares and the woman's crude words, what hurt most was the thought that Massimo had chosen the duchessa.

What if it was true?

"My sister didn't throw herself at anyone, and anyone who thinks differently is a damned fool!" Liliana's sharp words snapped Alessia back to the present.

They were surrounded now.

She held her head high. "Let them think whatever they like. They have to have something to amuse themselves with." She turned to her sisters. "Some people's lives are so miserable, they have to speculate on others' lives just to get themselves through. Come on, let's go."

Signora Savelli sputtered in outrage as they pushed past her. The others dispersed, giving the Silveris repenting looks.

"Well, at least—what is that? What is that?" the older woman screeched behind them.

"Rats!" someone screamed.

Everyone ran now, clearing the streets. A group of rats chased Signora Savelli, trying to run up her legs. The woman screamed and tried to shake them off, pulling her dress up to an unseemly height and running quite fast for her age. The cats followed, chasing after the rats.

Alessia whipped to Serafina, who smiled in satisfaction.

She met Alessia's eyes. "What? You said no snakes. Never said anything about rats."

Liliana laughed.

"Fina, don't hurt the poor woman," Alessia said with a shake of her head.

Her sister shrugged. "They'll let her go inside. Serves her right!"

Fiorella nodded and giggled, pointing at the old match-maker as she ran out of sight.

Alessia couldn't help but laugh too. She threw her sisters an appreciative look. "I don't know why I ever thought you needed me. Clearly, you all can take care of yourselves."

Liliana nodded. "We take care of each other."

"Always," Pamina added.

"She was lying about the duchessa, wasn't she?" Fiorella asked as they continued shopping.

"Of course she was!" Serafina answered for her.

Alessia only nodded, unable to speak. In her heart, she knew Massimo wouldn't let her down. Still... she was ready for him to return.

Back at home, Alessia and Liliana went upstairs to check on Mama. She was recovering from her latest vision, seeming much better than before. She listened as they told her about Signora Savelli and the rats.

She turned to Alessia. "Don't doubt him now, amore. You two are meant to be."

Alessia sighed. "I don't even know how it happened. Somehow, in one of these quiet moments, I fell in love with him."

She threw her arms into the air. "But it doesn't even make sense. I've spent my whole life just fine without knowing him and now... everything is different."

Mama smiled. "That's the way love usually works. Sometimes it comes when we least expect it."

"But that's just it. If you hadn't told me about your vision... would I still have come to feel the same? What if I've invented all this just to... I don't know, make sense of your vision?"

Mama snorted. "You cannot deny your own heart, Alessia. My vision had nothing to do with that."

A mysterious look crossed her face. "Besides, my newest vision was about Liliana."

Liliana frowned. "Not another wedding vision, I hope. Because you forget about that."

Their mother only shrugged in response, which made Liliana grunt in frustration.

"What is this?" Liliana asked, holding up a black vial.

Mama smiled. "Oh, that nice, handsome warlock left it. He said it was free of charge."

Liliana scoffed. "Oh, he did, did he? A healing tonic? Cinnamon and honey? Please. How basic. And he had the nerve to dismiss my recipe."

Alessia was too caught up in her thoughts to pay them much attention. When Massimo came back, she would choose him. No matter what that meant. Her mother was right, she couldn't deny her own heart.

Chapter 26

The Speech

"**T**hank you," Massimo said to the king's coachman as she stepped out of the carriage.

He turned to face the giant palazzo, a queasiness in his stomach. It was the day he'd been preparing weeks for. Today was the day he would go before the king and his council and ask for approval to court Alessia.

"The worst he can do is say no. Or throw me in the royal dungeon. Or behead me, I suppose, if he was really upset," Massimo said aloud.

Taking a deep breath, he tried to steady himself. Nodding in greeting to the king's staff, he made his way up the wide steps.

He was led straight away into the king's council chambers. Everyone was already there, waiting in their seats. Even the duchessa had come.

Massimo took his seat beside her.

She turned to him with a friendly smile. "Not nervous at all, are you, Count?"

"Of course not. I just have to explain to the king why I don't want to marry his chosen match for me. That should be easy, right?"

The duchessa squeezed his arm affectionately. "You can do this. Just speak from your heart."

"Right."

"Ah, Count Gallo, I see you have met my niece, the duchessa," King Carlo's voice boomed in the room, silencing everyone.

All eyes turned to Massimo and the duchessa. She turned to him as well, waiting expectantly. Behind them, the servants milled about, pouring drinks and taking away plates.

Massimo cleared his throat. "Yes. We've met. We've grown very fond of each other as friends," he emphasized.

The king frowned. "Francesca, what is this?"

The duchessa met the king's stare. "It's as he said. We've become friends, Uncle." She motioned for Massimo to continue.

Forcing himself to get through it, Massimo turned to the king. "As much as I appreciate your input, Your Majesty, I'm afraid this isn't a match either of us wants."

The king huffed. "No? And why is that?"

Everyone stared at him as if he'd lost his mind. Only the duchessa nodded, smiling encouragingly.

"I've fallen in love with someone else. She—"

"A noblewoman?" the king cut him off, his bushy eyebrows furrowed.

"Well, no. She's not. But—"

"Then you must find someone else," the king said with a wave.

Massimo sucked in a breath and faced the king once more. "There is no one else, Your Majesty. Not for me. I know that this is not proper. Believe me. I've grown up with such rules, but if I may point out, Your Highness, my very existence, by such society, is not proper. If you can have a fae count, I do not see why I shouldn't have a common bride."

One of the councilmen gasped. Another frowned, shaking his head at the king.

Massimo waited for what felt like an eternity as the king stared at him, digesting his words. He sat back against his large chair and glanced at his niece before staring at Massimo some more.

The expression written on the king's face was unreadable. Even the duchessa looked worried. Massimo did not find that reassuring.

This is it. He's going to take away my title.

"If the council should not agree, then I will politely surrender my title and all that applies with it."

The duchessa's eyes widened at this.

King Carlo gave him an odd look. "You'd give up everything for this match?"

"I would."

The king sighed and rubbed his forehead. "Very well then. You may wed her. This... commoner. If that is what you really desire. Why shouldn't our first fae count have a common bride?"

"But, Your Majes—"

"The king has spoken," the duchessa cut off the councilman.

She shook her head and met her uncle's gaze. "Now that's settled, I should hope you would extend such grace to your niece as well."

"You want to marry a commoner too?" the king asked, incredulous.

The duchessa shrugged. "I might. In the future. Who knows?" She glanced at Massimo, "I'm just thankful to have a gracious king who is open to such things. Should I ever want to get married, that is."

"Enough talk about marriage. Let's eat!" the king commanded.

* * *

"I can't believe you told the king no!" Dante exclaimed, sitting in Massimo's library.

"Well, I didn't say it like that," Massimo replied, taking a sip of caffé.

His friend grinned. "I'm proud of you. You found the courage to do what you wanted. Propriety be damned."

Massimo shook his head. "It wasn't like I started a rebellion, Dante. I just told him the truth."

"So, what will you do about all the politics and meetings you're supposed to go to? Will you have to keep traveling? How does your intended feel about that?"

Massimo shrugged. "Not so much now that all my affairs are settled, but in the chance that I am needed, I'll need a... representative, so to speak. Would you be interested? You'd be my personal page and representative. Go to the parties. Go to the meetings and such."

Dante's eyes widened. "Me? I'm flattered that you thought of me, friend, but I'm afraid I don't want the position."

"No? It's traveling and parties, mostly. I thought you enjoyed those things?"

His friend shrugged. "I'm growing tired of them. I think I want to settle down. You've inspired me, actually. I have a new business venture I have to share with you. Once we're done planning your wedding, of course."

"My wedding. Right. Well, I haven't proposed just yet, but that's next on my list."

"Minor details. We can still discuss the menu. The outfits. The venue. There is much to a wedding, Massimo."

A wave of uncertainty washed over Massimo. Everything was all worked out, just as he'd promised Alessia. She said she loved him. He had her letters to prove it, in fact, but what if she had second thoughts?

Dante, who'd still been talking, paused and frowned at his friend. "Are you well, Massimo? I have some tonic if you need it?"

Massimo shook his head. "I'm fine."

His friend gave him a forceful smack on the back. "Don't worry. She's not going to say no. You two are the perfect match."

Face sobering, Dante met his eyes. "Your Mama would love her."

Massimo found himself nodding. "Yes. She would. She would be so happy for me."

Dante grinned. "Yes. I'm happy for you as well, friend. You've found love at last."

"Yes, and now we can find your match," Massimo said with a teasing smile.

Surprisingly, his friend didn't protest.

"Well, I should write her. Tell her the news. Don't you think?"

Dante frowned. "Write her? No. You have to ask her in person. Make it special."

Massimo set down the paper he had picked up. "Yes. You're right. I'll tell her in person."

A smile spread across his face. He couldn't wait to tell Alessia the good news.

Chapter 27

The Proposal

The villa seemed to sense the importance of what was happening and hung back, watching the Silveris prepare. Mama made a quick breakfast of bread and jam and Pamina poured caffé into everyone's cups. Fiorella took it upon herself to braid everyone's hair, adding flowers from their garden.

Even Liliana sat patiently and let her sister work her magic, weaving lilies into her dark curls. The result was stunning and made Alessia's heart lurch. If she left Zamerra, she'd miss out on these moments.

"Are you alright?" Pamina asked gently.

Everyone turned to Alessia.

"Yes. Of course. Just anxious to see him again," Alessia replied, waving off her sister's worry.

Pamina smiled and clasped her hands together. "He's going to be speechless. You look beautiful. Like a fae princess."

Alessia laughed and shrugged off her sister's compliments. "It's Fiorella's magic," She swept a hand over the group. "I hope I don't have to fight off too many would-be admirers today."

Pamina's cheeks reddened in response. Liliana gave a sound of disgust and the youngest two were too busy whispering together to hear her.

"Mama, are you coming with us to the festival?" Fiorella asked, pulling Alessia out of her thoughts.

Everyone quieted and turned to their matriarch. She smiled at them and folded her arms across her broad chest. "Of course. I wouldn't miss the count's return."

Liliana frowned. "Is your head feeling better? I can make the tonic stronger, if you like."

"Oh, no. I feel much better. Thank you, amore."

Fiorella stood behind Mama's chair and wrapped her arms around her neck, leaning in to kiss her on the head. "I'm so glad you're better, Mama."

Mama smiled. "Me too."

With the final preparations finished, Alessia helped Pamina clear the table. A tremor ran through her hands. Massimo was returning today. She couldn't wait to see him. To kiss him.

Face warming at the memory, she shook away the image and turned to ask Serafina to ready Fabrizio, but she'd already left the kitchen. Liliana stood to carry out one of the crates of jams they'd made from the leftover strawberries.

"Fabrizio is ready," Serafina announced from the doorway.

Alessia bent to help Liliana with the crates. Together with Pamina and Fiorella's help, they loaded the wagon.

Outside, the sun shone brightly from a clear, blue sky. Alessia breathed in the crisp mountain air, her heart growing lighter. The problems of the future seemed so far away now. She didn't want to spoil the special day with her worries. Whatever would happen, would happen and she knew she couldn't control that, but her time with her sisters, if it was drawing to an end, she wanted to soak up every moment she could.

"Look!" Fiorella's exclamation caught her attention.

The cats and Gio went wild, rushing the gate as the sound of wagon wheels came closer. Serafina and Fiorella ran ahead, braids whipping behind them.

"Oh, don't mess up your hair!" Pamina called after them.

Liliana frowned. "Who is it?"

The gates opened and Alessia held her breath as Massimo drove in, a concentrated look on his face as he weaved the horse and cart in through the lively group of animals.

"Shoo!" Serafina waved them out of the way.

"Count Gallo!" Fiorella squealed with delight.

Alessia's heart skipped. Once again, Alessia was struck by his beauty. His hair was loose, falling in soft waves around his broad shoulders. He met her gaze, her skin burning under the intensity of his amber eyes.

"Count!" Mama exclaimed, motioning for Serafina to help with his horse and cart.

Massimo smiled and stood. "Thank you, but I'm here for Alessia."

He turned to face her once more, making her stomach flip-flop. "Will you take a ride with me, Alessia?"

A sheepish smile spread across his face. "I've been practicing my driving. I promise I won't drive us off the mountain."

"Oh, Santos," Pamina exclaimed, hand on her chest.

Alessia laughed. "I'm coming."

"Can we come?" Fiorella whined.

Liliana frowned at her. "You weren't invited."

Massimo gave them a sympathetic smile. "Next time. I promise."

Alessia gave Fiorella a reassuring squeeze as she passed by. Her sisters watched as Massimo helped her onto the wagon. She took her seat beside him and waved goodbye as he led them back out of the gate.

He took the turn sharply, making her crash against him.

Massimo grimaced and glanced at her. "Sorry. I'm still getting the hang of making turns."

Unable to stop herself, Alessia threw her arms around him and pressed her head against him.

"Whoa!" Massimo exclaimed, shaking the reins as the cart lurched forward.

He threw Alessia a nervous look. "Did you miss me as much as I missed you?"

She nodded, flushing. "I did."

"We'll see you at the festival!" Serafina called as they passed through the gate.

"Massimo, town is the other way," Alessia said with an amused smile as he drove the cart past their villa.

He glanced at her. "We're not going to the festival just yet."

"Oh? Where are we going then?"

"It's a surprise. You look beautiful, by the way," he said with a shy grin.

"Thank you. You too."

Massimo smiled, still staring at her.

"Massimo, the road!" Alessia said, gently guiding his hands back to straighten the cart.

"It's alright. We're here," Massimo said, eyes gleaming.

Alessia stared at the sloping meadow before them. "Here? Are you taking me into the forest?"

Her eyes fell on one of the massive oak trees near the meadow. It was one of the first trees Fiorella had grown with her magic. When she was barely walking. Her eyes grew hot at the memory.

"What's wrong? You don't like it?" Massimo asked, brow furrowed.

"Oh, no. It's not that. It's just a lot of memories here. Why did you bring me here, Massimo?"

He frowned and glanced around. "Happy memories, I hope?"

Alessia nodded, growing more curious. What was he doing?

Massimo let go of the reins and took her hands in his. His eyes met hers. "Alessia, I promised I would figure everything out, and well, I think I have. For the most part. But the rest, I think we should figure out together."

He took a deep breath before continuing. "I missed you so much. And Zamerra. This place has become home to me. So much so that I asked the king for a building permit. I don't want to live at Villa de Sole. I want to live here. With you."

"Here?" Alessia couldn't hide the surprise in her voice.

He smiled and squeezed her hands. "Yes. We're going to build a villa here. Right next to your family."

Alessia gasped. "Here?"

"Yes. Right next to your villa. Well, I guess your mother's villa now. You'll share one with me. After we wed, that is."

Tears welled in her eyes and a smile spread across her face. "Oh, Massimo! That is wonderful news. So, the king approved our courtship as well?"

Massimo smacked his forehead with his hand. "I meant to ask you that first. I'm getting this all wrong."

He shook his head and turned to her. "Let's try this again. Hello,"

"Hello," Alessia replied with amusement.

Massimo smiled. "Hello. I have a question I've been wanting to ask you..."

"Yes!" Alessia cut him off.

"But you haven't even heard the question yet."

"Er... I'm sorry. What is the question?"

"Will you marry me?" he asked, voice soft.

Alessia's heart leapt into her throat.

Massimo's face flushed. "Well, I mean, not right away, of

course. We have to court first. So, what I mean is, do you want to court me?"

Alessia laughed, and her eyes gleamed. She leaned over and kissed him on the cheek.

"That's a yes, then?"

She smiled and nodded. "Yes."

He sighed deeply and leaned in, lips hovering above hers. Alessia's heart raced. But before he could kiss her, the horse started moving, jolting them. Massimo grabbed the reins and looked at her. "I guess we should save the kissing for when we are safely down the mountain. Should we join the others at the festival now?"

Alessia nodded, unable to stop smiling. She laid her head against Massimo's strong shoulder as they made their way down to Zamerra.

Music and voices drifted across the plaza, along with the savory smell of meat and the sugary smell of sweets. It was a scene she'd seen a hundred times, but today it seemed all the more special.

Alessia waved to her sisters as they arrived. Several people gasped around them. Others stopped to stare, and she could hear the whispers starting already. That was just fine. It wouldn't be long before the king would publicly announce their courtship. Then the whole town would be talking.

The music paused as Massimo drove the cart toward the middle of the plaza. Everyone jumped out of the way. Alessia turned to see her mother and sisters following on foot with excited looks.

Massimo tried, unsuccessfully, to bring the horse to a stop. He gave Serafina a pleading look. She nodded and stared at the horse.

Standing up, he helped Alessia to her feet and turned to address the crowd.

"What are you doing, Massimo?" Alessia asked, feeling everyone's heavy stares.

"Excuse me, everyone! I have an announcement to make." His voice rose above the whispers.

Alessia's eyes widened. Was he going...

"I would like you to be the first ones to know. I've chosen my bride—Alessia Silveri," he said proudly.

Gasps sounded.

"Uh, this is where you clap," Massimo said.

Applause erupted through the plaza. Alessia's face warmed. She smiled as she spotted her family clapping proudly.

With Serafina's help, Massimo settled the horse nearby and led Alessia past the fountain.

"Let's go listen to the musicians!" Serafina exclaimed, tugging at Fiorella's sleeve.

They turned to Mama with hopeful looks, bouncing on their toes. Liliana and Pamina were setting out the jars of jam they'd brought to sell.

"Very well, but stick together and no trouble!" Mama could barely get the words out before the girls were gone.

Alessia watched them disappear into the crowd and turned to face Pamina and Liliana. "Don't you two want to dance, too?"

Liliana gave her a flat look, but Pamina glanced wistfully at the direction the girls had gone.

"Go, I can sell the jam," Mama said with a wave.

Pamina kissed her and headed toward the music. Liliana shook her head.

"You two go. Celebrate," Mama said, motioning Alessia and Massimo to leave. "We'll join you shortly," Mama added with a smile.

Alessia turned to her new suitor. "Will you dance with me?"

Massimo smiled. "I'd love to."

Alessia put her hand in Massimo's and pulled him through the crowd. They weaved in and out of the wave of people and headed for the center of town where the music had started back up.

Lively music filled their ears as they made their way through the throng of people. Strawberry perfume wafted by, along with the clashing scents of all the different food carts.

The excitement of the crowd stirred around Alessia. Laughter rang in her ears as they shouldered their way past everyone. Soon the notes of the musicians drowned out all the other noise.

As they made it through the crowd, Alessia spotted two familiar heads of red and brown moving along with the music. Pamina was there too, dancing with one of the young men from town.

The song ended, and everyone cheered. Next, a ballad started. Alessia and Massimo moved toward the middle of the dance floor and Massimo held her by the waist. His nearness made her body burn with need.

Alessia felt as if she was melting into his embrace. All was good. The villa was fixed. Mama was well. Her sisters were well. She didn't have to leave Zamerra. Best of all, she had a life with Massimo to look forward to.

"Can I kiss you?" Massimo asked softly, his eyes burning through her.

Alessia's eyes widened at his question. Nodding, she tilted her head up to meet his. He bent his head and claimed her with his soft lips. There were scandalized gasps and boisterous cheers. No one cheered louder than the Silveri sisters.

The End... or rather the beginning...

Epilogue

It was her wedding day and Zamerra had gone all out. Everyone did their part to decorate and prepare special foods and drinks. The count's wedding was a very prestigious affair, after all. Not only was he getting married in the little town, but he was moving there as well. Further up the mountain, but still a part of Zamerra all the same. All the townspeople were a buzz with the news.

A count in Zamerra is like having the king live among us!

He's even found himself a bride from Zamerra as well.

Zamerra is the place to find the prettiest brides, after all.

Alessia didn't pay attention to their whispers, nor did she care about their approval (which they did give heartily). All that mattered was that she loved Massimo and he loved her. Everything was perfect.

"You look amazing!" Fiorella said with a squeal.

Her other sisters nodded in agreement, all smiles and watery eyes. Mama stood with them and Alessia could see her wiping her tears in the mirror's reflection.

"Is it just like your vision, Mama?" Serafina asked.

239

Mama, too choked up to answer, shook her head. "No, *amore*. It's even better."

Alessia blinked, a lump growing in her own throat. She'd been so adamant that the vision was a mistake, and though she had never asked for details, she knew this was meant to be. She didn't need to see into the future to know what lay ahead. As long as she had Massimo and her family by her side, everything would be okay. More than okay.

"This is all happening so quickly. I can hardly believe it," Alessia said, staring at her reflection in the mirror.

They had only been courting for a few months, but Alessia felt as if she'd been with Massimo forever. As if they'd grown up together. He'd shared everything with her and she with him, yet she knew there was still more to learn about each other.

"Do *you* feel it's too soon? Are you uncertain about him?" Mama asked.

"I'm certain. I love him, but what will everyone think?"

Mama kissed her cheek. "It doesn't matter what anyone thinks, amore."

Serafina smiled wickedly. "They'll probably think there's a babe on the way."

Fiorella's eyes widened and Pamina's hand went up to cover her mouth. Mama merely shook her head at her.

Liliana frowned. "I hope you haven't been spreading such rumors."

Serafina gave her an indignant look. "Of course, I haven't! I just merely said what others have been wondering." She turned to Alessia. "It's not true, is it?"

Alessia's face warmed. She snatched the flower crown from Serafina's hands and put it on. "No. We've barely started court-ing. Santos. It's much too soon to talk of... babies."

A look of disappointment flashed on Serafina's face. Alessia couldn't help but smile, imagining what kind of aunties her sisters would make. The very best. And Massimo would be the best of fathers. She couldn't wait to start their life together.

The little church was packed with more people standing outside and peering in through the open doors and windows. A wedding in Zamerra was always a festive event, and his wedding was even more so.

Massimo had gotten the king's permission to hold it there and quite privately. Only Dante and his oldest, most loyal servants accompanied him. The rest of the nobility would have to settle for hearing about it from the papers.

Sweat clung to him as he stood at the church altar, the summer sun streaming inside. Excited voices clamored around him. Though Massimo appreciated their enthusiasm, he was ready to get the ceremony started. Then the party would begin, and he and Alessia would be free to escape.

Their new villa was ready and prepared for them, and he'd given the servants the night off so that he could have his bride entirely to himself.

His bride who was running late. A worried thought filled him. What if she was having second thoughts? The courtship had been so quick. Maybe it was too quick for her.

A soft purr sounded, and he looked down to see Lucia rubbing herself against his legs. Even the cat was dressed up with a fancy red bow tied around her neck. Serafina had worked her magic to get Lucia to agree to such a thing.

"You're going to have a mother now, Lucia. And perhaps in the future, brothers and sisters. I mean human siblings, of course. Well, that is, humans with fae blood and magic, I imagine."

Lucia blinked up at him, unfazed by his rambling.

The music began and Massimo looked up to see Alessia walking in. His breath hitched. She looked stunning in the white sundress with her dark curls unbound. A crown of flowers, no doubt made by Fiorella, sat on her head.

She smiled at him, and he smiled back. Everything was right with the world.

The ceremony was over quickly, and Massimo could barely remember the words Padre Leonardo had spoken, but he knew he would cherish this day forever.

Patrizio Foncello threw a grand party afterwards, and the streets were filled with good cheer and music. There were savory meats, a variety of salads and vegetables, and mountains upon mountains of desserts. Wine poured freely as everyone celebrated. It was an event, even bigger than their famous Strawberry Festival.

Massimo and Alessia joined in the merriment, dancing among the townsfolk until late afternoon. After a hearty lunch, Massimo had the carriage brought to take them up the mountain. It was quite the spectacle—one of the first carriages ever seen in Zamerra.

Dante and Liliana had worked their magic to enchant it so that it could make the trip up the mountainous passage safely. Serafina used her magic to coax Lucia inside and Fiorella's flowers adorned both the outside and inside, making it smell like lavender. Even Pamina had contributed, using her magic to bake them a tray of delicious tarts and a carafe filled with her special caffé.

A bottle lay in a bucket of ice In the middle of the carriage bench. Massimo picked it up as he slid in after Alessia.

"Is this the strawberry wine you promised me so long ago?" he asked.

Alessia laughed. "I'd forgotten all about it during our courting. I thought it would make a nice wedding day gift."

Massimo laughed too. "I forgot all about it as well, but in my defense, I've never really cared for strawberry wine."

"Oh, now you tell me," Alessia said with a teasing smile.

Massimo's heart lurched at the sight of her beautiful, happy face. Somehow, quite unexpectedly, he'd found his perfect match and he couldn't imagine a life without her.

"I think we should save this. If Fabrizio hadn't run away and caused that mess when we met, who knows if things would have turned out as splendidly as they have."

The carriage lurched and Alessia nestled closer to him, resting her soft head against his shoulder. "Do you mean to tell me our fate is thanks to my old horse?"

Massimo took her hands in his and kissed them. Her eyes met his. The brazen look she gave him made his skin flush.

A sigh escaped him. "I can't begin to tell you how fate works, amore, but I can promise you that I will love you forever."

Alessia leaned forward and planted a kiss on his lips. Heat surged through him at the contact. He deepened the kiss, holding her face in his hands. She was so soft, and he could taste the sugary strawberry tarts on her lips.

The carriage bobbed up and down as it struggled up the mountain. Lucia, who'd made the unfortunate choice to sit between them, was squashed and meowed pitifully, breaking their kiss.

"Oh, I forgot to tell you. We have a house elf now. You'll have to invite Bruno out to meet him," Massimo said with a smile.

Alessia frowned. "A house elf? But we haven't even moved in... officially."

Massimo shrugged. "I guess we are lucky."

She smiled and leaned into Massimo once more. "Yes, we are."

"Very lucky," Massimo added, bowing his head to kiss her again.

Lucia got up and moved to the other side of Massimo, casting them a long-suffering look. They were too busy locking lips and embracing each other to notice her.

Thank you for reading! Book two *'The Warlock's Bride'* is Liliana's story and features many of the same characters as well as some new ones.

Acknowledgments

A big thank you to my patient husband who made my cover! I can't even begin to tell you how many edits we went through. I'm so proud of him for diving in and following his creative passion. A thank you to my editor at Cate Edits for her help. This story would not have been the same without her.

Finally a big thank you to my family for their never ending support and all the readers who have inspired me with their kind words and loyalty. If you enjoyed the story, please consider leaving a review.

Thank you!

Also by R. L. Medina

The Silveri Sisters Series

Book 1: The Fae's Bride

Book 2: The Warlock's Bride

Book 3: The Goblin's Bride

Book 4: The Wolf's Bride

Book 5: The Druid's Bride

YA Fantasy

The Inner World Series

Prequel: Feylin

Book 1: Princess of the Elves

Book 2: Goblin King

Book 3: Fae War

Sign up at my website for a FREE Short story

GRIMM Academy Series

Book 1: Shifters and Secrets

Book 2: Vampires and Werewolves

Book 3: Witches and Wizards

Blood Moon Covenant Series

Book 1: Order

Coming soon...

Book 2: Allegiance

Book 3: Betrayal

About the Author

R. L. Medina was born in the Amazon, adopted and raised by two upstate New Yorkers. At age six, she vowed to hate reading forever. That hate quickly turned to love (or obsession) and by age eight she was filling every notebook with story after story. Now a mother herself, she juggles her time between a busy seven year old and the stubborn characters that demand her time. When she's not exploring all the Sci-fi/Fantasy worlds in her head, she enjoys life with her family in Florida.

Check out her website at www.rlmedina.com for a free story, giveaways, and updates!

You can also find her embarrassing herself on TikTok @thecrazybookdragon and the social media channels below:

Made in the USA
Middletown, DE
15 March 2024

51383586R00146